Anglers' Evenings

John Bartlett

Contents

ANGLERS' EVENINGS

BY

John Bartlett

"LET PATIENCE HAVE HER PERFECT WORK."

BY COLONEL JOHN I. MAWSON, PRESIDENT.

IF, in the fiftieth angling year of a Waltonian (the writer of these lines), the gentle word Patience has lost none of its true meaning, and influence

upon his mind and actions; if, through his many struggles, angling for the good opinion of his fellow-men, and for a position respected by his friends and acquaintances, he has ever found that word to have been an unfailing mentor and invincible auxiliary, can he act more honestly, and, as it were, more gratefully, than by acknowledging the friend to whom he owes so much, and without whose continual presence his exertions might have been fruitless.

Patience is that friend ?

Not content with the exercise of her own great qualities, she enlists, for the benefit of those with whom she dwells, the aid of her partner, Perseverance, equal in nobility to herself, so that " with Patience and Perseverance men do attain their desire."[1]

These lines being written by a Wandering Fisherman, with the best intent, are meant only for the charitable and uncritical consideration of his Brothers of the

1   Had she so dwell'd with the Fisherman of the title page, he would not have touched his line, and might have attained his desire.

Angle; and, lest it be supposed that he arrogates the title of Mentor, be it remembered that he is honoured with that of President, and that, although the saying of ye antient authorities, " the king can do no wrong," may not be of much value, your head officer, in the present case, claims that *he* cannot do much harm. Nay, even if his dissertation should raise a smile, such will, he believes, be only a Waltonian expansion of the facial muscles, acting sympathetically with the heart, and will correspond with the joyous look of an experienced Brother when he has safely landed a Two-pounder. Of a surety it will be so, for in each case he will have gotten something good.

The heart of the writer is too deeply impressed with the pleasantness of his office, and at the same time the importance of his exhortation, to desire to be considered Facetious, and he therefore dictates to his pen the following thoughts, advice, suggestions, wise saws, and experiences—real or supposed,—in the hope that the *good* in them, "when found, will be made a note of."

Now, BE IT KNOWN TO the members of the Manchester Anglers' Association, and never forgotten by them, that the spirit of Izaak Walton, speaking through the exhortation of their President, says: " Brothers of the Angle, one injunction I lay upon you—Let brotherly love continue."

It should also dwell in the minds of meditative men (and the same Walton says " Such be fishermen") that the man who wrote the great precept at the head of these lines, was a fisherman, and that, being such, he had, of a surety, been subject to many disappointments; doubtless he well understood his own exhortation.

Fishermen, above all others, have need to exercise patience and perseverance; for such is necessary, not only in their business callings, but especially in the pursuit of their pleasure; without such exercise they would simply be as other men, who may be without self-control, hasty in temper, and unstable ; and as such they shall not excel in the practice of their art. And let all consider the great and noble tone created in the mind by the practice of these virtues in the art of fishing. Sorely tempted to despond art thou, oh fisherman! how often inclined to rebel against the loved partner of thy bosom, when, returning weary and disappointed with non-success, and sorely puzzled thereby, thou seekest to be relieved, on floor of stone, of thy heavy boots, and dost find, instead of help, the flat and hollow-beaten iron, on fender laid before thy very eyes with ostentation cruel. Patience and Love! now for your boasted virtue! A smile, and then another, and then-   But some of ye are bachelors!—Well, then the hollow-beaten iron doth vanish, and with slippers on, and comforts in, the friend of patience rests,—with eyes on blazing coal he sits and thinks,—and thinks ; and next, at early morn, he wakes, with form and mind refreshed, and hopeful— nay, his hopes are certainties. Has he not, either dreaming or awake, found reasons for the—of yesterday ? (Failure he will not call it, he knows not such a

word—it is not British enough ; he cannot give it a name,—nor can I,—so let it pass.) Reasons he has found, thinks he has ; what matters it ? His mind is active,—he is content to try again, and so he does, and wins; and wins at many things in after-life—yet even when he wins not, he is content, for he can " try again."

But there are fishermen whose pleasure rests only in success, and they have a mighty pleasant way of describing the large baskets they have filled, or the larger fish they have missed basketing. Brothers, we wish them well—we wish them well. Your President hath met them at times in his fifty years' wandering, and hath now and then been mystified, upon being shewn most improbable flies, with undamped feathers, most innocent of guile, and newly tied on line. He thought it was not like Old Izaak, who would " with us have shared his fish, and shewn the flies that caught them."

Every true fisherman has learned, or found out, some speciality due either to his style of fishing, or the district to which he has devoted most of his time ; and rarely is such an one found to hide his knowledge,—rather does he burden you with the tale of his experience, much of which is necessarily your own.

Reciprocity is especially Waltonian, and often charms away troubles and disputes. The writer has known instances of strong antagonism and antipathy being dissolved during a quiet chat on the river bank after the request for interchange of flies, which interchange and dissolution were, most singular to relate, immediately followed by an interchange of "two nips of pale"; indeed, it is said, **they** also have been followed, several times, until four friends have been seen, instead of two men at enmity.

Mutual forbearance,—kind words,—considerate and kind tokens of good-will, cement, both on the river bank and Piccadilly, not only friendship, but that affection which often begins between men of the angle, and doth then continue, and ennoble both; and when good-will exists among men, so will Patience have perfected her work.

And now, the writer (having become thoroughly prosy) will justify and conclude his dissertation upon the virtues practised by true fishermen, by referring all men to the writings of Izaak the Good. Lastly—but remember as Firstly—

Do nothing in haste.
Use the best tackle.
Keep your head cool.
Your back and feet dry and warm,
And your heart in charity with all men.

Written at our Fisherman's Home, on the banks of the Irt, in Cumberland, and faithfully addressed to our Brother Anglers meeting at Piccadilly, in Manchester, this 30th day of June, 1878.

TROUT FISHING IN NORWAY.
BY ABEL HEYWOOD, JUNR.
PART I.—BERGEN TO LÆRDAL.

TEAMERS sail from Hull for Christiania, calling at Christiansand, every week, and for Bergen, calling at Stavanger, every fortnight. On the two occasions when I have visited the country I have made Bergen my port of debarcation, for two or three reasons. The first is, that the best fishing and most beautiful rivers are on the western side of the country, and I, like most anglers, am always anxious to use my rod as soon as possible; another, that when you have only a trifle over a fortnight at command, as was my case, you gain a day by sailing to the latter place, as the Christiania boat sails on Friday, and the Bergen on Thursday. A final reason is, that should you by any accident get delayed on your journey across the country from the west, it cannot be a worse affair than the loss of a week, whilst, in the other case, it may be that you will be delayed a fortnight.

We sail generally at from six to seven o'clock in the evening, and if the weather be very calm, as I have seen it, we may on the following day, as we pass over the great Dogger Bank, see fish, apparently whiting, by the score, in the bright clear water. On one occasion, when I was having a counting match with a friend, he taking all the fish he could see on one side of the bowsprit and I on the other, we had an admirable view of the under-water swimming of the birds known as divers. There were three of them right in our path, and when we got almost close to them they dived and were distinctly visible for some time, using their wings in water just as in air, and going almost as quickly in one element as in the other.

By half-past ten or so on Saturday morning we reach Stavanger, but for some hours before that time, we have been sailing between the mainland and the innumerable islands which stud the coast from the Naze to the North Cape, in calm water, where there is no fear of sea-sickness. This passage among the rocks and islands is most interesting, and occasionally exciting. In places, the ship goes through channels which seem barely wide enough for her passage, and turns and twists occur so rapidly in the course, that one keeps running from side to side of the vessel to see if she is not going to bump.

Stavanger is an important town, built at the extremity of a small fiord, where the tide is so slight, that houses and warehouses are built right down to the water's edge, and even into the fiord. These are all of wood, painted all sorts of bright light colours, and roofed with red tiles ; and the whole town being surrounded by wooded hills, has a most picturesque appearance, which the splendidly clear water of the fiord much increases. The water is so clear, that the boats which throng around the steamer do not seem to touch the water at all, for you can, see every part of them as clearly as though they were on land. There is a little cargo to land here, and while this is going on, you may go on shore to the Credit Bank and get your money changed, which will enable you, if you wish it, to start off from Bergen early next morning, instead of spending all Sunday there, waiting till the banks open on Monday. To one who goes to Norway for the first time, I should say, certainly spend a day in Bergen, it is a curious and interesting town, situated on a beautiful fiord, and a place, if trout were not in view, where even more than one day could be profitably spent. On my latter visit, when I had come to " know my way about" pretty well, my companion and myself agreed to waste no time in towns, and we left Bergen, where we arrived after midnight, by eight o'clock in the morning. We ordered carrioles to be got ready while we breakfasted, and the two curious little carriages drove up to the door soon after we had finished.

In the districts where there are no railways, and there is in Norway happily only one, the carriole is the only means of travel, unless you go on foot. This car-riage is in appearance something like a small sitz-bath, placed on the end of a pair of long slender shafts, and mounted on wheels. You sit in the bath with your legs stretched out before you, the seat not being more than a few inches high ; or you can rest your feet on a cross bar, or even dangle your legs between the wheels. There are no springs to the vehicle, but the shafts are long and slender, ending at the back of the bath, where a cross-board is placed, on which your luggage, if you have any, is tied. The journeys along the road are in stages, from " station " to " sta-tion," four or five to ten or twelve English miles apart. These stations are places at which you change your horses or carrioles, and at most of them you can get a bed and food, if you require them.

It is not advisable to go further than one stage with the same horse, even if the animal is equal to it, but perhaps the first ride from Bergen is an exception. The first two stages will be about sixteen miles, and this distance you will do for one dollar. Your drive is through scenery which you would suppose to be Scotch if you did not know it to be Norwegian, and, though beautiful and varied, has nothing par-ticularly noticeable about it, Garoens, the first station, is reached at about twelve o'clock. It is on the edge of a fiord, where the road terminates, and further progress must evidently be by water.

As soon as we arrived, we asked for the Day Book and booked ourselves, as it is always necessary to do, for the next stage, to Dale, a water journey of seventeen or eighteen miles. We found the peasants in the house eating out of one common dish, with one wooden spoon which was also common to the lot, and I had a little discussion with the men as to how long a boat would take to get ready. My stock of the native tongue is not large, and being on the first day unaccustomed even to the sound of it, I could make nothing out of them, but one was a practical genius, and leading me to the clock, pointed to two o'clock. "No, no," I said, and in turn pointed to the figure one, and, as I would hear no reason, I had my way, for soon after one the boat appeared.

We had three men with us to row, rather a curious number perhaps, but we got on well, and I soon found that pipes, like spoons, were held in common, for a solitary pipe kept circulating from mouth to mouth throughout the voyage. I cannot venture to say anything of the scenery through which we passed ; it is not a thing to talk about, and while you are being quietly. rowed along that fiord, it is not even a time to talk. The man who has sailed this journey bears away a remembrance of beauty and glory that will last his lifetime, but he bears it as a secret, which he can never impart.

It was after six o'clock when we reached the station at Dale, and by this time we were so far 'called back to the grossness of life, that we first of all asked for something to eat. They had nothing, neither eggs, nor bread, nor milk, nor meat— nothing but some " flad-bröd," a dish of raspberries, and some coffee; so we dined off these delicacies, and then began to think of supper.

At Dale, which I find in my journal described as" the most beautiful spot in all the world," a little river enters the fiord, and the custom of the country, as well as the necessity of the case, urged upon us the advisability of trying our angles on that calm Sunday evening. A little higher up the stream than the station a bridge is built, and below it is a fine pool where anyone can see that the fish will lie; but there are many people about, and I do not care to perform before an audience. I straightened my flies out, however, and in the process took two or three small trout; and then singling out a lad to carry my landing-net, I went a few hundred yards down stream, where the dimples and wrinkles on the surface of the water showed that deep rocks lay where the eye, in the twilight, could not see them. Here I threw out my flies, and instanter, away goes the line, making the reel sing out its delightful music. Whilst the fish runs unchecked I turn to my lad and joyfully call "stor fisk," which are the only words I know for "big trout." " Stor fisk," he replies, as glad as I. But it is no easy thing to have a lad who can hardly understand a word you say, handling your landing-net. "Gently," you bawl out, as you carefully wind your fish in, and in response, your assistant with a clumsy splash of the net frightens the trout away into the midst of the waters again, and there is your hope of supper and breakfast which was at your feet a moment ago, twenty yards out in the pool and still running. He has never shown himself, so the chances are he is well hooked, but you are bound to put some pressure on, for you do not know what he may be making for. At last he comes slowly in again, tamed this time, and the lad whom you have been shouting at in your own language, for you can find no other, more lucky than before, gets the net under him, and lifts out a nice sea-trout of a pound and a half. This might serve for supper, but there is still light enough to go on, and you cannot find in your heart to leave the pool. Again the flies dance on the surface, and another sea-trout, somewhat smaller than the first, comes into the net One more fish, about the same size as the second, is caught, and then it is too dark to go on, and we return to the station, or to another house close by, where, we are told, we shall find better beds than at the station itself. We are glad of the change, for the house is cleaner than the first, and every way in better condition. But we are not able to get our trout cooked after all, and once more feed on flad-bröd.

We are up before six in the morning, and while breakfast is getting ready, I go down to the river again with my rod, and am fortunate enough to land, after an exciting fight, a sea-trout of 23/41bs. This is my last success at Dale. A countryman who came up just as I landed my fish, persuaded me to fetch salmon rod and flies, and, while I went for them, caught with my tackle another trout, the twin of the one I had taken. I had no luck with the salmon, and had soon to go to breakfast, to which we had fish, eggs, milk, and cocoa (the latter we had brought with us), a sumptuous meal indeed.

I am a pretty ardent angler, and I do not think that anywhere but at Dale I ever gave up fishing in disgust But here, in the bright morning sun; as I raised my eyes from the waters to look around me, I really flung my rod away and vowed it a sin to forget for a moment, in the rapture of angling, the glories of the place I was in. That this enthusiasm did not last long it is needless to say; like the philosopher who throws away his money as vile dross, and, immediately repenting, stoops to pick up the coin, I resumed my rod, and my indifference to everything but fish returned.

From Dale, by land to Dalseidet is but five or six miles, then comes a like distance on the fiord, then carrioles again, and once more a trip by water terminating at Evanger, which we reached by two o'clock. Here is an excellent station where you can get capital food. At the very door of the house, a large river, which for some miles has flowed through dark pinewoods, rolls into the fiord, and here at the mouth of the rapid river, we tried, from a boat which the rowers could with difficulty keep in the stream, to spin a minnow for salmon; but the bottom was the only thing my friend or I caught We had not time to try further up the river, but Evanger would unquestionably be a fine place to stay in for a few days.

From Evanger a twelve miles stage takes you to Vossevangen, where is a magnificent station by the side of a fine lake, the hills around which are topped by snow that never melts. This place is midway between the two great fiords Hardanger and Sogne, and we are now on our way to the latter. Our host comes into the dining room while we are taking our evening meal, with a string of twenty or more small trout, four or five ounces in weight, which he said it had taken him an hour to catch; but I should not advise anyone who goes to Norway for fishing to stay at Vossevangen, however tempting the house and the fare may be. In our case we had no intention of staying, and an hour or two on the river next morning from about five o'clock, settled us in our determination to move on. Still we lingered about the place rather longer than was necessary, and it was near mid-day when we got our cart. The first station is Tvinde, where is a magnificent fall four or five hundred feet high; here we had a long delay before getting a horse, and it was four or five o'clock before we got away again.

After a drive of a couple of miles, the road began to skirt a charming river. The result may be easily imagined. The angling itch begins to make itself felt, and presently we can stand it no longer, but bribe the boy to pull up, while we see what the stream affords. In a short time I had four trout, then two at once, and by the time we got sight of Vinje, perched on the hill three miles away (the place we had made our destination in consequence of the attractions of fishing), I had twenty. Now, we were by a pool which I declined to leave, though it was beginning to darken, and my friend wanted to get on; so he agreed to take on the traps while I finished my fishing. I could then walk on to the station. The fish I took were not large, but I saw one rise constantly, just beyond my throw, which was larger than his fellows, and I determined to have him. As I threw towards him, my fly was taken once more, but not by my fish; then another trout comes in, but *mine* is still bobbing about there, suckling in everything that conies near him. After many tries I venture to advance an inch or two, pulling up my wading stockings with my left hand so as to keep the water, which is nearly on a level with the tops, from giving me that delightful foot-bath which most fishermen have experienced. Once more I throw with all my force, and this time am rewarded, my trout has taken his last rise and is now madly rushing about the deep pool, in vigorous but fruitless rage. Soon he is on the bank, a nice trout of three-quarters of a pound, not a large one certainly, but his capture was vastly interesting. I gave the lad a dozen fish as he came back, and carried home thirty-two. During the evening I got two together, twice over.

Vinje we found to be a wretched place, beautiful as is its situation. The station is a dirty little hovel with two rooms only, the upper one reached by a ladder from the bare ground, which is the kitchen floor. There was nothing in the house to eat, and no milk to drink, so we had to go to bed supperless. The beds were merely boxes of straw covered by a blanket and a sheet, but I never slept a sweeter sleep than there. As soon as we awoke we began to think of breakfast, and I went down our ladder to see what was stirring. The fire was burning on a sort of stithy, like a blacksmith's, but somewhat lower; there were no bars, and a big iron pot, containing a teapot, was suspended from the chimney—this is the way they brew their tea. Another pan was on the fire with milk in it (we had sent a lad up to the mountains to buy us some), and the old woman and her daughter were devouring one of our fish which had been fried in a third pan. They were busily at work, both eating off the same plate, and without the aid of spoon, fork, or knife. We are told that fingers were made before forks, and these two were evidently in a pre-fork age, diving their fingers into the dish as occasion required. When I stepped off the ladder the woman left her feeding, and taking hold of the frying pan, in which the fish were, spluttering, turned them over with a wooden spoon. Then, finding the spoon rather dirty, she licked it clean, and immediately popped it into our milk to ascertain if the latter was sufficiently hot. I had seen enough of the culinary business by this time, and returned up the ladder a sadder and a wiser man.

The day was thoroughly wet, and we had a long journey before us, so as soon as we could we left the sweet place. The first station is Stalheim, just beyond which is a marvellous cork-screw road, between two fine waterfalls which would delight our good President's eyes to see. From the foot of this road a fine level way runs by the side of a small river to Gudvangen, where is a capital station and scenery of the most romantic character possible. Right opposite the station, perhaps a mile distant, is the Keelfos, a fall 2,000 feet high ; and on both sides of the fiord, at the head of which we now are, the cliffs are from this to 5,000 feet.

From Gudvangen to Lærdal a little steamer generally runs, during the summer season, once or twice a week; but for some reason it was not running at the time of our visit. We were aware of this, and had arranged with two shipmates whom we saw on the road the previous day, to take a row-boat together as far as Frönningen, where we could meet the large fiord steamer. We dined together in the excellent station at Gudvangen, and learned from our host that there was no hope of obtaining food at Frönningen, there being only one house there, and that a gentleman's residence, the owner a very inhospitable fellow, who hated tourists, and had refused shelter even to ladies in a storm. The journey would take us some six hours, but as we should get food on the steamer we could manage without provisions till then. It was raining heavily as we started away; the clouds hung in great heavy masses on the hills, blocking out all prospect, and we were altogether dispirited at the journey before us. Just as we were " shoving off," our landlord came running down to say a gentleman who had just arrived wished to ask if he might go with us; our boat was full, but he would sit in the bow and would be greatly obliged if we would take him in. Of course we agreed, and a large Norwegian gentleman in ponderous mackintoshes made us a bow and stepped on board. He, like ourselves, was out of spirits and sat silent for some time; but after a while the sun shot out as rapidly as the gas is turned up at the pantomime, and with the same effect on the performers. Our four rowers held up their heads and put more power into their strokes; our new friend shook himself clear of his mackintoshes and addressed some playful remarks to us which we did not understand ; all our English tongues became loosened, and we were able to turn our eyes to the glorious scenery we were slowly passing through. It would be idle to attempt to describe this portion of the marvellous fiord. No painter ever depicted it—no panorama could ever hold it By your side the rocks, towering up now 2,000 now 5,000 feet, go straight into the water, which, within a yard of them, would float the largest ship in the world; over on the other side it is the same. Yet, steep as the precipices are, they are not bare rocks, for scanty trees and herbage clothe them wherever a cranny offers support for a root; nay, on the ledges where the eye can see no sign, we are told that human dwelling-places are built, though there is only one break-neck path, and that down to the fiord, from which the wretched inhabitants draw their only means of subsistence. Now and then you get at the foot of the cliffs, a field or two, where the stream which usually tumbles over the rocks straight into the fiord, has made itself a channel; here you will always find dwellings, and probably a plain whitewashed church. But for these occasional signs of man, the place is " as God made it," and such a place as no one can pass through unmoved.

Our rowers kept steadily on, only once stopping to take some bread and cheese, and an hour before the steamer was due, put us on the little landing stage at Frönningen. By this time we were good friends with the last comer, and between Norwegian and German, got on pretty well with him in the matter of talk.

We had nothing to do, and our hour hung heavily, but at last eight o'clock came and we got ready for the steamer; then a man appeared who said it would not come yet—it must be late. Soon it became dark and cold, and we were sick of our position. Some of us tried to go to sleep on the logs, others tried running races along the narrow planks, but darkness put an end to the sport, and all became thoroughly miserable once more. At last a servant girl came down from the house we had long been casting longing looks towards, and an Englishman sug-gested to our Norwegian friend that he should try and get her to bring us some hot coffee. He agreed to help us, and accosted the damsel. She departed and returned, but without the coffee. Again our friend addressed her, and again she returned to the house. Once more we heard her coming after a long absence, and this time, what a reward for our waiting! we were invited into the house. As we entered, we were received by a young lady, who apologised for the absence of her father; but when we saw the table, we thought it as well that the cur-mudgeon we had been warned against should be away. On a dark, polished board were spread all the delicacies that a sub-stantial Norwegian house affords—dried meats and fish, sausages of various sizes and hues, fruits, fresh and dried, wines, and beer. Clearly we had fallen on our feet this time. At the pleasant sight every eye twinkled, and we quickly settled into the places our kind hostess bade us occupy. Every plate was filled, every glass charged— but, as the first mouthful was impaled on our forks there came a hurried footstep on the wooden stairs, and a grating voice bawled in at the open door " Dampen er kom ! " (the steamer is here). These words suggested a particular form of blessing on the interrupter of the feast, which I fear rose to every lip, though politeness kept all silent. There was no help for it; we must go as hungry as we came, and we quitted our Tantalian feast with the best grace we could assume. In miserable plight, and in single file, we marched disconsolately away. Our good hostess gave her hand to each as we left, and received our " tousand tak " with sorrowful eyes, though meth-ought that the comicality of the scene half provoked a smile to her lips, and when the last of us disappeared I doubt not that she burst out, as did we all, into peals of merriment Our jolly friend, to whom we had *nearly* owed so much, screamed in his laughter as we walked down the dark way to our old quarters, and, victims as we were, every One of us joined in the fun as heartily as though we were amused at someone else's expense. From the little pier we rowed out into the fiord, and waved a large lantern to attract atention, Then the steamer came up, looking inmense in the dark distance. On board we finished our interrupted meal, and after a sail of a couple of hours were landed at Lærdal.

As we neared the end of our journey, and again reached a town, we found the portrait of our stout friend in every shop window, and learned that he was Björnsen, the foremost man of letters in the country. This explained the whole of the Frönningen mystery. When we asked him to beg the coffee, he no doubt also communicated his name, which had the " open sesame " effect I have recorded.

Lærdal introduces us to a new district, a new class of scenery, and better fishing. And here, if you please, we will rest; it is a fitting place at which we may break our journey, and when we continue it, I promise you that we shall get more trout than we have so far succeeded in catching.

PART II.-LÆRDAL TO CHRISTIANIA.

Lærdal is a considerable village at the extremity of the fiord, with three hotels; too popular and populous a place for one in search of an angler's "sweet retirement;" and as soon as practicable after our arrival, our little cavalcade of two moved out again into the open, towards Haeg, some two or three stations distant The road traverses what may be termed a pass, of great beauty, through which flows a river, which has to a fisher, attractions almost equal to the beauteous landscape itself. Such a stream is not to be found out of Norway. Its water is as absolute pure, and gleams with colour as bright, as the sky above it; the average width of the stream is some forty or fifty yards, now flowing in deep unbroken current, now constricted by huge rocks to only a dozen yards or so, and rushing through its channel in a bounding mass almost sufficient to rive the very, rocks themselves; then dashed in its uneasy bed by a thousand rocks and boulders, it urges on for a couple of miles, with a roar that will allow you to hear nothing else when you are anywhere near it.

By this glorious river runs the road, all the way from Lærdal **to** Haeg, at one time perched far above it, at another sinking down almost to its level. Where the road is highest, and where a shy from your horse would plunge you over a perpendicular cliff into the roaring waters beneath, your protection from the edge is not a solid wall, but some big stones placed at the edge of the road, a yard apart. Here, your stiff little horse, which rejoices in the situation, is sure to set off at full gallop, and to stay not till he reaches level ground at the foot of the road's declivity, or is pulled up by the next rise. The interest of the situation is even increased by the manner in which your horse is harnessed to the carriole; it is done in such a manner that the breaking of a peg, about as strong as a common clothes peg, would upset the whole conveyance, free the quadruped from its encumbrance, and hurl you to destruction.

As we go along by portions of the river where angling seems practicable, we make enquiry from our boy as to whether we should be allowed to fish there, but are met with an unintelligible sentence in which the word "Smith" inevitably appears. After many tries, we discover that Mr. Smith owns all the fishing hereabouts, but being unable to use his own rod on more than a fiftieth part of it, he is specially careful to keep the whole to himself. See, there on the other side, is Madame Smith, the great man's wife, fishing away like a man ; and after a time, we meet an Englishman, with a salmon rod over his shoulder, whom we take to be the greedy Smith himself, and who gives us much inward satisfaction by informing us that he has found the fishing very bad this year.

Midway between the second and third stations is a little village, Sæltun, where the river is owned for half a mile or so by a native farmer. This length breaks up Mr. Smith's preserve, which is both above and below the village. The farmer is not far to seek; there is a red nightcap by the river side, bobbing about the rocks, which is probably his. As we go down towards the red beacon to enquire, we find the wearer of it busily engaged in the capture of fish—I must not call it fishing. He is stationed over a small but deep pool, a sort of by-wash from the foaming, roaring torrent which the river here is, and being protected by rocks which break the strength of the current, there is a nice quiet eddy, where the salmon, wearied with their boisterous passage up the broken waters, come in to take a rest. Here the red-capped wizened old farmer waits, and as he sees a salmon enter (the water is clear enough to see to any depth), he lowers a great four-barbed fork on a staff twelve feet long, as far as he thinks safe, then gives an awful prod, you see the shaft furiously shaken from below, and up comes a salmon, which the farmer immediately offers to sell you for a " specie " In Norway I have always found that when anything is said to you which you do not wish to entertain, the best way is not to understand it; this is on the same principle that it is sometimes well to be afflicted with deafness, as you are then enabled to refuse to hear applications for subscriptions, and other unpleasant things. So I did not understand what the old man meant when he offered to sell me his fish, for I did not want it. However, he heaped coals of fire on my head by offering to let me fish as much as I liked in his part of the river ; he even went with me while I fished, and asked me to share his meal when the time for feeding came. Oh, that Mr. Smith should know this! At dinner he sat at one side of the table and I at the other, and both helped ourselves from the same dish, which contained a salmon all mushed and jammed together as though it had been prepared with a " peggy," in a" peggy-tub." The wife, who was no less hospitable than her husband, pointed out with her finger, the curd which one only sees in fresh caught salmon, as the tit-bits of the dish. Then I had some drink brought, of a bright canary colour, and had to pretend to drink some, but being a teetotaler I was afraid to take a gulp. If the old fellow would only have turned his head for a minute, I would have slapped the stuff out of the window, and made-believe that I had drunk it, but he was too polite for that, and I had to explain as well as I could that I did not quite like it.

Between this and Haeg the river is a perfect marvel of beauty, and one succession of delights to an angler. On the occasion of my first visit—this meeting with Mr. Red-cap occurred on the second—we made out from bur boy, that a mile or so above Sæltun, where the river stretches out into a wide and gently flowing stream for some four hundred yards, we might defy Mr. Smith, and fish away. The lad seemed to know nothing about trout, so far as we could understand, but assured us that "lax," *i*.e., salmon, could be caught of great size, for he held out his right arm to the full extent, and placed his left hand on the top of the shoulder, to show what we might expect. This set us all (there were three of us) ablaze, and we immediately offered the lad a " mark " to stop and tend the horses while we caught some " lax."

The bribe (Io1/2d.) was sufficient; we bounded from the carrioles and immediately began to put our rods together. My friends, less ambitious than I, put up trout rods, and used smallish flies, but I, anxious alike to try a new rod and to catch a salmon, took out my largest rod and a gaudy yellow fly, about the size of a canary. Before I had fished five minutes I got a trout of a pound weight on this huge fly, and then I fished for some time without success, but whenever I turned my head towards my friends, I found them engaged with trout, so that after half an hour, I could stand it no longer, abandoned my brand-new salmon rod, and took to my faithful, single-handed trouter. My time had come now, and as long as we stayed—it was eight o'clock in the evening when we commenced—I caught trout of about half a pound weight nearly as fast as I could land them. We were obliged to leave in the height of our success, for our lad had become impatient, and though the light held out, as it would all night, it was getting late. Each with a nicely stocked basket, we mounted our carrioles once more, and with the lightest of hearts drove on to Husum, the next station, where we stayed the night. There is a capital house here, and the people, who were in bed when we arrived, made no demur at getting up and cooking us a meal.

In the morning we found the river much too rough to fish ; there is not smooth water enough at Husum even to have a bath in, and our morning tub was taken only knee-deep with the crystal waters swirling around our legs. We sadly wished to go back to our last night's ground, but prudence overcame our desire, and we went onward, towards Haeg. Midway between the two stations, near an old blackened wooden church, of most extraordinary and interesting construction, and said to be a thousand years old (the famous Borgund Old Church), the river is a sweetly rippling stream of forty yards breadth, with pools and streams and scours in perfection. Here we alighted, and sent out traps on by the lad. Our rods had not been taken down from the last night, so immediately we were in the river, and immediately taking half-pound trout. That day is marked in my memory with a white stone; soon I had two great ones on—an event that often happened afterwards—but I only landed one. Before noon came, my basket was quite full of the brightest, cleanest, handsomest, and noblest trout the eye ever looked upon. Then a child from a little wooden cottage by the stream, whom I disturbed at her play, runs away from the stranger, but is coaxed back by the offer of a fish, and I gladly empty my pannier into her little apron, and under a load as heavy as she can bear, she struts back home. There is a fine deep pool here, about which I linger for some time, and soon comes back my little maiden, with a dish of wild strawberries in return for the fish.

A little further on towards Haeg the stream widens out into a lake, by the side of which we walk, chatting over our successes, until we reach the river again, and from this, almost every foot, for four or five miles, may be fished. Once more I empty my creel, this time to a native who speaks English, having been in California, and for the rest of the day he bears us company, carrying and using my landing-net. I gave up fishing before I reached Haeg, for I was carrying my third basketful, and we were all hungry Our new-found companion told us he could take us where the fish were larger than here, and we agreed that after dinner we would set off with him for Breistöl, high up in the mountains, which we did at about ten o'clock p.m., arriving there at half-past two. We had no darkness, but a gentle twilight with a ruddy orange coloured sky overhead for about two hours, and long before we reached our destination it was broad daylight. The good people of Breistöl, like those of Husum, made no demur at getting up and making us some coffee, indeed, everywhere when we came in at the small hours, as we often did, there was the greatest readiness to oblige us.

Norway is not a land to lie abed in, and by six o'clock I walked down to the river for my bath, rod in hand. Before returning to the house I got two fish, one three-quarters, and the other, one and a half pounds weight, and immediately after breakfast one of two pounds, and then I raised one which I had seen playing about in the middle of the pool; this was a good one, and my line flew out merrily, but only to come away again, as soon as the fish stopped running. Thinking to come to him again, I left him alone and went higher up the stream, but one of my friends following an hour after, got a rise from me and the fish at the same time, and killed my trout, a magnificent fellow of two and three-quarters pounds. During the day I was accompanied by our pilot, the Californian, who again used the landing-net for me. Perhaps his English may be taken as a specimen of the current language of California, it was full of oaths and foul expletives, which were uttered with the conviction that they were in perfect good manners. The result was rather peculiar, and after the novelty of the thing wore off, decidedly unpleasant.

We were here in quite another climate from yesterday, the snow was all around us on the bare hills, and the water of the river icy cold. The weather was hot, so hot that I took a plunge during the morning into a lake from which the river flows; but a very few strokes satisfied me. In the middle of the day, when we met together for lunch, my basket would not hold another fish, and I had left my large ones behind, In all I had eighteen trout, and the average weight was thirteen and a half ounces. The afternoon added only three or four fish to the number, the trout refusing to rise as it grew colder. My friends had not the same fortune as I had, but the united baskets were quite large enough to satisfy reasonable mortals. At eleven o'clock at night we got back to delightful Haeg, situated among towering hills and falling waters, and here, had we been wise, we should have spent all the time that our journey over to Christiania allowed us. There is no place along the route I am endeavouring to describe that will repay the fisherman so well as this, where the river is so admirably suited to his requirements, and where the quarters are so good and so cheap. As an illustration of the latter quality I will give my first experience of the place. We arrived, as I have mentioned, in the evening, and had a meal, then drove to Breistöl, and slept a night on the hill top, returning to Haeg the following night, where we took another meal, slept there, had breakfast, and paid one mark, that is Io1/2d. each. But prices are higher now in Norway, as elsewhere, than they were, and Io1/2d. will not go so far as it did. Still it is cheap enough, and if what I have mentioned costs you half a crown, you may pass on and be thankful.

The river immediately behind the Haeg station widens out into a large pool, several hundred yards long, and fifty or sixty wide. At the head, a considerable fall tumbles over the rocks in dazzling foam, and for a long distance the water is charged almost like soda water, with bubbles of air. Here, on the morning after our second arrival, we took our bath. The pool might have been made for the purpose ; at its margin, ten yards behind the house, is a sloping rock, going straight down into deep water, where you may take your header from any height you please, and a few yards below is a little beach where you can walk pleasantly out. A plunge into the soda water, and you soon find that it will be well not to get far out into the current, for even here you rapidly drift downwards, and the broken waters are not far off. After such a luxurious bath as one who loves the water, as an angler should, can never forget, we land at our little beach and lazily commence dressing. What is the luxury of *undress* ? Where is the pleasure in lolling on the rocks unbooted, and clothed only in trousers and shirt? Luxury indeed it is; there is a feeling of liberty about it, a freedom from the commonest restraint of our lives, that is delicious, and makes us linger and linger. As we lie steeping in the warm sunlight, or sit negligently chatting on the good fortune which has brought us here, what is it that we see dimpling the surface of the water, where a few moments ago we, like so many grampuses, were rolling and plunging ? Trout, of course! Fetch the rod; it is there in the house, only a dozen yards away, all ready for use. A cast of the flies goes over the charmed circle; at the first throw a brilliant half-pounder is fast, and in a minute or two, beautiful still in death, is lying on the grass. Perhaps there is another. Out go the flies again, and after two or three casts we have a brace towards breakfast, and by a quarter of an hour has passed, another brace to it. This, too, before we are dressed! Where else is fishing like this ?

Our Breistöl trout came in very opportunely ; a family of English people we met here were delighted to have a basketful, and the people of the house were nothing unwilling. I have sometimes thought that the Io1/2d. paid for our lodging must have been the amount they made us debtors, after giving us credit for the fish we left them.

From Haeg, the road is a steady ascent to Nystuen, where the summit of the hill (the Fille Fjeld), 3,500 feet high, is reached. As we have got higher we have several times seen a curious animal, the lemming, which is not unlike a little guinea pig, and which the natives regard with great aversion. It comes in swarms from the far north, only once in three or four years, and the creatures spread themselves over the high grounds of the south. They travel, it is said, in a straight line, turning neither to right nor left, and establish themselves so rapidly and simultaneously over a district, that the country people say they come from the clouds, and I was gravely assured by a strapping fellow we engaged at Nystuen that this was the case. The lemming seems quite inoffensive, though it barks like a little dog when you assault it, and for this reason the Norwegian name for it is "lom-hund," or "pocket dog." From Nystuen we descend to Skogstad, and then proceed to Tune, reaching the latter at dark; it is a black dismal looking place at night, almost enough to make you afraid. Close by the road-side is a grand lake, called the Little Mjösen, which gleams with a terrible aspect in the almost total darkness. It has grown cold too, and we are glad as we enter the courtyard, to see the glare of a fire. The station is like most of them. There is a large room with bare board floor, bare rafters, and bare board walls. The furniture consists of two beds, two chairs, a roughtable, a dark wooden clothes-press, and a diminutive washing place. But if this simplicity is any disadvantage (and far from that, I look upon it as the greatest addition to enjoyment), it is soon dispelled by the entrance of the evening meal, and then comes sleep, as peaceful as that of the just. In the morning, as I stroll down to the lake for my bath, how mistaken I find I have been in my impression of the place. What a land it is ! How great and good should all those be who live in it!

As I return, the words of the Psalmist rise to my mind with a meaning they have never had before :—" Let the floods clap their hands; let the hills be joyful together." I accosted a lad on my way back, and asked if he knew the height of the hill over there. " Jeed veed ikke," " I know not," he replied, " but perhaps it goes up to heaven." This was chaff, no doubt, but the truth was never so unwittingly spoken.

As I ascend to the station I get the finest view of the scene. The mountains on the other side of the lake, high and precipitous though they be, are no longer gloomy and frowning, but are lit up and gleaming in every shade of purple and gold ; bare rocks tower upwards to the clouds, dark precipitous woods slope down to the water's edge, and here and there a glittering white " fosse," bred of the snows above, pitches over the precipice, or roars down the abyss. On our side of the lake, the road skirts the water as far as I can see, which is no great distance, for a bend in the lake appears to bring it to a sudden termination, and to enclose the landscape in a vast amphitheatre of loneliness,

The landlord of the station at Tune, who is a member of the Storthing, sadly wanted us to stay, telling us of big fish to be got up the mountains, and even saying that bears were to be shot in his fields ; but like the wandering Jew, we ***must*** go on. A gentleman whom we met afterwards some distance further on, told us that the hope of killing a bear induced him to stay at Tune, and he waited out all one night in the hopes of getting one, but he only succeeded in frightening himself almost to death, lest the bear should come and eat him instead of a carcase, which the brute was said to have killed, and which he would be sure to return to devour.

The next stage is to Oylo; the road for a long way runs close to the lake, and the journey is one of the most beautiful of the land stages we have travelled; next came Stee, which we did not reach till afternoon, and being rather lazily inclined we decided to stay the night at. The place, like Tune, is near a lake, into which a river runs, about a mile and a half away. We found a rickety boat not far off, and at about seven o'clock rowed over to the river to fish it. By ten o'clock, when we stopped, we had each a dozen fish of a half a pound and over.

The next journey was to Fagernoes, only a short day again; we reached it at four in the afternoon, and for the first time since we landed in the country, had dinner. The station, or hotel it now is, is a very excellent, and after some of the rough quarters we had been in, luxurious one, but the place is the head-quarters of the flies and mosquitoes of the country. Here they come in their thousands; it is the only disadvantage of the place. But there are advantages to outbalance the plague of flies. The station is again on the margin of a fine lake, surrounded by hills clad from summit to water's edge with fir and birch, a delightful mixture of verdure. A fine river flows into the lake half a mile away, and the fishing is said to be excellent, though I must confess that on my two visits I have not found the trout in the humour. On the evening I am speaking of, I did, however, get one of two pounds, and a few smaller ones.

Next we went on to Frydenlund, where we were informed there was good fishing in one of the two rivers on the far side of the lake, which is one of the same long chain on which Fagernoes is situated. The river is some distance away, and we lost much time on the lake before reaching it, so that it was evening again before we were fairly at work. It rained heavily all the time we were out, and I do not consider that, under the uncomfortable state of affairs we encountered, we gave the place a fair trial. Many fish I know I lost through the wet line sticking to the rod and refusing to run out; however, when we stopped I had twenty-five trout, the largest of them a pound, and the average about the usual one of half a pound. This river is very large, and seems to be well filled with fish, but my only experience of it is the few hours I have spoken of. A friend who has stayed three days at Frydenlund, tells me that he always did well in the river, getting, with smaller fish, a fair proportion of one and two pounders.

This evening's fishing was the last I had, and from what I have seen, it is, I should say, the last good fishing on the Fille Fjeld route; the character of the scenery after this entirely changes ; you have no more high precipitous rocks, roaring streams, or brilliant falls, the valleys widen out until they are miles across, the hills become lower, the streams gentler. There is plenty of water, but though I tried the river at several places, I got only small fry, and as fish of a similar size are brought to table, I think there are not many large ones to be had.

The journey is not yet over, but its interest is in great measure gone. The country we have to pass through for the rest, though beautiful enough, is not to be compared to what we have already seen; and, therefore, with all speed we may urge on to Christiania. There is a choice of several routes, each full of attractions. Those I have taken are, first one by the Mjösen Lake, and on the second journey by another lake, the Randsfiord.

I was singularly fortunate in the time chosen for my journeys. On the first occasion, I arrived in Christiania on the day of the festival of the unification of the kingdom by Harold Harfaager, a thousand years ago. All the town was decorated with flags and banners, all work suspended, all the people in the streets, and at night a display of fireworks was given before the king's palace, and music and dancing enlivened the public squares. With the history of this festival I am not acquainted, but there must be a singular reverence for the past in a people who can celebrate with such rejoicing as we were witness to, an occurrence a thousand years old. I think we should have some difficulty in getting up in England any enthusiam in honour of the deeds of King Alfred.

On the second occasion, when I entered Christiania by way of the town of Drammen, I found there a most interesting exhibition of all the products of the country, from the North Cape to the Southern point, including minerals, skins, timber, corn, harpoons, and even fish hooks and trout flies.

I should mention before closing that from reports I have had from friends who had travelled over the same ground, and also from the experience I have had myself, in the two visits I have made, the trout fishing is somewhat precarious. It is not always so superb, as I found it on my first visit. That visit was made in the month of July, and the season was mild and fine. My second journey was in August, when the weather was much colder, and the fishing very inferior. I found the trout on the second occasion in quite different water to the first, and the spots where I had been most successsful yielded few fish. Still I had such sport as I have never met with in England, Wales, or Scotland. Two friends, who, since my visit, at my suggestion, took this Fille Fjeld route in July, reported only indifferently of. their success ; one, who is an experienced angler, saying he had only got a few trout, and those of no size; and the other, who I fear is no fly-fisher at all, saying he did not think there were any fish in the river, for he never saw any. Still, I can scarcely believe that my friends and I caught the whole of the trout when we were among them, and if another summer I should have it in my power to choose my own holiday ground, I should without hesitation seek the same scene I have endeavoured to introduce to you, and where I had a few days of such fishing as I never had before, and in all probability shall never have again.

THE ANGLERS JOY.
BY W. W.

LET misers hoard their yellow store,
Let sailors tempt the raging main,

Let soldiers wade thro' fields of gore,
Ambitious prize to gain:
Let statesmen plot and courtiers fawn,

Give silly sots their wine;
But give to me the rolling stream,
The rod, the reel, the line.

O, ye who seek in worldly cares,
Content or peace of mind,
Come learn ye from the angler's art,

The bliss you cannot find.
It is not 'neath the gilded roof,
It is not in the hall,
Nor is it in your gathered gold,
The pleasure sought by all.

It is beside the wimpling stream,
Within a peaceful glen,
Where silent nature tempts to stray
Afar from toiling men—

When sailing clouds obstruct the sun,
And dripping showers descend,
Beside a breezy, haunted pool,
Where leafy alders bend.

How sweet, with gliding step to steal
Along the margent green,
Alone, or with a silent friend
At gentle distance seen—
To drop the fly with skilful hand

By stones with moss grown grey,
Where, deep beneath, the eager trout
Awaits his floating prey.

To see, amid the waters brown,
His gleaming sides appear,
And mark him dart, with many a bound,
The stinging barb to clear;
But soon the music of the reel,
Grows slow, and fainter still,
Then tired, reluctant to the strand
You guide him at your will.

Not less the bliss to mark at times,
With eye to nature keen,
Unnumber'd beauties, all disclosed
As shifts the verdant scene :—
The water-craw upon her stone,
With breast of virgin snow—
The heron, from her station scar'd,
With flagging wing and slow.

To hear the mavis from the shaw
Salute his brooding mate,
Or view the dimpling flies that play
Unheedful of their fate.
Wherever strays the willing foot,
New scenes and fairer rise ;
Where'er we look, to bank or stream,
New pleasures meet the eyes.

Fair Annan ! on thy blooming banks,
The summer's day has past,

Till evening hush'd the ruddy scene
In purple folds to rest—
While still I wander'd by thy side,
And drank of joys my fill;
What joys so pure as those we find
Beside a murmuring rill.

THE MIND OF FISHES.
BY F. J. FARADAY, F.L.S.

ASUITABLE introduction to an inquiry concerning the mind of fishes, would be a careful account of Locke's ***Essay on the Human Understanding,*** followed by a consideration of the metaphysical investigations of Kant, Hegel, Coleridge, and the other eminent men who have made the nature and qualities of mind the subject of profound contemplation. For, it is self-evident that it would be advisable, if possible, to know thoroughly our own minds before presuming to express opinions concerning the minds of our fellow-creatures.

An exhaustive analysis of nervous tissue, with a comparative examination of the ganglia of the various classes of the animal kingdom, and a tabulation of the proportions of brain substance in each order, genus, and species, would likewise seem to be appropriate to the task.

A sympathising friend lately suggested that the science of optics ought to contribute much towards the elucidation of the subject. The eye of a fish is a special construction, and the relations of the molecules of water to light are different from those of the uncombined atoms of air My friend illustrated the importance of this line of inquiry by observing that a noted fisher (a member of this Association) is fully persuaded that a fish sees a fly as a spider—and supposes it to be such. The deep philosophy of this suggestion is apparent; for the question naturally arises, supposing that the fish takes a fly for a spider, what would he take a spider for ? The line of speculation thus opened is absolutely infinite, and it is clear that valuable knowledge of wonderful possibilities would be evolved by diligent thought in this direction. We may reasonably assume that, under the conditions of aquatic life, a fish must see things under a different light from that under which we see them, and hence may have a peculiar series of primary ideas. The pulsations of ether which, we are told, constitute the declining light of the setting sun, and the melodies of the musician, all bring thoughts, to us, or awaken them in us. But we are conscious only of a small series of the ethereal waves. What are the psychical effects of those vibrations which are imperceptible to humanity, though possibly sensible to other organized beings ?

The inquiry need not be restricted to physiological examination and physical speculations. Much might be inferred from facts coming within the range of human observation. The writings of naturalists and anglers from the remotest periods of ancient literature, down to these modern days, would probably furnish many anecdotes of the manifestations of intelligence by the denizens of the watery world, which would belong to the border domains where analogies between their experiences and mental processes, and our own, might be perceived. Such a search would doubtless modify our prejudices, and might even yield a rich and surprising mass of testimony, but probably its most important result would be to show us how restricted after all is our scope of observation. Little must be our knowledge regarding the life-history of creatures dwelling in a portion of the world very much larger in extent than that occupied by terrestrial organisms.

But an attempt to pursue these various branches of the subject, with patience and diligence, would be unsuitable to the present occasion. I shall, therefore, restrict myself to a few general reflections attributable to the period when I officiated as curator of the Manchester Aquarium. These may serve to elicit more important contributions to the science of the subject from anglers. For a pursuit so essentially observant, and affording such breadth of opportunity for cogitation, as is that of the angler, should be productive of considerable acquaintance with the phenomena of ichthyological psychology.

It is perhaps not an exaggerated statement that there exists a stronger tendency

to reject the idea of mind in regard to fishes, than in regard to any other living creatures. One gentleman, to whom I have mentioned my theme, has taken it for granted that I shall merely endeavour to produce a treatise in the vein of Charles Lamb's
celebrated ***Essay on Roast Pig,*** while another has candidly expressed his belief that
the notion of intelligence in the scaly tribe can only be associated with mental aber-
ration in the human subject This prejudice has found proverbial expression. Thus,
when a man is known by his friends to be excessively partial to alcoholic recreation,
he is sometimes said to "drink like a fish," a comparison suggesting that a fish is
rather given to sensual indulgence than to intellectual pursuits. Again, if a man's
eyes have the lack-lustre appearance which is often believed to indicate stupidity,
he is said to have " the eye of a fish;" and when an honest attorney has in hand a case
which contains too much principle and too little law, he speaks of it in confidence,
and in a derogatory sense—as being " rather fishy." But if proverbial phrases often
owe their currency to their innate truth, do they not also often merely prove the
subservience of human intelligence to unreasoning wit ? The philosophical angler
is free from vulgar prejudices; his mind is not trammelled by hasty assumptions.
The patient disposition which the experience of many hours spent in watching the
shadows on the water generates, and the knowledge of the frequent astuteness of
his prey, tend to preserve him from conclusions which, in the minds of the many,
are essentially dogmatic, and are, therefore, not tolerable in good society.

It may be contended that the voice of authority is on the same side as prejudice
in this case ; and of this I fear there can be no doubt. The great Cuvier places fishes
very low down in the scale of vertebrate intelligences. He says of them :—

Breathing by the medium of water, that is to say, only profiting by the small-
quantity of oxygen contained in the air mixed with the water, their blood remains
cold; their vitality, the energy of their senses and movements, are less than in mam-
malia and birds. Thus their brain, although similar in composition, is proportionally
much smaller, and their external organs of sense not calculated to impress upon it
powerful sensations. Fishes are, in fact, of all the vertebrata, those who give the
least apparent evidence of sensibility. Having no elastic air at their disposal, they
are dumb, or nearly so, and to all the sentiments which voice awakens or entertains,

they are strangers. Their eyes are, as it were, motionless, their faces bony and fixed, their limbs incapable of flexion, and moving as one piece, leaving no play to their physiognomy, no expression to their feelings. Their ears, enclosed entirely in the cranium, without external concha, or internal cochlea, composed only of some sacs and membraneous canals, can hardly suffice to distinguish the most striking sounds, and, moreover, they have little use for the sense of hearing, condemned to live in the empire of silence, where everything around is mute. Even their sight in the depths which they frequent could have little exercise, if most of them had not, in the size of their eyes, a means of compensation for the feebleness or the light 5 but even in these the eye hardly changes its direction, still less by altering its dimensions can it accommodate itself to the distance of objects. The iris never dilates or contracts, and the pupil remains the same in all intensities of illumination. No tear ever waters the eye—no eyelid wipes or protects it—it is in the fish but a feeble representative of this organ, so beautiful, so lively, and so animated in the higher classes of animals.

This, with more to the same effect respecting the other senses with which we are endowed, constitutes a strong case against the fish ; and it is becoming that we should bow with reverence to the opinions of the great Cuvier. Nevertheless, a few suggestions on the other side will be harmless, and may have a temporary interest and utility.

We do not sufficiently consider how very little we know of the modes of communication between fish, or of the forms of their external impressions and the manner in which these are received. Having had no experience of what living in the water is like, are we not rather hasty in our estimates of what a fish can, and does, think ? Persons who have been rescued from drowning have told us that the mental consequences of prolonged immersion are very peculiar; the memory appears to be wonderfully quickened, and the rapidity of thought is so great, that every past incident of a man's life is vividly realised in a moment. May we not accept this as an illustration of the fact that there *are* peculiarities ? The vision of a fish, moreover, must be very remarkable. It was long supposed that a fish could not hear; there is the old rhyme,

If a fish could hear as well as see,
Never a fisher would there be.

But there is considerable evidence against the supposition that a fish cannot hear. Carp and other species have been taught to come for their food at the sound of a bell or a whistle, and I find in the *Angler in Wales,* by Thomas Medwin, an account given of fishing on the Ganges, where the Hindoo is actually said to attract fish to his net by means of a musical instrument. In his *Harvest of the Sea,* Mr. Bertram says that the oyster-dredgers at Cockenzie keep up a wild monotonous song while the dredging is being carried on, believing that it charms the oysters into the dredge :

The herring loves the merry moonlight,
The mackerel loves the wind;
But the oyster loves the dredger's song,
For he comes of a gentle kind.

My own observations do not confirm their assumed ability to hear. I have often tried to attract the attention of fish in the Aquarium by tapping on the glass, or striking the framework of the tanks in which they were confined, but almost invariably without success; and even when there has been an appearance of success, it has always been doubtful whether the fish have not seen my moving hand, and thus been influenced by vision rather than by hearing. A noiseless wave of the hand has caused shoals of a hundred or more to wheel with the regularity of a column of infantry, but with far greater promptitude, the motion being to my dull perception simultaneous. Dr. Carpenter describes the ear of the fish as being moderately developed, and containing some curious little bones, technically called otoliths. As the processes by which the fish obtains and communicates ideas appear to differ materially from our own, may we not imagine the possibility of his. having abstract conceptions of a somewhat different character from those which are the basis of our rationality ? Is it possible that he has somewhat different mathematical axioms, for instance, from those which are intuitive with us ? Is he acquainted with space of four or more dimensions ?

We cannot realise how a fish can talk ; the notion of conversation in the water seems ridiculous. But the fish clearly does communicate with his fellows in some way which, however different from conversation as we understand it, practically serves the same purpose. Fishers of perch know that there is an end to their sport if they allow one to escape from the hook. If a perch be drawn smartly out of his native element, every member of a party may be successively captured, innocent of evil, and led on by an inquiring disposition (which surely is an indication of intelligence), each fish follows his vanished companions, and falls a victim to his love of knowledge. Not so, should one of the captives return to his companions. By some means he makes his experiences known, and the others, without any positive knowledge of their own, realise the importance of his abstract infor-mation, and disappear from the scene. *We* require for the communication of *our* ideas a gram-matical language; the fish communicates intelligence without the aid of language. Clearly the phenomenon indicates some process which, for want of more accurate knowledge, we may provisionally say is included in the domain of mind, but which appears to lie outside our powers.

It is difficult, if not impossible, to define that which is simply different from anything which we have experienced, We are also predisposed to estimate all pow-ers by our own powers, and to deny the possibility of anything which does not appear to be mentally comprehensible by us. But philosophers are now earnestly inculcating the doctrine that we must assume that much which appears irrational, is not necessarily opposed to reason, but merely transcends the axioms which at present constitute our reason. We are actually Conscious of ideas which seem to represent undeniable realities, and which yet involve an impossible contradiction, and are in fact unthinkable. Our mental organization cannot realise space as having an end, because we immediately ask what is beyond the end ? On the other hand we cannot realise the notion of space without an end; we talk about it, but it has no real meaning to us. The mathematicians find that they have to deal with what they are obliged to call " imaginaries." Commenting on the apparently contradictory results sometimes attained, Dr. Spottiswoode says:—

Suppose that we are gravely told that all circles pass through the same two imaginary points at an infinite distance, and that every line drawn through one of these points is perpendicular to itself. On hearing the statement we shall probably whisper, with a smile or a sigh, that we hope it is not .true ; but that in any case it is a long way off, and perhaps, after all, it does not very much signify * * * * Omitting details as unsuited to the present occasion, it will, I think, be sufficient to point out in general terms that a solution of the difficulty is to be found in the fact that the formulae which give rise to these results are more comprehensive than the signification assigned to them ; and when we pass out of the condition of things first contemplated, they cannot (as it is obvious that they ought not) give us any results intelligible on that basis. But it does not, therefore, by any means follow that upon a more enlarged basis the formulæ are incapable of interpretation; on the contrary, the difficulty at which we have arrived indicates that there must be some more comprehensive statement of the problem, which will include cases impossible in the more limited, but possible in the wider view of the subject.

I venture to submit that in regard to the phenomena of intelligence in the lower animals, it is possible that we require an enlarged basis, a more comprehensive interpretation of the formulae we use. Those profound observers, the Ancients, had a way of getting out of difficulties of this kind by provisionally relegating them to the supernatural. The origin of such a doctrine as that of the transmigration of souls may be fairly held to indicate their recognition of the inadequacy of the significations attached to their formulae, and at the same time their wondering consciousness of the association of manifestations of intelligence with the most varied forms of life.

But let us descend from these transcendental considerations, and direct our attention for a little to some of the evidences of mind in the fish according to our narrow conceptions of the formulae, and the restricted area of our experience. In the average human mind the notion of water has in it something opposed to the idea of quickness of intellect. It is undeniable that outside this Association, the water-drinker is regarded as one whose mental development takes place under unfavourable conditions, and whose ideas partake rather of the nature of instinct than of that fresh originality, that expansiveness, which characterise the mental calibre supposed to be associated with a right appreciation of the juice of the grape. The notion of dilution is opposed to that of force ; the idea of clamminess to that of vitality ; and the feeling of external dampness to that freedom from irritability, and that good-natured temperament which are most congenial to the healthy exercise of the mind. Many persons who came to see the fish at the Aquarium expressed their disappointment at the apparent insipidity of the exhibition by likening the excursion to a visit to see scales and cold water. Such reports were very unjust to the fish. For my part I learned to look upon the odd thousands who inhabited the tanks with something of a brother's eye. Possibly the feeling that the only difference between me and the others, was the fact that I usually had the biggest tank to myself, quickened my appreciation. There is nothing like similar experiences for promoting sympathy and mutual understanding. The season was one of the most rainy for many years past; the tanks round about me were always leaking, and the floor and the atmosphere had a cellar-like humidity. Moreover, there was no prospect but liquidation ahead. But if it be considered that in regard to the subject of the present discussion these conditions, by approximating the tone of my mind to the mental temperature of the fish, tended to exaggerate my esteem for them, it must also be remembered that the fish had compensating disadvantages. I conceive that the tanks must have been found by them vastly inferior to the deep blue sea, or the willow-fringed, mossy-cushioned, and ranunculus or lily-dotted stream. No doubt this had a depressing effect upon the fish; they often looked as though they were attending their own funerals. They were seen under lugubrious circumstances, and must sometimes have found it difficult to keep up their spirits. Still, they seemed to me to succeed wonderfully well, and greatly increased my opinion of their strength of mind.

Decided evidences of memory were displayed ; for at four o'clock in the afternoon, when hungry, they collected about the surface of the tanks, waiting for the hand that fed them. They had no watches, and their appetites varied according to other conditions ; but when they were hungry they did not forget that four o'clock or thereabouts would bring food, nor did they forget whence it would come. They were not always fed at four o'clock; for various reasons irregularities occurred ; but the fish kept their appointments with the keepers. I have seen fish full of fun and laughing, not with the mouth and lips, but with that most kindly and intelligent of all laughter, the laughter of the eyes, which twinkled with overflowing frolic-someness. I have seen a crab caress his lady-love, and with the quickness of thought deal a fierce blow at an approaching rival with the same nipper. I submit that such promptitude of application to totally different purposes indicates precision of idea, freedom from confusion, and clearness of head. I have seen a novel problem also presented to a fish which I have been unable to solve, but which the fish has solved, and in a marvellously ingenious manner. I have also seen fish apparently struck with admiration of human feminine beauty, and if there be any truth in the story that the " heavy, dull, degenerate mind" of Cymon was quickened by contemplating the charms of Iphigenia, does not the presence of similar appreciation in the fish suggest similar responsiveness to educational influences.

From women's eyes this doctrine I derive :
They sparkle still the right Promethean fire :
They are the books, the arts, the academes.

The blenny is one of the most remarkable of organized creatures, and is always attractive from its playfulness. My predecessor at the Aquarium, Mr. Saville Kent, records some interesting anecdotes of this fish, which, he justly observes, fully re-deem the character of intelligence implied by its looks. Mr. Kent describes the in-genuity and faithfulness with which the male fish defended the spawn, on a ledge specially selected, from the greed of the other blennies in the tank. More over:—

While the female was depositing her spawn, an operation which extended over several days, her brave little knight was seen on several occasions to descend to the bottom of the tank, and hurriedly snatching up food dropped there for the public good, return aloft, and place it at the disposal of his lady-love.

Mr. Kent properly cites this as an instance of' attachment, forethought, and sagacity," qualities for which few persons would be disposed to give a fish credit[2] I have myself seen the same fish display liveliness and playful fancy resembling those of a kitten. On one occasion I had some freshly caught blennies placed in a tank from which other fish had been removed. They immediately examined their new abode industriously, and one little fellow quickly espied a crevice about half way up the side of the rock-work, which was almost exactly his own shape, even to the extent of two lateral recessses corresponding to the pectoral fins. He examined this with much interest, bending his head from side to side, like a bird on a rail, and at last fitted himself into it, and looked around with evident pride. Ever afterwards he appropriated this recess. He would retire to it from play, as I have seen a tired child retire to a favourite corner. One or other of his companions would sometimes in his absence steal into his loved retreat, much as I have seen a child take possession of another's neglected doll; but as the owner of the doll, though perhaps not wanting the article at the time, would nevertheless resent such unsanctioned appropriation, so the blenny would leave his play, attack the invader, and, having driven him from the crevice, ensconce himself therein, and with almost a toss of the head survey the assembled company with an expression of countenance which said plainly " This belongs to me." What an immense gulf there is between such spontaneous and erratic fancy, and the forces associated with atoms and molecules! It was the blennies who manifested that appreciation of feminine beauty to which I have alluded. They were generally indifferent to the presence of spectators. On the occasion in question I had the honour of conducting a number of young ladies, pupils from one of our principal schools, round the exhibition. It is necessary to say that the young ladies were merging into womanhood, and were exceedingly good-looking. No sooner had we arrived before the blenny tank, than one of the fish, happening to turn his head, caught sight of the unusual spectacle, and instantly rushed to the

2   In connection with this subject an interesting anecdote has been com-municated by the President of the Association : At Irt Side, Cumberland, near the President's " Fisherman's Home," there is a fine gravel bed, and for some time a number of ducks were seen " rooting about" on this, and trying to reach the deeper parts by diving—no doubt after salmon spawn. One morning the ducks were observed in a state of great commotion, and all but one flew to the bank. The one left was seen struggling in the jaws of a salmon, who, says Colonel Mawson, " was no doubt defending the female during the deposition of the spawn." The captive cluck succeeded in making her escape, but afterwards none of the birds would return to the place.

front. Other blennies, attracted by his sudden movement, turned round and followed, and speedily every blenny in the tank (there were some hundreds in all), was pressing his nose against the glass, and a row of gleaming eyes was seen, expressing such intense and unmistakeable admiration and amazement that some of my fair companions actually blushed.

A remarkable indication of intelligence was given by a large skate, a fish belonging to a species usually betraying little activity. This fish, as you are aware, is of the shark tribe, and has the mouth situated on the under surface of the head, while the sides are spread out into a large expanse of fin. A portion of food thrown into the tank fell directly in the angle formed by the junction of the glass front and the bottom. The fish, which generally lay amongst the shingle, floated to the food and endeavoured to seize it This he was prevented from doing by the position of his mouth and the proximity of the food to the glass; what I may call his snout pressed against the glass so that the mouth could not arrive at the food unless the snout passed through the glass. He made several ineffectual attempts, and then lay perfectly still, as? though thinking. Seeing that the creature was hungry, and having no expectation that he would be able to arrange matters without assistance, I was about to instruct the attendant to change 'the position of the morsel by means of a pole, when the fish saved me the trouble. Raising himself in a slanting posture, so that the head inclined upwards and the mouth became visible, he waved his fins as a duck does her wings when she comes ashore, and thereby created a current in the water, which lifted the food from its position and carried it with perfect precision to his mouth.

The more this incident, simple as it at first sight appears, is thought about, the more remarkable it will seem. It may be said that the action proceeded from inherited instinct; that some remote ancestor of the skate, accidentally placed in a similar difficulty, accidentally discovered the way out of it But this would only remove the problem farther back; for the original skate must have mentally noted cause and effect, and have registered them in the abstract in his physical mind for future use. But do we ourselves profit by such transmitted experience ? Have we not each of us to learn life's lessons for ourselves ? And if this had been a case of transmitted instinct similar to nest-building, would not the ultimate solution have been the first and immediate method adopted by the fish ? The very idea of choice pre-supposes the power of judgment. That the fish immediately in question accidentally attained the result is a quite unwarrantable supposition. There was no indication of accident; there was every indication of deliberation, of abstract pre-figuration of the end to be achieved. It may be said that it was a case of reflex action. If by this is meant the reflex action of the mere machine, there is no analogy; the machine supplied with motive power runs along the rails as ordained by its construction, and if an obstruction blocks the way it does not turn aside and avoid the threatened evil, but continues, even though its own destruction be the consequence. If by reflex action is meant some more occult influence of external conditions on the nternal organism of the creature calling forth a corresponding action which is always of necessity beneficial, and in the interest of the actor, the fish would have just as good a right to say the same of *our* brightest inspirations and most sagacious proceedings. It matters not whether the mind was in the fish or round about it, the action was intelligential.

" The mullet," says Ovid, ' with its tail beats off the pendent bait, and snatches it up when thus struck off." I do not know whether any modern anglers have had experi-ence of this sagaciously cautious act. It is commonly reported, however, in books on fish and fishing, that a shoal of mullet when taken in a net will often escape by leaping over the margin into the open sea. It would appear also that this proceeding is not exactly a case of inherited instinct, since it is usually one daring fish (fitted by nature to command) who leads the way. If he succeeds in effecting his escape, the rest avail themselves of the idea and follow like a flock of sheep going over a hurdle. If the net is too high for a leap the fish will endeavour to creep under it; and failing in this attempt he will carefully examine every mesh in search of a defective place. Mr. Couch records that he has seen a grey mullet, after trying all other methods of escape, deliberately retire to the greatest possible distance from the barrier of net, and then dash furiously at the meshes in an endeavour to break them. This fish has also been known to leap, when hooked, from the water, and fall with its full weight on the line, clearly with the object of breaking it. When captured for the Aquarium, mullet were always exceedingly active, and struggled to the last to effect their escape; but once in their new home they adapted themselves philosophically to its conditions, and became tamer than most other fish, even feeding from the hands of the attendants.

"The pike," says Ovid again, "taken in the net, though huge and bold, sinks down, crouching in the sand which it has stirred up with its tail. * * * It leaps into the air and, uninjured, with a bound it escapes the stratagem." The cool self-possession of this fish, combined as it is with extreme voracity and remarkable quickness of action, has often seemed to me to indicate singular mental control, and therein to present a useful lesson to the human observer. Watch a pike chasing minnows! The apparent unconcern of their existence, until he has one fairly cornered, shows a methodical mind triumphing over appetite. Should his one sharp bite fail to snatch the prey, he betrays no chagrin, but swims slowly round as though nothing had happened, until another opportunity presents itself. There seems to be something allied to the distinguishing qualities of a superior mind in this patient perseverance and freedom from excitability after disappointment.

In a paper read before the Literary and Philosophical Society of Liverpool in 1850, Dr. Warwick communicated a remarkable anecdote of a pike. The author was walking one day near a pond at Dunham, the seat of the Earl of Stamford and Warrington, when he startled a large pike, which, in darting away, struck its head against a tenterhook in a post. The fish rushed about apparently in extreme agony. At last it came to the surface in an exhausted state, and the Doctor succeeded in capturing it, and observed that the head had sustained a slight fracture, and that a portion of the brain was protruding. By means of a tooth-pick he pushed back the exposed portion of the brain, and re-placed the fish in the water. The pike seemed much relieved, but presently it appeared again to suffer pain, and came voluntarily to the side, when the Doctor again took it out of the water, and, with the help of a keeper, contrived and fitted on a slight bandage for the wound, again launching the fish after thus dressing it. On the following day Dr. Warwick again visited the pond, when presently the same fish came to the side, and in the words of the Doctor, "literally laid its head at his feet."

The sticklebacks are nest-builders, and some curious anecdotes are told of their ingenuity in this respect when under confinement. The basse, or sea-perch, is said when hooked to double back under the boat, and endeavour to cut the line against the keel, or it will seek to gain a fixed point in order that it may be able to drag the hook from its mouth. The tame cod-fish pond at Port Logan, Wigtonshire, is well known. Mr. Buckland records some amusing experiences in feeding these fish, which took the mussels from his hands. Such anecdotes of the intelligence and educational capacity of fish might be very greatly increased. But even in describing what has been seen, we must remember how much has not been seen, partly because of the medium in which fish exist, and partly because of the prejudice against their claims to the possession of any intelligence at all. In consequence of the observations which large public aquaria have latterly made possible, opinion on this matter is being considerably modified.

If we are to accept the latest theories of the evolutionists, which in this respect harmonise with the record of Moses, who doubtless learned a good deal on the subject from those sagacious scientists, the ancient Egyptians, animal life originated in the ocean; it is in the water, therefore, that we must look for, at least, the raw material of mind. It is true that the physiological character of the brain of the fish indicates a low order of intelligence, both on account of its smallness and its shape. Of all the vertebrata, the cerebral hemispheres of fishes bear the smallest proportions to other parts of the structure. The brain of the carp is said to be proportionately the largest, and this fish is described by Walton as " a very subtle fish." Dr. Carpenter has the following on the brains of fishes :—

On opening the skull of a fish we usually observe four nervous masses (three of them in pairs) lying one in front of the other, nearly in the same line with the spinal cord. Those of the first pair are olfactory ganglia, or the ganglia of the nerves of smell. In the shark and some other fishes these are separated from the rest by peduncles, or foot-stalks. (A similar arrangement is seen in the olfactory ganglia of man.) Behind these there is a pair of ganglionic masses of which the relative size varies considerably in different fishes (thus, in the cod they are much smaller than those which succeed them, while in the shark they are much larger) ; these are the cerebral hemispheres. Behind these again are two large masses, the optic ganglia in which the optic nerves terminate. And at the back of these, overlying the top of the spinal cord, is a single mass, the cerebellum ; this is seen to be much larger in the active rapacious shark, the variety of whose movements is very great, than in the less energetic cod. The spinal cord is seen to be divided at the top by a fissure, which is most wide and deep beneath the cerebellum, where there is a complete opening between its two halves. This opening corresponds to that through which the oesophagus passes in the invertebrata; but as the whole nervous mass of verte-brated animals is above the alimentary canal, it does not serve the same purpose in them; and in the higher classes the fissure is almost entirely closed by the union of the two halves of the cord on the central line.

Thus it will be seen that the cerebellum, which is supposed to be related to the purposes of motion, is largely developed relatively, while the cerebrum, which is supposed to be the peculiar seat of the intelligence, is scarcely perceptible. The cerebrum is also generally inferior in size to the optic ganglia.

It is true also that the fish is a cold-blooded animal. The heart consists of only two chambers, one auricle and one ventricle, and the circulation is consequently feeble, and is not highly oxygenated. A leading physiologist has lately expressed an opinion that the irrigation, or blood supply of the brain, is possibly of more importance in determining intelligence than the size of the organ itself. As I have before remarked, we are accustomed to associate ideas of sluggishness with cold-ness. This circumstance, therefore, seems also to be strongly against the assumed intelligence of the fish. It is not my intention to lead you into a discussion of these abstruse physiological problems. I may, however, in conclusion, mention some pos-sibly compensating advantages.

Before the fish is condemned as devoid of intelligence, it should be remem-bered how much he accomplishes with very inferior appliances. Let any man con-sider how he would get along through life if reduced to the position of a person in a sack-race. If one of my hearers will imagine himself to be thus bound, I am sure he will feel that under such conditions more than ever would depend upon his intelligence: in other words, his head would become a more important member of his system than before. If an ordinary man were to be hooked by an angler, like a fish, he would be able to liberate himself by means of hands or legs, and he would instinctively use these appurtenances. But the fish, having no such convenient appliances, has to rely entirely upon his wits. How well, even with such manual deficiency, and opposed to constant danger, he succeeds in supporting the burden of existence, sometimes for very lengthened periods! There is an instance on record of a carp maintaining himself for ninety years ; and, as readers of Izaak Walton know, it is said to have been demonstrated that the celebrated " Frederick the Second Pike " lived at least two hundred and sixty-seven years. How many members of our own species, unblessed by early parental training, launched upon the world without education, would be able to support themselves without assistance from the Union or the State, or the charity of friends or relatives, for even the shorter period ?

Observe that, destitute of such vulgar and obvious muscular appliances as arms and legs, and of a large cerebrum, the fish is mainly dependent upon a wonder-fully lively spinal column, which, if not absolutely brain matter, is at least closely akin to such, and upon relatively large optic ganglia, embracing a visual arrangement as yet little understoood, but evidently of singular power. The fish is indebted, therefore, rather to nerve tissue than to muscular or brute force. And as intelligence, so far as we can analyse it, seems to exist largely by impressions of external things, may we not suppose that the peculiarity of its organs of sight enables the fish to dispense with a very elaborate organ for calculation ? That by getting complete and correct ideas to begin with, he has no need for intricate machinery for subsequent sifting and comparing operations ?

And with reference to the coolness of his blood, may not something also be said in the fish's favour ? Experience teaches us that it is not when subject to the impulses of passion and the generous dictates of hot-blooded youth, that the mind is most free and most judicious. It is when familiarity with "the pranks o' mankind" has developed in a man the cooler condition of middle life, and produced in him a permanent average of equanimity,—in short, when he is adapted to the temperature of his environment, that the mind is most clear, calm, and philosophical The fish is always adapted to the temperature of his environment.

And consider finally how favourable are the conditions of fish-life to contemplation. It has been said that the mind is most free and active when it is least conscious of the presence of a body. Supported in a medium in which he is cushioned without corners, which yields with perfect elasticity, and which he cannot feel; capable of transporting himself whither he will by a mere tremor of his spinal column ; what hindrances can there be to the free flow of his ideas ? If Shelley was justified in speaking of the sky-lark as a "blithe spirit," an "unbodied joy," surely the terms are still more applicable to the fish, calmly suspended in *his* medium without even the necessity of using a pair of wings! And think of the time he has for reflection! Does he not often

Under the shade of melancholy boughs Lose and neglect the creeping hours of time ?

I have seen him motionless for hours together, suspended beneath the shadow of a rock, his large eye gazing into vacancy, and I have said, " What *can* he be doing but thinking ?" At such a time may not his thoughts soar, unconscious of the " muddy vesture of decay" which Shakespeare says " doth grossly close us in ?"

And deep asleep he seemed, yet all awake,
And music in his ears his beating heart did make.

Let me add that I do not feel that any of the possibilities alluded to in this disquisition need interfere with the angler's pursuit. So long as the fish eats us whenever he gets a chance, it seems only fair that we should continue to eat him.

ROD FISHING OFF THE ISLE OF MAN.
BY E. G. S.

LIKE many of our pleasures, that of angling is enhanced by anticipation, and by retrospect. What angler, whilst making his way to the river side, has not thought,

" Now I'm sure to get a monster today;" "I know that *this* fly will be a killer, and that I shall make a capital basket," and other equally consoling and flattering things of the same nature? How often has the monster never come, or if he has come, has *gone*?—gone with some six or seven feet of very carefully selected casting line, which you had boastingly said was, " though fine as gossamer, strong enough to hold a horse,"—gone, too, with three of the favourite flies which were to do such wonders. But on some cold winter's evening, in the company of a genial friend, you narrate your fishing experiences, and allude to the particular day when you were " broken " by " that big fish." How you then enjoy the retrospect, your pipe and glass become pleasanter as you conjure up scenes of many days past, and together compare notes until the solitary stroke of the clock on the mantel-shelf tells you that " the wee short hours " have come, and that it is time that you " turned in."

On a lovely evening towards the end of August, I found myself ensconced in comfortable quarters looking over the beautiful bay of Ramsey, and in this bay I purposed trying what I could do with the rod.

Ramsey is rapidly becoming a favourite summer resort for those who like a quiet sea-side place, at which can be had the advantages of fine scenery, capital boating, fishing, and bathing, with reasonable charges. The principal drawbacks are the difficulties attending the landing of passengers. The steamer can only go into the harbour at or near high water, and the passengers have frequently to be landed in boats. This entails considerable delay and inconvenience, as the officials will insist upon tumbling a certain quantity of luggage into each boat. As my party was a large one, the baggage was proportionately large, but ultimately it was all tumbled into the boat, and, on the top of a pile of boxes I was rowed from the steamer up the harbour in a sort of triumph. I mention this because the inconvenience would be greatly reduced if one or two boats were kept exclusively for luggage, and the others for passengers, separate gangways being used. If the matter is taken up by the visitors to Mona's Isle, it is very probable that before long this much-desired change will be made. .

The beauty of Ramsey Bay is so well known that I am not going to attempt to describe it, and shall simply say that, between Point of Ayr, the northerly headland of the bay, and Maughold Head, the southerly point, about nine miles, there is ample room for the fisherman to try his skill. For rod-fishing, the rocks to the south are decidedly the best ground, and my first attempt at sea-fishing with the fly was from the rocks at Port Lewaigue. I cannot say that I was particularly successful. The rocks are some height above the water, and the foothold is not of the best, so that if I had managed to hook a good fish it is a question whether I should have landed him, or he would have landed me—in deep water.

I understand that good fishing may be had from these rocks with a strong rod and line, using sand eel or other bait, but I never tried it, so cannot speak positively. Finding fly fishing from the rocks a failure, I determined to try it from a boat, and accordingly I consulted Looney, who is the principal pleasure boat proprietor in Ramsey. He is engaged in many other profitable undertakings, and by the visitors is regarded as a sort of "enquire within upon everything." Anyone going to Ramsey cannot do better than consult Looney for such information about boating or fishing as may be required, and certainly from my own experience of the ways of that active little man, he will find any information which Looney can give imparted most cheerfully. The end of my conference with Looney was that I engaged a boat for a week, and determined to fish diligently. That afternoon, after hiring a couple of " sea urchins " to row, and having seated my wife com-fortably in the stern of the boat, with the landing net in her care, we pulled off for Maughold Head.

I would advise anyone fishing with the rod on the sea not to fish from too small a boat. No great speed is required,—in fact the boat should just be kept moving,— and the "way" on a moderately heavy boat is much steadier than on a light one. In addition to this the sea sometimes becomes rough in a very short time, and in a small boat this means a wetting, and probably compels the fisherman to make for the shore just as fish may be well on the feed. The boys, of course, are anxious to have a light boat, as it may, perhaps, be a little easier for them to pull (though I very much question this), but for comfort I advise the selection of a boat tolerably broad in the beam, and having, at least, one strake more than the generality of rowing boats are built with. It is also an advantage to take one or two large stones, which, being fastened to a rope by the ordinary timber hitch, with an additional hitch at one side, and dropped over the stern, will act as a drag, and prevent the boat drifting too fast, in case a strong tide is running or too much wind blowing. This device, however, is not often required, if you get hold of boys who will row as they are ordered, but if they won't do so, then the stone over-board is a more powerful argument than many words. The boys I had rowing for me were pretty obedient, so that in a short time we were on the fishing ground, and then, as I had got my tackle into order, the word was " easy all," and the flies were thrown on the water and allowed to trail, for I had determined to try "whiffing," as it is called, until I got to know the ground.

It may not be out of place here to give a description of the tackle which, after many trials, I found most suitable for general sea fishing. It is the common impression that any sort of tackle is good enough. Many times have I seen the amateur angler fishing for "what he could get" with a line something like a signal halyard, at the end of which was tied, in the most marvellous complication of knots, a hook, either as small as he should have used if he had been fishing for stickle-backs in a pond, or else as large as a conger hook, and baited with all sorts of wonderful bait. Even the professional fishermen are no exception to the rule, though now and then you will find one who has been converted and learnt to "fish fine," with the result of making much better hauls than those who insist upon following the old-fashioned method. There is no greater mistake than to use rough, coarse tackle for sea fishing, whether with the rod or the hand line. Doubtless a very large quantity of fish may be taken with any sort of tackle when they are on the feed, but the experience of those who have tried fishing with fine and carefully-made tackle is, that even when fish are not greedily feeding, twice the number may be taken. Sea fish, of course, are somewhat unsophisticated, and have not had the careful training of the wily trout in the Dove or other well-fished Derbyshire streams, but we must give them credit for not being stupidly blind and unable to see a line like a cart rope, or a hook about the size of an anchor, on which has been placed a microscopic portion of mussel or dead fish.

Perhaps the best lines for sea-fishing with rod are the dressed lines manufactured by the Manchester Cotton Twine Company, and I should advise anyone fishing in Ramsey Bay to have at least sixty yards on his reel. I always, when in a boat, fish with two rods, the one a trolling rod, with a moderately pliable top, and the other a strong trout or a grilse rod. The lines should, of course, be of proper thickness for the different rods, that is to say, an ordinary trolling line for the trolling rod, and a fine salmon line for the fly rod. The ordinary check reels should be used.

The trace for the trolling rod I make as follows, and though it may appear somewhat peculiar as to the way in which the leads are placed on it, I feel sure that for sea-fishing it is much the best. In the first place I have the "Field" leads mounted on strong treble-twisted salmon gut or gimp, using only a short length of about three inches, with a knot at each end, and the usual loop. The best way to make this is to make the ordinary casting-line loop (which in this thickness of gut or gimp makes a tolerably large knot), and not to cut the end too short, but to leave about the third of an inch, which should be wrapped with well-waxed thread. It is well to have two or three of these mounted leads of various weights, so that the trace may be altered to suit the state of the tide. One of these leads I put on immediately below the reel line, having first attached a brass swivel to the reel line by a *knot,* and I then attach three feet of treble-twisted salmon gut with loops at each end as before. At the end of this treble-twisted salmon gut I loop on another brass swivel, smaller than the top one, and to it I loop two feet of double-twisted salmon gut, on which I have mounted a *very* light " Field " lead, which is kept on this particular portion of the trace by a *small* brass swivel attached to the lower end. To the lower loop of this small swivel is fastened about two feet of single salmon gut, the hook (a No. 4 Limerick) being tied on with the ordinary gut knot, so as to make a perfectly clean run for the last three feet of the trace. Thus a trace of seven feet in length, gradually tapering from the reel line, to the hook is made. I think it preferable to use tinned hooks, as they do not rust, and are nearly the colour of the bait usually used in trolling.

The reason for using two leads placed as I have explained is this, that the heavier lead close to the reel-line enables you to keep the proper depth, while the light lead three feet from the bait steadies it and ensures much more easy and attractive spinning than can be got by the mere bait streaming behind, ***when you are trolling*** *slowly*. In a variable tide-way, and in sea-fishing, slow trolling is very much the most killing. As a rule the best fish are taken with the troll, and it is a very good plan if fish are not taking well, to spin the bait, by sinking and raising the point of the rod slowly, and so slightly varying the speed and depth of the bait. Some persons advise that the speed of the bait should be varied by an occasional spurt of three or four strokes, but the variation of speed can be attained with so much greater delicacy by working the rod, that I much prefer it.

Undoubtedly the bait of bait for sea-trolling is the sand launce, commonly, but erroneously, called the sand eel, the former being the **Ammodytes Lancea,** and never exceeding the length of seven inches—the latter being the **Ammodytes To-bianus,** and reaching, when full-grown, the length of 12 or 13 inches. The Manx name for the sand launce is "The Gibbon." At low tide they are obtained in great quantities by being forked out of the sand, into which they wriggle to a depth of three or four inches. At spring tides the boys and girls may be seen by dozens at the water's edge, turning up the sand and gathering the gibbons in large quantities; for, not only are they a bait which almost all sea' fish will take greedily, but they are also regarded as a delicacy for the table, and when fried in oil or butter in the same way as whitebait, they are certainly most excellent eating. The natives also cut off their heads, clean them, and dry them in the sun, and afterwards fry them in the ordinary way. They may generally be obtained fresh for 2d. per quart; and of course for bait, the fresher they are the better. Mr. Willcock, in his able and exhaustive book upon sea-fishing, speaks of the killing properties of the *live* sand launce as a bait, but for my own part I never use a live bait, and I do not care to inflict unnecessary pain even upon sand launces. The only advice of dear old Izaak's, which I don't care to follow, is, that as to the treatment of a live frog as a bait for pike, and I always think that the Father of Anglers meant to convey some hint as to the cruelty of this when he carefully pointed out how the unfortunate frog has to be put on. the hook "as though you loved him." Most good fishermen are able to spin with the natural bait, and will, therefore, have no difficulty in mounting a sand launce according to their own particular fancies; but as my remarks may be addressed to some who have never "spun," I will tell them my own way of putting on a sand launce as a spinning bait A single hook properly baited is, to my mind, much more convenient than the most elaborately got up triple-hook, with lip-hook, tail-hook, and all the usual paraphernalia of spinning baits, and equally killing. Of course it must be remembered that I am speaking of trolling for sea fish; but having tried all sorts of arrangement of hooks, I may add that I now never use anything but a single hook, and I find that with it, properly dressed, I seldom miss striking, or landing, my fish. The hook should be passed through the sand launce from right to left just behind the eye, and then a turn should be taken and the bend of the hook passed through the back of the bait from left to right about an inch below the eye, so as to leave merely about half an inch of the barbed end of the hook projecting from the side of the bait. Before passing the hook through the back of the bait, the sand launce must be "gathered up," so as to give it the least possible curve. If these instructions are carefully followed the bait will spin so as to look like a bar of burnished silver, and will prove most attractive to nearly all sea fish.

If sand launces cannot be obtained, a very good substitute is a scar about four inches long cut from the side of a mackerel, and if this bait is used it is an advantage to have a small lip-hook wrapped on the gut about two inches above the ordinary hook. This plan may also be adopted if any difficulty is experienced in mounting the sand launce in the manner I have explained above.

Artificial spinning baits may be used, but though I have tried several I have not found any of them answer so well as the sand launce, whilst the danger of the triple tail hooks catching in the tangle or seaweed is much greater than if a single hook is used ; and I know from experience, that when strong tangle is caught by the spinning bait, the chance of recovering it is only small. A good imitation of the sand launce can be made by lashing about six inches of small india-rubber tubing to your hook, one inch of the tubing being left whole and slipped over the shank of the hook, and the remaining five inches being composed of the tube divided into two halves by cutting longitudinally with a sharp penknife. A little twist given in the cutting will cause the artificial bait to spin very fairly. This is a very economical bait, as, of course, by taking care in cutting the tubing (which may be bought for about sixpence or eightpence a yard), seven inches of tubing will make two bait— one inch at each end of the tubing being left untouched to form the head portion to be slipped over the shank of the hook, and the remaining five inches in the middle of the tube being divided across diagonally, will of course give five inches of tail to each bait. If the angler desires to try other artificial bait, he will have no difficulty in obtaining an almost endless variety at any good fishing-tackle makers, but the bait I have mentioned are, in my experience, the simplest, the cheapest, and the best. *Experto credo.*

I must now explain the tackle used on the fly rod, and also the flies which I found most killing. The ordinary flies for sea fishing may be obtained at most fishing-tackle shops, and are generally dressed on Limerick hooks of various sizes. The wings are composed of white goose feathers, or white and red feathers with bodies of white or red wool; but many other variations may be made on these with advantage. Any half-worn grilse, sea trout, or salmon fly may be used, but the fly which I found the most killing was one which I had dressed to my own pattern. It is dressed with rather large wings of goose feathers, dyed the brightest possible yellow, and the body is made of scarlet wool wrapped round with a little bit of gold tinsel. It is a very showy fly, and after trying it in all sorts of weather, as tail, middle, and bob fly, I can, without boasting, say that in whatever position it was placed, it was taken in preference to any other of the established pattern flies, by three fish out of every four that I caught. So great a success was it that at the request of many anglers in the Island I gave the pattern to Miss Linton, Market Place, Ramsey; I have also given it to Mr. Mitchell, of Market Street, Manchester, from either of whom the flies may be obtained. For anglers who dress their own flies, I would simply say that these flies, and, in fact, all sea flies, should be dressed on salmon gut. The trace for sea fly-fishing should be about seven feet of strong salmon gut. If you are likely to have much casting it is better only to use two flies, and it is an advantage to place a moderately large split shot at the head of your tail fly in order to sink it a little, as few sea fish are taken quite on the surface of the water. If, however, you are "whiffing," or trailing your flies, you may use three, but they should not be more than a foot from each other; in fact, in sea fishing I think you can hardly have your flies too close together. There is one fly called the " shaldon shiner," which I hope to try for myself, and which is described by Mr. Willcock as "a kind of imitation of the dragon fly. The body is as thin as possible, being nothing but flattened silver wire, a small brush of scarlet feather or the tail, a little green, blue, and red dubbing out of an old Turkey carpet for the shoulders, and bright blue wings, to which add half a dozen fibres of goose feathers in front. With this, fishing at the mouth of a river, harbour, or in the pools just inside, you will probably take a sea trout or two, or even a salmon, particularly if you fish at the beginning of the ebb tide. Make it on a '9, '10, or '11' hook. In the Taw and Trowbridge estuary at Instow, North Devon, the fly in use is made with white and grey feathers and a silver body, and with this, great sport is frequently obtained." The fish taken by the rod in Ramsey Bay by the fly are mackerel, pollack, and coal-fish ; and by the troll I have taken rock-cod, sea bream, and wrasse. The whiting pollack, which is known in the Isle of Man as the " calig," is a fish which affords great sport, and may be got on the coast weighing from a quarter of a pound to eighteen or twenty pounds. It is called in Scotland and on the north coast, the " lythe," whilst the coal-fish, known in the north as the " saithe," is by the Manxman called the " bloggan," and has been known to attain a weight of thirty pounds. Both these fish are to be taken off rocky ground, and over the large beds of tangle near the shore ; and as they are strong, and struggle hard, they afford plenty of sport It is necessary to use a gaff to land a " calig" or " bloggan " of above seven or eight pounds. A cheap gaff may be made by filing down the point of a large conger or bonita hook, and lashing it to a stout wooden handle of from two to three feet in length.

Amongst the first things that a sea fisherman has to do, is to get to know the situation of the rocks and beds of tangle, the set of tide, and other matters of the same sort. This knowledge he will gather by an hour's quiet chat with the local fishermen, who, over a pipe, will in the most obliging way give all the information they can. Let me, however, point out that Manxmen are a fine, hardy, independent set of fellows, who do not care either to be chaffed or condescendingly patronised, but who never hesitate to take any amount of trouble to assist those who ask it in a manly, straightforward way. I have visited the island for many years, staying there sometimes for weeks at a time, and in no part of the United Kingdom have I found greater civility or kindness.

The situation of rocks and tangle beds, most of which are to the south of Ramsey harbour and town, is soon learned. There is one large rock, called "The Carrig," about a mile and a quarter S.E. from the harbour, and about half-a-mile from the shore, which was some years ago the scene of a wreck, some of the timbers of which now lie at the bottom of the sea, close to the rock. It is covered at about three-quarter tide, but when the top is. visible it may be considered as a good fishing ground. This was the first place that I tried, and I had not been fishing many minutes before I rose, and struck a " calig." A few more fish were taken, but, as they were small, I determined to go still further south, and fish about fifty or sixty yards from the rocks. Accordingly " the boys " bent to their oars, and away we shot from the Carrig to Table-land point. I was fishing with two flies to one rod, and to the other an artificial Devon bait, and I may as well say that with the latter I only took one fish (and that a very poor one) during three hours' fishing. As we rowed away I let out more of my fly line, and shortly had my reward, for I felt a tremendous pull, and the line ran off the reel at lightning speed, " Easy, boys," and whilst my wife reeled *up* the trolling line I played my fish, which was making the rod (a strong two-handed green-heart rod of Farlow's) bend in a way to try the temper of the top piece. My trace was one which I had used for trout fishing, so I had to humour my fish, which for ten minutes or so seemed to be making for every point of the compass. Foot by foot I got him in, and, as my wife sat ready with net in hand, there was a great splash, and I saw that there was more than " a him "—there were two fish on. Short work it was to bring them up to landing distance, and the net being quietly put under them, two exceedingly large mackerel were taken out of the water and dropped into the boat. The ten minutes' playing those two mackerel on somewhat fine tackle was as good a bit of sport as I ever experienced, and to such anglers as have not fished for mackerel with the fly and rod, I can only say " Do so once and you will do it again." "Pull on, boys," and after a short time the music of the reel again was heard, and a fair-sized calig was soon in the net. "We've overrun the mackerel," I exclaimed; "Pull back, and let us try for another." This was done, and after taking two or three small calig, we got amongst the mackerel again, and soon had a few good fish. As we now had got a first-rate appetite to enjoy our freshly caught fish, and the afternoon was pretty well over, we pulled ashore, and so ended my first day's fishing. The description of my afternoon's fishing so acted upon my friend Urmston that he arranged to go with me the next day. He had been out with me a day or two previously, fishing for trout in the Sulby River, but without any great success, and he looked forward to having much greater sport with the calig and bloggan than he had been able to get with the wily trout. By the advice of Looney I took some " gibbons " with me in order to try a change, for I determined to fish in every way I could until I found out the most killing method. We had the same boys with us as on the previous day, but I found that one strong young fellow would manage the boat very much better than two boys, and I afterwards took " Robert," whom Looney recommended, and whom I found one of the handiest and most civil young fellows that ever got into a boat.

Our second day's fishing was a decided improvement on the first, but we did not get a single mackerel. We got a good number of fair-sized calig, and at last my friend, who was using the "gibbon," whilst I was using fly, got a tremendous pull. "That's either a good fish or tangle," I exclaimed, but on easing the boat we soon found that it *was* a good fish. Urmston's rod and tackle were light for the work, and the fish had to be played very carefully. However, patience is a useful virtue, and after some minutes the broad yellow side of a fine calig could be seen gleaming in the water, and before long an 81b. fish was safely basketed. From that time Urmston became an enthusiastic rod fisher, and I was convinced that though with the fly a larger *number* of fish might be taken, *the big fish* were only to be tempted with the gibbon.

Here is a piece of advice for anglers: When fishing from a boat never be induced to take with you a friend who is not either fishing himself, or thoroughly interested in your fishing. If you do so you will find most probably that just as you are getting on grandly, your " passenger " will complain that his " legs are getting cramped," or that " the seats of the boat are dreadfully hard," and ultimately that " he wishes he could get ashore." Of course you have to put him " ashore," and in so doing lose perhaps an hour of the very best state of the tide. My remarks may appear ill-natured, but I can speak from experience that a non-fisherman is about the most unsatisfactory company you can have on a fishing boat, Another piece of advice which I again give is—learn the ground *thoroughly*. A rocky shore varies so much with the state of the tide, and so much good ground may be fished at half water during a flood . tide, which it would be useless to go to at ebb tide, that the trouble of getting to know the ground thoroughly is more than repaid by the extra success in fishing, whilst the annoyance of getting your spinner or flies caught and broken in the tangle may be avoided. I may say that half ebb is about the best time for pollack fishing, though the half flood tide is nearly as good.

Perhaps it was my feeling with regard to " passengers " to which I have given expression just now, which induced me, one glorious day early in September, to start off about three o'clock in the afternoon, taking only "Robert" with me to pull the boat It was a day I shall long remember. There was hardly a cloud in the sky, and the sun was shining with dazzling brightness on a sea literally as smooth as glass. Certainly it did not seem a very promising day for fishing, but I had determined upon a plan of operation which, though an experiment,' I hoped might be crowned with success. " Now, Robert," I said, "let us try the Carrig, keeping a good way out, and row slowly round, gradually getting nearer in." " Well, sir," replied Robert, " you mean to try them properly to-day. Them Mr. L.'s were out all day yesterday. There was three of them at it, and they got over three dozen, but none of them very big." (I should here say that my rod-fishing had induced some other visitors to try it as well.) " All right, Robert, we'll see what we can do, but it's not a very likely day." I have explained that the " Carrig " is an isolated rock, round which there is good pollack fishing. We went slowly round the rock, and so clear and smooth was the water, that looking over the side I could see every leaf of the tangle slowly waving below, and now and then the fish darting about or "hovering" like lazy well-fed trout in a pool. "Not much good to-day, Robert, I fear; but let us try another round a little nearer the rock." Quietly, with hardly a motion of the oars, Robert kept the boat slowly moving. I fished, as usual, with my trolling rod, baited with the "gibbon," out on the starboard side, which was the side farthest from the rock, and consequently in the deepest water, whilst I fished the water nearer the rock with my fly rod "whiffing," as it was too smooth to cast. I got three or four of what Robert called "humbugs" with the fly, and was just inclined to leave when the reel of my trolling rod. made its well-known music. "That's a proper fish, sir," said Robert, and so I found it, for, though I had a strong rod and strong tackle, I had hard work to keep him from getting into the tangle. A big pollack, when hooked, sometimes comes to the top of the water with a rush, but more frequently he makes a run of from ten to forty yards, and, unless checked and got well in hand, will get down into the tangle and "thread the needle" amongst the tough stalks, when you and your fish will very soon part company. I had got to know the ways of "the critter," but this "proper fish" took out some fifty yards of line in his first rush, the greater portion of which I took back as soon as possible, and then he sulked, and, hanging like so much dead weight, refused to be moved. " Pull away from the rock, Robert, and slightly towards the fish," I said; and this order being promptly obeyed, I got on better terms with my fish, and had the boat in a position for checking the rushes which he would probably make towards his harbour amongst the tangle-covered rocks and old timbers. At length ' he moved, and rapidly too, but I had him well in hand, and after checking some half dozen vicious rushes, I saw the side of a fine fish gleaming brightly in the water. He was a pollack of ten pounds weight, in magnificent condition, and certainly had died game.

I then determined to carry out a plan which I had formed of fishing the little creeks and crannies at Maug-hold Head, and so rowed quietly a couple of miles south from the Carrig to another detached rock called the " Stack," On my way I got one or two more fish,including a nice rock cod of about four pounds weight. As I have before stated, Maughold Head is the headland which forms the southern boundary of Ramsey Bay. It is composed of wild crags and rocks, which in some places rise to a considerable height, and there is deep water up to the very edge. Under the shadow of the rocks was the place I had determined to fish, as I knew that it could only be fished on a perfectly calm day. If there is any wind there is sure to be a sea running at one side or other of Maughold Head, sufficient to try the seaworthiness of a boat and the muscles of the rowers. However, this day there was not a ripple. As we rowed along about ten yards from the rocks, the cormorants, which were sitting in scores on the ledges above, would tumble into the sea or scatter oft over the water as fast as they could go. The scenery was grand in the extreme, but I had not full time to admire it, as my attention was pretty well taken up by the rods. I had three hours' fishing along these rocks, and had finer sport than I anticipated. On one occasion I thought that I had "a monster" on my fly rod, but it turned out that I had three fish, one on each fly. Luckily for me, that on my bob fly was not a large one.

The others were good fish, and, on landing all three, which I succeeded in doing, I found that they weighed together about nine pounds. Just as I landed them, a sea bream of about three pounds was taken by the gibbon, which had got a good deal too deep in the water, so that I had variety in my fishing. "We are going to make a rare fishing of it yet, sir" said Robert, and sure enough we did, for I took fish with the fly very rapidly. Such as were small I threw back into the sea, trusting that they would profit by the lesson, and remember that certain yellow or red flies had stings in their tails. As we were going slowly back over the ground which we had been fishing, I struck a big fish with the troll. "Another good one," said I, for the rush was that of a strong fish ; but suddenly he stopped, and in a second or two afterwards away came the line, leaving the hook and gibbon behind. " How's that, Robert ?" said I, for I had been treating the fish "tenderly." "Conger, sir," said Robert, " there's a many of them hereabouts, and that's just a conger's trick." And so I fancy it was, for when I reeled up I found that the gut had been bit clean in two. The damage was soon repaired, and before I gave up that evening, many another good fish was in the boat. As the last rays of the sun sank in the west we pulled straight away for home, and, on our arrival at Ramsey beach, we counted the " basket." I found that in about four hours I had killed thirty-one fish, and returned to the sea about a dozen more. The thirty-one fish weighed nearly one hundred pounds. After taking one or two for my own use; the rest were borne away by Robert, who, in a sort of triumphant way, upon wishing me "Good night," exclaimed, " They'll have hard work to beat that fishing, sir." Such was my experience ; for though I was out several times afterwards, and had very good sport indeed, I never had so large a take of fine fish. One rough afternoon afterwards I got some very good ones, the largest of them a pollack, in splendid condition, and measuring nearly a yard long, but my calm afternoon's sport with Robert was such as a man cannot expect to have often.

If in this paper I have been somewhat egotistical, I would, by way of apology, remark that angling anecdotes must of necessity be of a personal character, and that a fisherman's advice, to be of any practical good, should be confined to what he has tried and found to be of service. I have done my best to make my instructions clear, and I can truly say that whatever I recommend I have tried and found to answer; and that this paper has been written with a wish that it may not only afford an hour's amusement, but may be the means of giving many an angler as good sport and keen enjoyment as I derived from rod-fishing off the Isle of Man.

A CONGER STORY.
BY EDWIN WAUGH[3].

"I GUESS thou'll not remember thi uncle Jonas ?" " Well, I can just remember him, Robert;' but it's as mich as th' bargain." " I dar say. . . . Him an' me wur particular friends. We had a rare do together i'th'Isle o' Man once, twenty year sin. There wur thi uncle Jonas, an' me, an' Jone o' Simeon's, th' bazzoon-player. Jone had a wood leg, shod wi' iron. We o' set off together to th' Isle o' Man ; an', when we geet theer, we went straight across to a place co'ed Port Erin, at th' west end o' th' islan'; where there wur very good fishin'; an' it's a terrible place for conger eel, an' o' sorts o' big fish. Well; one day we took a boat, an' a boatman, an' we went out a-fishin' i'th' bay,—wi' strong lines, an' great hooks, ready for aught that coom. An' while we sat theer, danglin' th' lines o'er th' edge o'th' boat, thi uncle Jonas began a-jokin' Jone about his wood leg. ' Jone,' he said, if this boat happens to upset thou'll float lunger than me.' ' How so ?' ' Thou's so mich wood about tho.' 'Well, but,' said Jone, 'I think thou'll ston as good a chance as me—if I have a wood leg ' How so ?' ' Because thou'rt so well timber't at th' top end.' But while they wur agate o' their fun, thi uncle Jonas felt a great tug at his line. ' Hello!' cried he, what the devil's this ? Come here, lads !' Th' boatman went and geet howd o'th' line. 'Aye,' said he, ' this is a conger ; an' a big un, too! I hope it'll not break th' line! By th' mass, how it tugs! Gently! It's a big fish is this ! Let him play a bit! It's comin'! Eh, what a mouth ! Ston fur! Here it is!' It wur a tremendous size; an' as soon as we'd getten it o'er th' edge o' th' boat it flew fro' side to side, snappin' savagely first at one, then at another on us. 'Look out!' cried one. 'Punce it!' cried another. 'It's a devil! cried another. 'Mind; thou'll upset th' boat! Heigh, Jone; it's comin' to thee! look out!' Jone took aim at it with his iron-shod wood leg ; but he missed th' fish, an' sent his wood leg

3   Mr. Waugh, though not a member of the Anglers' Association, was kind enough to send the above humorous sketch before publication, to be read at one of the " Evenings," and has further increased the indebtedness of the Anglers to him, by allowing them to add it to the present volume.

slap through th' bottom o' th' boat, reet up to th' knee. 'Theigher!' cried thi uncle Jonas ; ' thou's shapt that grandly, owd lad !' ' Poo me up!' cried Jone; ' Poo me up, some on yo; I'm fast!' 'Howd; stop!' said thi uncle Jonas; 'thou munnot tak thi leg out! We's be drown't!' ' Drown't or not drown't,' cried Jone, ' I mun ha' my leg out o' this hole!' ' Thou mun keep it where it is, I tell tho, or else we's ha' th' boat full o' wayter in a minute 'An' how long am I to cruttle down here,' cried Jone, ' wi' my leg i' this hole ?' Then he gav a sudden jerk, an' he skrike't out louder than ever, 'Oh, poo me up, this minute!' 'What's to do now?' 'Th' conger's getten howd on me beheend ! Talc it off!' An' sure enough it had getten fast howd o' th' soft end of his back,—and theer it stuck. 'For pity's sake tak it off!' cried Jone. 'Oh; don't poo so hard; let it get loose of itsel'! Prize it mouth oppen! Oh! I cannot ston this 1' ' It's no use !' said thi uncle Jonas,' it'll not let goo!' ' Then cut it yed off!' cried Jone; 'an' poo ashore as fast as yo con,—I'm bleedin' like a cauve 1' So we pood ashore as fast as we could, wi' Jone's leg stickin' through th' bottom o' th' boat; but when we were gettin' near lond, Jone's leg coom again a sunken rock, an' snapt reet off close to th' boat ' Theer,' said Jone. pooin' his stump out o' th' hole, 'thank God for that,— sink or swim! Now, then, tak this thing off my hinder end!' So wi' much ado, we manage't to cut th' conger oft, close to th' yed; but th' yed stuck fast to th' owd lad's breeches when done. An' thi uncle Jonas had to carry Jone on his back fro' th' boat to th' alehouse, wi' his brokken stump, an' th' conger's head hangin' beheend him. An' when th' folk at th' alehouse seed us comin', they shouted fro' th' dur-hole, an' axed what luck we'd had. ' Luck!' said Jone; 'look at th' back o' me, here! I've had a bite, if nobody else has!'"

AN OCTOBER DAY AMONG THE GRAYLING.
BY DAVID REID.

THERE is probably no river, in these times of polluted streams and close preserves, offering such advantages to Manchester anglers as the Derbyshire Wye. This lovely water, and the vale through which it flows, are indeed difficult to surpass. Salmon fishing has its triumphs: and to wave the wand o'er some northern stream, capturing the speckled beauties in Nature's wilds, and breathing the invigorating air of the moorland and mountain, is also glorious ; but these are more difficult to obtain. On this water both the possession and the opportunity are within the reach of us all, and a quiet day amongst the graceful grayling here is a treat that stands by itself.

The Wye extends for our purpose from the fine old town of Bakewell to the village of Rowsley, about four miles by road, but by the river-side probably twice that distance. It may be described as consisting of two nearly equal parts, Haddon Hall marking the division. These may be spoken of as the upper or semi-artificial portion, and the lower or natural river. In the upper part (for the purposes of irrigation and the improvement of the fishing) art has been most judiciously employed in banking up the river by means of weirs, the result being most satisfactory, especially from an angler's point of view. Here will be found those long silent reaches which appear to be a peculiarity of the Wye, and in which grayling abound. The lower portion comprises broken water, high banks, and deep pools, and is rather the home of the trout than the grayling. The whole of these waters are fishable if a ticket be obtained either at Rowsley's famous old inn, the "Peacock," or at the sign of the " Rutland Arms " at Bakewell.

Of Haddon's classic vale, through which our water meanders, a word must be said ; for I take it that a true angler and worthy disciple of our common master is also a true lover of the beautiful in Nature. Visit the Wye at whatever season you please, the valley will charm you with its beauty. Though on our October day the emerald brightness of spring is not to be seen, and though the golden sheen of summer is gone, yet the autumn tints are there ; and though the birds of summer have departed, the watchful heron and ever-wary wild-fowl will keep us company. The fair landscape will fill us with rapture— winding stream, fertile plain, wooded copse, hills crowned with verdure, and, closing in the scene, the time-honoured towers of Haddon. Are you an angler-naturalist ? The wealth of insect life (your quarry's food) that swarms around, will reward your thoughtful gaze. Are you with antiquarian thoughts imbued ? The shades of the mighty dead from far past feudal times will accompany you in your musings, or more honoured still, the form of Dorothy the Fair may glide in imagination by your side, and shew you how to become "a complete angler."

This water is a proof of what careful preservation will do. The stock is assisted by artificial breeding so far as trout is concerned ; the grayling have to look about for themselves. From Bakewell to Rowsley there is not only always a fair amount of fish, but in some places the river is comparatively full. Of the takes of fish, I have it on credible authority that in 1874 a gentleman, then residing at Bakewell, took out of this river, between January and December, upwards of twelve hundred fish ! Of ordinary takes I have also proof of thirteen brace of fish in one day followed by eleven brace the next day. On good fishing days, given all the essential conditions, six to eight brace may be averaged. And what fish to be sure! Bright, silvery, and beautiful to behold—fish well brought up, in fact, highly educated, I promise you; fish that will test your skill, both to hook and afterwards to basket. I need scarcely add that upon this water there is nothing allowed but fair fly-fishing ; no ignoble death to these lordly fish by vulgar worm or treacherous minnow ; no vile grub, or bait of any kind. These October fish must be taken only by the fly and " with brains, sir."

As regards flies, the small hackles, red, dun, and black of an angler's book ought to be good killers always, and provided they be good hackles, and used by a work-man, I do not doubt that they will hold their own against the local flies. The local flies, however, are beautiful specimens of the fly-maker's art. Many anglers may hold fast to the famed bumbles, and believe that they are the best all the year round. I do not go so far as this, but, unquestionably, they must occupy a foremost place in every angler's stock for Derbyshire fishing.

My own cast, an " all the year round " cast, is a small-winged dun for point; first dropper, a dun bumble; second dropper, the little Derbyshire red; top dropper, the stone midge. This cast I use as a standard. Of the excellent qualities of the small black fly (the stone midge) I have only recently been made aware. I use for point-fly, in early spring, a large dun ; in March there is nothing like it I remember well my astonishment when first told of this on the Wye. The take in one day in spring was eight brace of the finest grayling; and this on a non-rising day, as I thought. I vary the cast in summer by using for a point-fly, either the dotterill hackle, the sand-fly hackle (the corn-crake of the north), or the small yellow-winged dun. These three flies represent that numerous class, the duns and browns that cloud a summer water. The colour and the fine, silky, sensitive hackle that is on them are the attractions. This cast is not only used by me on the Wye, but on Clyde and Tweed I have found them very satisfactory; and in September I used with success the dotterill and sand-fly for a sea-trout cast at Galway.

As regards the procuring of flies, Mr. Ogden has an agent at Bakewell, Mrs. Shenton, who keeps the toy shop in the Square. It is well to look at the stock; many a good idea may be picked up by so doing. Mr. Hensberg also, the civil and obliging keeper of the water, who lives in the ivied cottage on the hill (a good fisherman and ever ready to help with a word of counsel), has always a stock of suitable flies.

When on the stream, begin at the first weir-pool below the bridge. Mine host of the " Rutland " says it contains more fish than any other pool on the river, but as to catching them—that is another matter. From this pool down to the stepping stones, near the rookery, there is about a mile of water of the choicest kind—a stream slowly gliding over gravelly shallows. Be particular to fish the deep silent pools at the ends of the shallows. Leaving the first pool, you come successively to the second and the third weir, then comes the mill stream junction (where is a glorious shallow), next, the island, with its swim, and then the rustic bridge pool. All these are good places, and this description thrice repeated will apply to almost all the water from this point to the stepping-stones, where, in the course of a couple of hours, we will suppose you have arrived with two or three brace of fish in your creel. The catch of thirteen-and-a-half brace before-mentioned, was chiefly taken out of the water we have now passed. From this point to Haddon the river widens considerably, the water becomes rougher, and the pools are larger and deeper. By some fishers this part is considered the cream of the water, and by the time the angler arrives here his success for the day is pretty clearly indicated. The holds are many, and the fish plentiful, and such as delight the angler's eye.

Again, be sure to try the pools. These constitute one of the peculiarities of this stream, and it is casting on these that proves what the fisher is capable of—all the art he possesses, the finest casting, the most delicate tackle, the longest throws are required[4]. If the cast be clumsy, there is a splash, and all is over—these Wye fish will have none of you. But if the contrary—a stream of silvery light glances, and a thrilling tug that goes to your very marrow is your reward. Then, angler! ply him skilfully, and deal with him tenderly, "as though you loved him." Thus, on and on, refreshing yourself from time to time under one of the fine old oaks that adorn this water side, while the music of the stream soothes you with its sweet melody. If accompanied by a brother angler, all the better; here you will compare notes touching your experiences, and of " the fish you might have caught." There are some losses and disappointments in life anent which speech is useless; but you moralise about the fish nevertheless. Possibly, a snatch of melody will be interposed, your companion taking up the burden; or queries may be asked concerning the brethren of the angle who passed you during the morning with friendly nod and cheery Compliment. Who was the rosy-cheeked angler with slouched hat (covered with casts of flies), rough coat, and superb meerschaum ? Ah! he can throw a fly deftly, and 'tis said he is a rev. Canon of a Cathedral in a great manufactoring city, and well-known for his urbanity and good fellowship. He may be seen wending his way to a certain railway terminus with grave aspect and trim attire; but, once here, away goes the cleric! and out comes the angler. And that other well-built, cheery Englishman, who had the fight with the big fish which you helped to land—know you not who he is ? One who deservedly stands high in the esteem of his profession, and well-known amongst our city's best men ; in all probability he has this morning ministered to both mind and body's ailments. Heavy be his creel and light his heart! And those other two, surely they are from the big city ? Right again—one from Imperial cares relieved, the other from moving a world by his pen. " The best of all good company" meet here ; divines, statesmen, philosophers, the professional man, and the honest tradesman.

---

4   The very fine pool at the end of the island at the rookery is a most excellent hold for fish. A member of the Association had once a famous catch here, viz.: one small boy. The little fellow had a narrow escape. It was all but over with him, but, fortunately, he was landed, and the joy of the angler when restoring that lad to his widowed mother in the village far surpassed the pleasure afforded by even the heaviest creel of fish.

Thus, having refreshed yourself with an angler's lunch, you make another start with wrist in good trim, and the determination that no more misses shall be yours. Now, also, the fish are settling down steadily to their work, and so you angle on and on, over pools and deeper rapids than before, by rushing currents beneath overhanging banks, again and again adding to your pannier and losing also many a prize. Angling under the bridge at Haddon, perhaps bright eyes may be watch-ing your movements, and merry criticisms, in which even the jackdaws will seem to participate, may be freely bestowed. Of course you will lean your rod against the yew-tree hedge, and rest a moment at the old cottage under the ivy-covered porch, where a last rose may be still blooming. And you will taste the cup of barley wine, and afterwards angle on until the day is declining, and your last fish is taken near Vernon's embattled towers, now gilded by the beams of the western sun. And as you gaze upon the hills, you will pleasantly remember that they are the barriers that hide the classic Dove, whose stream Cotton, the father of us fly fishers and old Izaak's dearest friend, fished, and you will be thankful for another good day, feeling the truth of our master's saying, that " God never did make a more calm, quiet, and innocent recreation than angling."

Several peculiarities of this water have arrested my attention. Firstly, with reference to fishing up and down stream. Why it is, I do not know, but fishing down stream, throwing long and fine lines, seems to be the right mode on the Wye, so far as grayling are concerned. My experience is certainly in favour of this mode, and I have conversed with old fishermen whose experience corroborates mine. Is it that the unusual clearness of the water and the keen sight of these fish require that the angler should use a long line ? Is it not possible also that the grayling at times love to take a fly considerably under the water and floating down the stream ? I have also wondered again and again why fish do not rise well here, save in clear, low water. It is perfectly surprising to an angler to come across a splendidly clear, though full, high water, and have no sport. Again, the condition that ensures good sport on other streams, namely, when the river is clearing after a flood, seems here to have entirely the reverse effect, no rising taking place at all; and when, by chance as it were, you do hook a fish, it is basketed without a struggle, as if it were sick, its behaviour resembling that of a trout hooked in mid-winter, or after spawning. The only reason I can suggest is, that it is possible the road-washings which enter the river, and which contain a large quantity of lime, affect the fish. If the water is in a milky condition, it is indeed a sad state of things for the angler. If this reason be the right one, it will partly account for the fact of the best fishing being when the. water is low and clear.

Should the fisherman be so unfortunate as to meet with the conditions referred to, he should put on two large bumbles (or, say, the dotterill fly), stand at the head of a deep pool, and sink and work the fly exactly as in fishing for salmon. Possibly these flies have a resemblance to insects creeping on the bottom, and hence tempt a fish or two. This a hint from an old fisherman ; I have tried it, and found it to be successful.

An October day amongst the grayling may be followed by an October night round the hospitable board of the " Rutland." The very mention of this calls up visions of delight. What tales of adventure by flood and fell! what fraternal interchange of experiences! while music lends her aid, the calumet of peace is enjoyed, ambrosial pleasures abound, and the spirit of our Father Walton prevails.

NOTE
ON THE GRAYLING AND THE POLLAN.

BY HENRY SIMPSON, M.I). The author of the foregoing paper having had his attention called to the large quantities of so-called "grayling" which appear on the slabs of the Manchester fish-dealers in the autumn, was at first under the impression that these fish came out of the Derbyshire rivers, and was consequently somewhat alarmed with regard to the prospects of his favourite sport on the Wye and kindred streams. Further inquiries, however, elicited the fact that the "grayling" of the fishmongers are obtained from Loch Neagh in Ireland. Specimens of the fish in question were obtained from the Fish Market, the dealer admitting that they were "pollan" or "powan" in Ireland, but "grayling" in Manchester. Specimens of the

Bakewell grayling were also obtained, and likewise a fine grayling caught in the Dee by Mr. Eaton, and the whole were submitted to Dr. Simpson, who furnished the following note on the subject :—

"There- is a certain amount of superficial resemblance in the silvery look of the pollan to the colours of the grayling; but it is not borne out by close inspection. The scales of the pollan have not the glistening nacreous sheen of those of the grayling, and they are browner—as if sprinkled over with brown dust. The pattern formed by the coalescence of adjoining scales is different in the two, and the lines along the side are more distinct in the grayling than in the pollan. The latter has not the pear-shaped, or, rather, perhaps, the lozenge-shaped eye of the former, nor the large and very remarkable dorsal fin which distinguishes the grayling. Both belong to the *Salmonida,* and possess therefore the small adipose fin; but while one is of the genus *Salmo,* the other belongs to the genus *Corcgonus.* One takes various baits and the fly boldly, while the other, so far as I know, is only obtained by netting. One is a river and the other is a lake fish, and both are well worth cooking. No doubt many of the members of the Association have noticed the extreme brittleness of the grayling as compared with the trout if the neck be broken on taking them out of the landing-net."

FISH OUT OF WATER.
BY CRABSTICK.

I WAS, one May, spending the week I have hitherto been fortunate enough to get for the 'I spring fishing, at Crook, by the Tweed, with three old friends—Selborne, Dunn, and Black. We were, except Selborne, hard-working anglers, doing our work with a will, and giving as good an account of ourselves at the day's end a here and there one. Selborne we chaff, and say he is lazy, though we know that is not the word that describes him, for when we return at night, with baskets laden as best we have been able to load them, has he an empty creel ? How many a botanic prize, that our otherwise-occupied eyes have overlooked, does he not haul admiringly forth ! How many winged creatures, that have been invisible to us, do his bottles not contain ! How many pebbles, in which his eye sees beauties unknown to us, as his tongue recounts them in language to which we know no approach, has he not brought home! How many birds has he not observed, how many animals watched? Nay, how many things Selborne has done that we have not done, let us no further enquire. I only know that at night, though his creel is the lightest, his heart is probably the happiest, and his head the wisest.

Well, on the evening in question we are all seated in the cheerful coffee room at Crook, anxiously waiting the advent of our dinner, when two "objects," about the last to be looked for here, are observed on the highroad, slowly sauntering hitherward. " Good gracious:" cries Dunn," two swells, as I live." It was true, they **were** swells, of the first water, and as our dinner comes in they enter the room. They have velvet cut-away coats, faultless trousers, patent boots, spotless linen, sparkling rings, whiskers, and mustachios—the latter trimmed to the utmost nicety—and hair carefully arranged with a straight, clear parting running from the middle of the forehead to the back of the neck. One is dark and the other fair, but they both have the touch-me-not air which, as a well-known and illustrious author says, " is more easily imagined than described." How intolerably mean and shabby did my rough frieze jacket and my long stockings feel! How I hid the latter away, like the mean sneak I felt myself to be, at the sight of those faultless breeches! All of us seemed, like Adam and Eve, to have become suddenly aware of our nakedness; but we soon rallied, and after the soup had disappeared, brave old Selborne even ventured a remark on the weather, and succeeded in getting a somewhat indignant reply from one of the two whiskerandos. Nothing daunted, he plied them again, and by the pastry came had made such progress, that he positively asked them if they had come there " a-fishing." At this question I blushed my deepest red, Dunn put his napkin to his face, and Black opened eyes and mouth in amazement. Fancy these exquisites come a-fishing! It is poor, rough, common people like ourselves who go fishing, not pomatumed and perfumed tailors' models like these. Poor silly Selborne, we did not take you for such an ignoramus ; you might as well ask if they have come butterfly-catching like yourself. Selborne got no answer,—how was it to be expected, he would ?—but seeing a hesitancy in the aspect of the darker swell, he asked, regardless of our digs under the table and our winks and gestures above it, if they were fond of fishing. "Yaas, vewy," said one, and they sauntered out of the room as magnificently as they had entered it. " I knew they had come here to fish," said Selborne triumphantly; but *we* knew better, and that they had only made this answer to get rid of his importunity. "Well, you'll see to-morrow," said Selborne, " who's right"; and then we dismissed the swells from our minds, and fell into the pleasant conversation that is only to be heard at an anglers' inn.

Next day we were out early, as usual, but Selborne said he would wait about a bit; and wait he did, till the noble swells descended, or condescended, I might say, to take their breakfasts. Then Selborne, with his book, sat him down on the low stone wall in front of the door, under the shade of the trees which were just coming into leaf. At about eleven, our velveteens appeared, arrayed as yesterday, more gorgeous than Solomon in all his glory. Rods were produced (they were really going fishing) all glittering with brass and varnish, and Selborne says (and he is to be believed) eighteen feet long at the least, and of the description labelled in shop windows, " general rods." Reels and lines come next, and there is a discussion what is to be done with them, but at last, after many tries, they are fixed in their places, and the lines run through the rings. Then come—what ? Hair lines ? No. Flies ? No. Long gut casts? No; floats! floats painted green and white!! This was too much for poor Selborne, and with a howl of despair, he seized his own rod, which was leaning against the porch, and rushed down to the river. At night, Whisker & Co. were in the same faultless dresses, but their spirits seemed somewhat damped. " Well, how have you gone on ?" said Selborne, " much sport ?" " Aw, we've done pretty well; we've sent our fish off to London." " Have you really, now ? How did you get it all carried ?" was the reply.

This was too much, and with a savage gesture, and something that sounded like " low fellows," our gentlemen walked away. We saw no more of them. They did not enter the room again that night, and we were out long before they came down the next morning; but when we returned, we learned that they had followed their fish.

ANGLING IN THE IRWELL:
A RECORD OF MEMORIES AND HOPES.
BY EDWARD CORBETT.IS

TIS sixty years" since, when in my early days, the idea of railway travelling yet undevelopedand the fouling of streams comparatively infrequent, my angling facilities were limited to a few ponds near home, where, with frequent catches of the beautiful stickle-back,' or Jacksharp, we had an occasional prize in the form of a dace, or a Prussian carp perhaps two ounces in weight. The report of such a catch was sure to bring a gang of fishers to that pond. As to river-fishing in those bye-gone times, it was what salmon fishing is now to the trout fishers of Manchester, a thing to be thought of, and possibly to be had some day.

The Bolton canal was a stage in advance of the pond fishing. I have seen a row of ten or twelve men within easy-speaking distance, -each earnestly watching his three or four rods with hair lines and quill floats ; one of them perhaps with a silk line and two lengths of a very superior and costly article called gut at the end. These with wasp-bait, or worm, or maggot (gentles we did not know), were successful in catching a few dace, gudgeon, and eels.

But old traditions of some ten or twenty years then gone, told of good fishing in the Irwell. We heard of the time when fine salmon were caught opposite the New Bailey—itself now no longer "new' but a vanished structure,—and we are told of many trout and other fine fish that had been common. Fisherman's Rock in Hulme had its history of wonderful catches. But all these accounts were for a time—say about the years 1820-22—tales of what had been before the gas-waste was put into the river.

About the year 1819 I have, from the New Bailey Bridge (now called Albert Bridge), watched the fish on the shoals at the lower sides of the piers, and seen innumerable fish both there and at the packet station near the old barracks (then opposite the New Bailey). These were chiefly gudgeon; but other fish were seen rising to flies, and so numerous were the flies that the air was lively with swallows and house-martins; and the " Old Quay boys " used to stand on the bridge and whip them down, with a long, heavy, short-handled whip, adroitly throwing the lash so as to kill the poor birds. It was a favourite amusement for us to count the swallows' nests along the Salford Crescent, and there were two or more in every window of the cotton mill at the river side opposite the New Bailey. There are no nests there now to be counted.

Some ingenious man found out that gas-tar would make a cheap black paint, and instead of its being put in the river it began to find a use, and by-and-by was actually sold for money—a great result in those days.

I have seen the river so covered with gas-tar (the varying tints of which were somewhat admired as they passed), that no real water-surface could be seen. But we heard of the offence given by this tar to the once famous Warrington salmon, and to the sparlings which used to be brought thence. These fish became scarce, as the use of the new light caused increasing defilement, and ultimately they disappeared. The demand for gas-tar was not equal to the supply, and, therefore, a larger quantity of gas refuse was put in the river—gas-tar, gas-lime, ammonia water and all, went in.

About 1824-6, gas-tar ceased to be an unsaleable article, the river was less polluted, and the fish began to show (especially above town). We school-boys spent part of our holiday times in going up the river from Pendleton, and trying various favourite spots with carefully prepared bait; and generally we were so far successful as to bring home from six to twenty fish for two of us. We usually went in pairs, furnished with maggots by Robert Ackerley, of Hope Tower, Salford, and with lines and hooks by Peter Sharratt,- Postmaster, Windsor Bridge, One favourite spot was half way between Douglas Mill and Agecroft Bridge, where the water from certain works came into the river from the Bolton canal. Here we generally caught one or two "shoalers."

These shoalers I believe to be the " graining." They are a fine fish of good flavour, like a herring in size, form, and colour, and not so broad as a dace, nor so thick as a chub. They are described in Webster's Dictionary as "Graining (Leuciscus Lancastrietisis), a small fish found in England and Switzerland." We caught them in the rapids generally; the Clifton Aqueduct, the channels in the rocks for half a mile above, and the outfall of sundry tunnels from coal mines and other places, being favourite spots. We often caught dace and chub, but seldom large ones.

The beautiful reaches of river beginning with the approaches from Pendleton by the footpath from Brindle Heath, near Douglas Mill weir, with the high lands of Irlams-oW-Height on the left, the sweep of Scar Wheel on the right, and the ancient racecourse site and buildings at Kersal Moor above; the broad quiet river before and the footpath through the meadows to Agecroft Bridge, mantled with ivy; steep rocks with trees on the eastern bank, forming a back-ground to the picturesque Kersal Cell, with its broad meadows; the whole crowned by the woods of Prestwich and the high lands of Stand ; these form a picture fresh on the retina of memory, though more than fifty years have passed since it was first, and frequently presented to me in all the varied tints of the season. The yew trees of Kersal Cell grounds, budding all over with their spring shoots of light green, backed by the older foliage, gave me my earliest ideas of the beauty of these evergreens. I had only seen them in their darker tints. It was only then that I began to find that not only yews, but many more evergreens, had more than one tint and more than one aspect in the varying seasons.

Agecroft Bridge was then a favourite study for painters, and the bridge was one well worth seeing either from below or above, from the west bank or from the east, the west bank of the river giving us a different class of prospect from that seen on the east. Broad meadows on the left; noble trees on both banks; the Hall (Irwell House when Squire Drinkwater lived); and the hill-sides covered with trees. There were no boards about trespassers to be seen, nor even a notice saying," This beautiful land on sale for building plots." Here was the broad rock on which we often spent an hour, and tried it on all sides; in shallow, in deep, in swift, in slow, in sun or in shade, always with patience and hope, and generally not without some finny prize.

A little higher up the stream we had steep rocks for some distance on both sides, and many favourite pools, runs, and shallows in the stream ; and then we came to the Bolton Canal Aqueduct. Above this, for about half-a-mile, we had again many beautiful views; not much varied except by the trees, the river course being very straight; but at the half mile, on the western bank, there came a very fitful stream from a tunnel through a steep rock, with a descent of some three or four feet to the river. In the eddies of this stream, and at its margin, we spent many hours and caught many fish. It was a sort of Rubicon, seldom passed, though sometimes we stretched our courage to go to the famous Ringley Weir. The tunnel was a wonder. Where did the water come from ? Why did it not always come ? These, and many similar questions puzzled us. One day, six of us had worked our way from the first rapid at Agecroft to this place.

Having had little or no success below, in the* numerous places tried, we had made a push to get here. Arrived, we found, instead of a rushing stream and a foaming waterfall, a mere trickle from the tunnel mouth. It was proposed that as there were no fish to be caught, and no water was in the stream-bed, we should explore the latter. So away we started into the dark tunnel, feeling our way with our bundled-up rods. Step by step we went, in single file, for such a length as seemed to us near a mile (really nearly a fourth of that distance), during the major part of which we saw before us a slight gleam of daylight. This itself was a puzzle, as we knew well that we were going towards the high lands of Clifton. We arrived at length at the southern end of the passage, and found ourselves at the bottom of a deep shaft or well, full of curious and inexplicable machinery, made chiefly of oak Long we looked at it to make out what it meant. Many years afterwards we came to know that it was a means of drawing water out of the Clifton coal-mines, the machinery being worked by the water of the river from above Ringley Weir, and the whole having been designed and constructed by the well-known Brindley, the engineer of the then famous aqueduct at Barton-on-Irwell. On that memorable Saturday afternoon we got a spattering of knowledge of this place, and it came in company with a great rush of water that soon began to flow into the tunnel by which we had arrived. We, of course, beat a retreat, going back more rapidly than we came ; but it took so much time that the water, which had not come to our ankles in our "up journey," wetted us above the knees during our return. We gladly welcomed the daylight as we arrived at the river side. Four of the six retreated all the way home, frightened, and indisposed to try more fishing. Myself and one companion tackled up again, and before we left caught several fish. The river, in those early days, was seldom seen by us beyond Ringley; but above, it had many beautiful lengths. All are now marred by some of the many uses to which the river side is devoted. In later years, I have seen many other parts of the river, and certainly few streams have originally been more varied and beautiful than our Irwell and its tributaries.

Even at this day, with a little license of omission of shafts, mills, and other works, or by taking the prophetic view of some eminent men and replacing the above-named objects with broken walls, ivy-covered roofs and shafts, with other such poetic arrangements; and improving off the rocks and trees the perpetually recurring grime of continual smoke, clothing the dead branches with verdure, and putting in a few anglers fly-fishing, the lover of the picturesque may yet find miles of beauty full of precious " bits," or broadening into grand views of lake, river, and mountain. We call the lakes " razzervoirs," and the mountains are "nobbut hills," while the river itself is but an open drain ; yet in a ten miles' walk from Manchester to Bolton (by river nearly twenty miles), or in a five miles' walk by the brook-side above Bolton to Turton, or by Wayoh and Bradshaw Brook to Entwistle, or from Prestolee to Bury, or from Bury to Haslingden, or branching off towards Tottington to Holcombe, or from Rochdale up the valley by river instead of by rail to Shaw-forth, or along others of the numerous tributaries, the artist may find such combinations of river, road, rock, and ruin, with back-grounds of hills and trees, as will give him years of work for his pencil. With such skill as an architect is required to apply in restoring a ruined old cathedral or monastery, he might paint back the views and produce a Lancashire of a century ago, or possibly a century hence, styling the picture " View on the Irwell, 1780 " or " 1980," according to his fancy. The river and its tributaries are really yet worth exploring, even in search of the picturesque, and many a fall, and turn, and rapid, give such views as only require the conversion of the stream itself to purity to become eminently pleasing.

This chief defect, the impurity of the water, is, however, now so perceptible, not only to the eye but also to the nose, that it would be advisable for our seekers of pleasure in this district to provide themselves with some of the preparations of carbolic acid, or with some other good antiseptic, before inhaling for any length of time the odours of these tributaries.

It has not been my fortune to explore the banks of the Dead Sea, but a sad sight it must be if it exceeds in deadness the sight I once had of the Irwell when engaged on professional work. I had to go in a row-boat from Manchester to Runcorn by river, or by "cut" where the navigation is shortened by canals; all along there was evidence of the direful effects of the polluted condition of the stream. There was scarcely a blade of grass or a bunch of rushes near the river itself; and only such trees as were high enough above its banks to keep most of their roots out of its reach, and luckily so placed as not to be destroyed at the top by chemical fumes, had preserved their leaves and lives. Excepting these, a very few rats, and now and then a melan-choly-looking sandpiper, who, no doubt, kept to the river side, not from choice, but from family tradition, with an occasional lock-gate keeper, and those few others of the genus *homo* and genus *equus,* who earned their living in connection with the navigation, there was not a thing with life to be seen. Indeed, the navigation itself is almost destroyed by the persistent river pollution, so many tons of rubbish being put in, that the dredging is a very serious and almost overbearing cost.

One of our greatest treats in my boy-days was to walk down to Mode-Wheel lock, there to meet the packet-boat, sail down to Warrington or Runcorn, and buy some Eccles cakes at Warrington. Returning by the boat the same day was some-times practicable, but more frequently we had to return by one of the Liverpool coaches, which placed us nearer home at Pendleton. On these packet-boat jour-neys we always, or nearly always, disturbed some angler who was fishing from the towing-path ; though, of course, fishers were more numerous on the bank where they were not likely to be disturbed.

It would require many journeys now to find one man fishing in this stream. Even the mouth of Glaze Brook, once famous for its bream, has lost its prestige; and only the Mersey and Bollin retain at their outfalls sufficient purity to keep eels and gudgeons alive.

About 1825 I became acquainted with practical fly-fishing, and made flies that caught fish. They were generally a sort of hackle, made of a starling's breast-feather, with a body usually of black silk, but occasionally a little scarlet wool. The first knowledge I had of the effect of this wonderful art of fly-fishing was on seeing a man with two flies, at work where a stream was coming into the Irwell, about one hundred yards below Agecroft Bridge. He caught almost at every throw, and often brought two fish to his basket. He caught some forty while I stood by, and told me he had over a hundred ; they were about two ounces each in weight—shoalers, dace, roach, and a few chubs. Of course I was converted to fly-fishing, but I generally kept a reserve of requisites for bottom-fishing, and pursued my way, with or without one or more companions, as far as Ringley Weir-hole. There we generally caught some fish, and at sundry places on the way we had more or less success ; often bringing home ten or twelve fine fish, either graining, chub, or dace; occasionally only gudgeons and minnows. When the others would not rise, and we had to try the bottom, we did not refuse the loach. Sometimes we got an eel, and sometimes a perch. I have often seen the bottom-fishers with a good lot of eels; and once I remember a man showing me a fish which, from memory, I estimate to have been about three or four pounds weight; I think it must have been a bream, but its silvery-white scales looked too bright for that dull fish. The scales were large-sized, and the man called it a salmon ; I did not, but it was a fine fish, and he had caught it in Ringley Weir-hole, within an hour of my seeing it. I went to Ringley Weir-hole at once, and after a patient trial of about two hours, was rewarded by a settled conviction that there was not another fish like the one in question left, and that it must have eaten all the little ones. Yet it was not a pike, or a trout, or a grayling; it may have been a chub.

The last time I went to try the upper part of the Irwell I saw the only pike I ever saw in that river. It was about twenty yards below Agecroft Bridge, and I was on a small island of sandy gravel. The fish was about the size of a herring, and swam round me, looking as if it was seeking food. I caught no fish that day. I think it would be about the year 1830. I had before this fished and caught fish in some other streams, notably the Irk at Crumpsall and Blackley, the Medlock at Ardwick, and the Derwent at Rowsley. On a day kept as a fête day on account of the passing of the Reform Bill, some time late in 1832, I went with a companion to fish in the Mersey below Irlam. We caught very few fish; but we saw some ten or twelve men at various favourite holes, each of them with a good dish of fish beside him, some twelve or twenty in number, very uniform in size, and mostly dace about as big as herrings.

This is the last of my remembrance of fishing in the Irwell, but I had previously seen and caught fish at Mode-Wheel mill-tail, at the Crescent, Salford, the weir below the Crescent, and various other places. Perhaps about 1828 I saw a man catch a trout nearly two pounds weight at the mill-tail below the Crescent, Salford, and I once met a man with six trout caught in the Irwell, at the foot of a small streamlet near Kersal Moor; but I never caught a trout in the river myself. I knew by sight an old man who got his living (according to his own account) by fishing in the streams around Manchester. I once saw him at Agecroft, fishing above the bridge, and he had two or three eels. I had some confidential talk with him, and found that his basket was more frequently weighted with hares and rabbits than with fish, and that fishing was with him only a cloak for poaching. About the year 1840 a salmon was caught, nearly dead, above Warrington ; it was about eighteen pounds weight. The latest Irwell fishing I have known was about 1850, when some people used to fish in Peel Park. They caught some fish, but I do not know the species.

And now for the future of the Irwell. There have been put into it, as refuse, several materials which, with the progress of science and invention, have been found capable of better uses, and of these I will name a few. Gas-tar was put in ; it now sells for thousands of pounds per annum, and forms the basis of many important trades. Ammonia-water was so wasted, and it is now sold and used. Gas-lime was also freely put in the river before a better use was found for it. Cotton waste was put in—I have seen the river white with this material; we have now a group of traders called cotton waste dealers, who have an Exchange of their own. Dye stuffs have been redeemed from waste to a large extent, but they yet form a great portion of the river's pollution. Soap has been very largely put in, and in some cases profitably kept out and converted into fine tallow candles and alkalies. Metallic and chemical refuse, coal, ashes, and cinders are yet thrown into the river. And last, though not least, the valuable article called sewage is still put into the river, to an extent causing a loss, in my belief, of more than a million pounds a year to South Lancashire. At Wrexham, and many other places, it yields a clear profit to the sewage farm of more than £10 per acre per year. The increase in the revenue of land so improved in South Lancashire, to the extent of twenty miles by twelve, would exceed a million a year, and the sewage of the town would improve such an area very materially, without nuisance from over-irrigation. Science has so far advanced as to show that it is profitable to keep sewage out of the rivers, and legislation must proceed to prevent the abuse of the water-ways of the country. Then we may hope that the Irwell will again be a bright stream with trout and other fish in it, swallows and other birds over it, patient anglers not disappointed of sport beside it, and the poisoned area along the whole length of the stream restored to its original atmospheric purity. Smoke may be as effectually done away with as other wastes have been. Then we may hope also for other improvements not so remotely connected with these as may at first sight appear; and as the filthy gas-tar has given us the beautiful aniline colours and the valuable carbolic acid, so other wastes may be utilized, until everything is put to its best use; and finally, through the operation of the much-despised utilitarianism and trades' profits, we may arrive at the highest attainable pitch of civilization, when our towns will be lively with vegetation, our streams replete with fish, the air resounding with birds, and ourselves living well-spent lives in a well-governed country.

These thoughts of ancient and of future times,
Rouse my old fancy till I think in rhymes.
Great changes have been, since my boyhood's days !
Oil lamps and candles gave our brightest blaze !.
Wells, pumps, and running brooks gave water clear!
Baths, little known, town's water scarce and dear,
Coaches and packet-boats our locomotion
On roads and rivers, sailing ships on ocean,

Our news from Hamburg taking weeks to come,
East and West Indies full six months from home !

Changes may come ; our streams be all reformed,
Our lights electric, every house well warmed,
Gas-fuel, water, time and power laid on,
Sweetness and health brought home to everyone,
Our towns all smokeless, and a nation freed
From soot and dust the " great unwashed " succeed !
Our hills and mountains' beauteous lakes and streams
Be rills and fountains fit for poets' dreams !

Some time ago, 'twas about " 'forty-four,"
When my dear father's age had reached four score,
I said, " If my life should extend to eighty,
I hope to catch a trout, or small or weighty,
In Irwell, twixt the Bank Mill and Mode-Wheel,
In a pure river, where 'twould spin my reel."
I live, and have lived, in an age of wonders,
Each one arrived at through a stage of blunders.

Our once pure Irwell, now a stream of ink,
Is one black blunder which should make us think.
Science must work, when carelessness is rife,
And change each foulness to a spring of life.
The filthy gas-tar now has glorious sheens,
In dyes of beauty, classed as anilines ;
Gas-lime now brings to lands increased fertility,
And, turned to grass and milk, has gained utility ;
Ceased from its waste as poison to our fishes,
It makes the grass grow as a farmer wishes.
The refuse yet to be reclaimed is sewage,
Which we may hope in this, or some near new age,

Will prove an increase to our farmers' crops,
A profit to our towns, and in our shops,
Ourselves or our successors soon may find it
In some new form, on counter or behind it.
Town's refuse is a large and nauseous thing,
Containing elements that ought to bring
Wealth to our people, plenty to our fields,
(Bricks, mortar, and cement it also yields),
Eau de Cologne may fail, and folks prefer well
Some grand new perfume, perhaps an Eau de Irwell !

And when the rainfalls pass from hill to sea
Along a course from all things foul made free,
We then may find our inky, stinky river,
"A thing of beauty, and a joy for ever."

NOTE ON THE CHEMICAL CONSTITUTION OF FISHING WATERS, AND OF THE IRWELL.

BY CHARLES ESTCOURT, F.I.C., F.C.S.

Believing the subject to be of considerable importance, not merely as indicating the effect of purity as contrasted with impurity in our rivers and streams, but also in connection with the natural history of fish, I have undertaken for the Association a series of analyses of famous or well-known fishing waters. As the Association has a sort of proprietary right in one river (the Dovey), I have begun operations with that river.

Two samples were taken from it on the same day (September 10), and within twenty minutes of each other at the same spot, just below Dinas Mawddy. They presented the following difference in constitution, caused by the fact that the river was clean and low when the first sample was taken, and that, owing to a sudden thunder storm, it had become milky white, and had risen three inches when the second was procured.

DOVEY.

	BEFORE RAIN.	AFTER RAIN.
	Grains per gallon.	
Total solid matter	2'38	3'10
Mineral Matter	110	no
Suspended Matter	0'00	72
Loss on Ignition	1'28	1'28
Hardness, Degrees	1'8	
Chlorine	'53	
Ureal Ammonia	0'0007	
Albd- ditto	0'0042	

It will be perceived that the only difference between the milky and transparent condition of the river may be ropresented by the total solid matter. The milky sample holds in suspension only 0'72 of a grain per gallon, notwithstanding its great show of muddiness. It may not be uninteresting to compare with the Dovey, two Manchester waters, one pure and the other polluted.

	Thirlmere.		The Irwell.
Total Solid Matter	3'10	...	48.30
Mineral	115	...	35.00
Suspended Matter	0'00	...	11.20
Loss on Ignition	1'95	...	13.30
Hardness	1'50	...	16'00
Chlorine	0'44	...	5'26
Ureal Ammonia	0'0009	...	0'3192
Albd- ditto	0'0042	...	1344

THE ANGLERS FLOWERS.
BY CRAVEN.

NOT lonely is the angler's mood,
Although he must in solitude,
On moorland bank, in verdant wood,
With stealth beguile the finny brood.

For friends of many a bye-gone day,
Still greet him on his silent way :
Not words, but glances soft and gay,
A thousand things at once do say.

The crowfoot, bearded leaves between,
Makes dimples in the water's sheen ;
Like white-smocked playmates these
I ween, Laughing from out their cradles green.

A country maiden in the wood,
Coquettish, and yet understood,
Anemone beneath her hood,
Once more the fisher's heart doth flood.

Or, by the edge of fragrant groves,
As o'er the bank he gently moves,
Sweet Cicely hid, her presence proves,
For Viola-like, unseen she loves.

And as he hies through bosky dell,
A riper kindness weaves her spell;
Veronica her beads doth tell,

And prays the fisher may speed well.

Nor less shall Orchis, regal-hued,
Exalt the triumph, when out-strewed,
With radiance from the West imbued,
The spoils upon the mead are viewed ;

Or, through bright Ob'ron's honeyed horn,
From branch of woodbine lightly torn,
Across the sea-green waves of corn,
A fairy note of praise be borne.

NOTES TO "THE ANGLER'S FLOWERS."

Verse 3.—***Ranunculas aquatilis.*** A peculiarity of this plant is the capillary character of the submerged leaves, the floating leaves being broad and 3—5 lobed.

Verse 4.—***Anemone nemorosa,*** the wood anemone. The half-pendulous corolla resembles a country maiden's white hood.

Verse 5.—***Myrrhisodorata;*** common name, "Sweet Cicely." In the early part of the year the flowers are concealed by the profuse foliage, but its presence is revealed by the fragrance it emits when pressed beneath the foot. The allusion is to Shakspere's Viola, who

"Never told her love But let concealment, like a worm i'th' bud, Feed on her damask cheek."

Verse 6.— ***Veronica,*** called after the saint of that name; common name, "Speed-well."

Verse 7.—The purple meadow ***Orchis,*** growing on the mead where the fisher counts his " take."

Verse 8.—In fairy mythology the horn-shaped flowers of the honeysuckle are said to be used as trumpets.

THE WENSLEYDALE YORE
AND ITS TRIBUTARIES.

BY THOMAS HARKER.

THE Yore, which I call my native river, has its rise a mile or so from Hell Gill. The Eden has its source about half a mile north-west of this, and the Swale rises at Hen Seat, about half a mile from the sources of Eden and of Yore. The Swale is the largest tributary of the Yore, and joins it near to Borough Bridge. From this point to Richmond it contains a great many coarse fish—pike, perch, dace, and chub. Above Richmond Paper Mill, the trout fishing is said to be very good, but not having fished this river, I cannot give much information respecting it and its tributaries. I will, therefore, leave it for what I trust will be of more interest—Wensleydale and its river.

We will begin our fishing tour at Ulshaw Bridge, about four miles below Leyburn. It is my intention to conduct you from this point to the source, taking side walks to notice each tributary in its turn. At Ulshaw Bridge the river Cover joins the Yore. This is an excellent trout stream. It has its rise at the head of the beautiful little valley of Coverdale. On the north bank we find all that remains of Coverham Abbey, founded in 1214, by Ralph Fitz-Robert With respect to the fishing in the Cover, whenever I have been fortunate enough to find it with a good water, the sport has been good, the trout taking the fly or spinner freely. My brother-in-law, the Rev. R. F. Dent, has reported to me some excellent takes. Dr. Cockcroft, of Middleham, fishes the Cover more than any other man, and takes good baskets ; reports of his takes often appear in the *Field.* A trout has been killed this season (1879) in the Cover, weighing two and a quarter pounds.

Along the main stream we wend our way up to Middleham Bridge, passing many fine pools for pike, perch, chub, barbel, &c, for these deep sluggish waters contain principally coarse fish. From Middleham to Wensley Bridge the fishing is good, the distance being about two miles. The best fish I have ever taken here would weigh a pound. We have here a fine view of Middleham Castle, or rather what remains of it, for it is falling fast to ruins. It stands on the high ground on the south bank, and was once the residence of Richard the Third. On the north bank we have the market town of Leyburn. The great attraction here is the Shawl, a splendid natural terrace, beginning half a mile west of the town. On reaching Wensley Point the landscape unfolds itself. You are stationed on a rock with the valley of the Yore extending far away below ; east and west the broad river winding through meadows and between pretty villages. When fairly on the Shawl, the view is magnificent.

At Wensley Bridge, we have, on the north bank, the village of Wensley, one of the prettiest in the valley, with a fine old church of the time of Henry the Third. At this church I was married, quite twenty years ago, so that it must be evident that I was here somewhat successful as a fisherman, in more ways than one, and that the trout and river were not the only sources of attraction to me. Passing along from Wensley Bridge through Bolton Wood and Park we leave, on our left, a portion of the river strictly preserved by Lord Bolton for his brother, the Rev. Thos. Orde Poulett, Rector of Wensley, who is a very good fisherman and kills heavy baskets with the May-fly. While here it is well to have a look at Bolton Hall, the seat of the Bolton family ; and afterwards push along the river-side to Redmire Falls, a most delightful spot for the fisherman, as he looks round and realises the full beauty of the falls with the towering wooded bank. On the north bank is the picturesque hamlet of Redmire; and on the south, away from the river, is West Witton, another interesting village. It was here, just above Redmire Fall, more than twenty years ago, that I first met the celebrated Wensley dale fisherman, Peter Percival. Mr. Dent and I had been flogging away for some time, when we came up to Peter sitting waiting for the flies to come on the water. He smiled at our efforts, and said in his dry way, " It's na use ; ye ma as weel thra yer hats in. Wait a bit, they'll rise in about an hour." After resting and refreshing from our flasks, we began fishing again, and fished through Thorsby to Burton beck foot. I noted well the style of this learned man of the rod (for I found he knew where the fish lay) landing a fine trout here, and a fine grayling there, and so on until we had a good basket of fish. By a process not unknown to fishermen, Peter's fish got into our basket, and we made our way to the inn at Redmire, where we had left the horse and trap, and drove away for home, trying to persuade ourselves that we had been very successful. When we arrived home the fine trout and grayling were turned out on to a large dish. " Well, you have done well," said one ; but another, more sceptical, suggested that to get a dish like that would require a silver hook, and then to finish us off the lady of the house inquired if we "had seen Peter on the river ? " For many years I visited this portion of the river in company with Peter, and rarely went home without a fine lot of trout. The length is now strictly preserved by Sir William Chaytor on the north bank, and Mr. Pilkington, of Blackburn, on the south.

About a mile north-west of Redmire stands Bolton Castle, long the lordly abode of the Scrope family. It was here Mary Queen of Scots was imprisoned by her loving cousin, good Queen Bess.

We must not pass Burton Beck without a word. It has its rise at Bishopdale Head, and takes its name from the village of West Burton on its south bank. The trout are very numerous in the beck, notwithstanding the wash from some lead mines. Salmon come into it to spawn in great numbers, from the Yore, to the village of West Burton being quite a favourite place with them. Another good trout beck runs down Waldon, a solitary valley quite out of the way, and having only a farm house here and there. Mr. Dent and I had a very successful day here four or five years ago. We fished the beck after a heavy fall of rain, with my favourite spinner, and killed forty-five trout weighing about fourteen pounds. It was early in September, and the fish were in fair condition. Coming back to Yore we proceed to Aysgarth Falls, and find good water for fly all the way. The scenery is grand, and many a delightful day's fishing has been ended here. The railway is close to the river, which is about a mile from Aysgarth village on the south side ; and a similar distance from Carperby on the north side. The first fall is too much for the salmon ; they have never been known to get up. Peter Percival told me how he once took a salmon, about eighteen pounds, in a rock-bound pool below the fall. The fish, after being hooked, rushed under a shelving rock, and Peter could not get him out; so he decided in the evening to leave his rod well-secured, with the reel arranged so that it would run, and went home to bed. Early in the morning, just before daylight, Peter again visited the pool and found his rod just as he had left it, with the fish still fast to his line at the lower end of the pool, and as he said in his own dialect," I tuke good care he didn't get back to his haad (hold) again."

Leaving Aysgarth Falls, three in number, we now press on to Askrigg, the distance being about four miles. There is good fishing all the way. A favourite length is Daw Water, about a mile long. I like to fish here with a good east wind blowing right up the river ; under these conditions I have caught many a good dish of trout. Beyond this length, broken water recurs more frequently. On the north bank Nappa Hall, once the residence of the family of Metcalfe, is passed. On one occasion James the First was the guest of Sir Thomas Metcalfe. The river Bain flows into the Yore not far from the station at Askrigg. I must not forget to draw your attention to a village on the south bank. Wurton is only interesting because the writer of this is a shareholder in a lead mine there, and he has more calls of £2 per share than dividends of that sum. The moral is:—Don't take shares in lead mines : firstly, because very few mines pay, and secondly, because they tend to spoil our beautiful trout streams. I trust that the act for the prevention of the pollution of rivers will compel all miners to filter the lead and impurities out of the wash-water. On the north bank is Mill Ghyll beck, not remarkable for the number of trout to be found in it; but if the stream be followed up for a mile or so, the water-fall of Mill Ghyll, considered by many to be the most beautiful in the valley, will be arrived at. This fall well repays the time and trouble required to reach it. Returning to the Yore, we see on the south bank the village of Bainbridge, through which the river Bain passes. Two miles up this stream is the largest natural lake in Yorkshire—Semerwater. It has a circumference of about three miles, and its greatest depth is about forty-five feet. It contains some good trout, and also bream and dace. Above Semerwater, the valley divides into three—Cragdale, Roedale, and Bardale. In these dales, and in others on Semerwater side, there are waterfalls at Roedale House, Park Scar, High Blean, and Barnet. At Low Tors near by, the lake pours down from a height of about eighty feet, in three zig-zag falls of varied and picturesque form. A week might be spent fishing and exploring these dells. " Long, long ago, while the Apostles still walked the earth, a poor old man wandered into Raydale, where a large city then stood, and besought alms from house to house. Every door was shut against him, save one, an humble cot without the city wall, where the inmates bade him welcome, and set oaten bread and milk cheese before him, and prepared him a pallet whereon to sleep. On the morrow, the old man pronounced a blessing on the house and departed ; but as he went forth, he turned, and looking on the city, thus spake :—

> Semerwater rise, Semerwater sink,
> And swallow all the town;
> Save this lile house
> Where they gave me meat and drink.

Whereupon followed the roar of an earthquake, and the rush of water ; the city sank down, and a broad lake rolled over its site ; but the charitable couple who lodged the stranger were preserved, and soon by some miraculous means they found themselves rich, and a blessing rested on them and their posterity."[5] Sailing on the lake on a fine, bright, summer's evening, by means of a strong faith the roofs and chimney tops of the doomed city may even yet be seen.

Again taking up the rod, and having reached Yore's Bridge, we begin to fish up to Hawes, a distance of four miles, which I class as the best fishing in the river. About three miles is nearly all stream fishing, but a mile from Hawes we come to a very deep part of the river, Sandy Wheel, in which many of the largest fish are found. Trout weighing four pounds have been taken at this point, and my father tells of a trout having been caught here, by a Dr. Balderson, weighing twelve pounds. I have not had the good fortune to kill any trout over a pound in weight, but, we may remember for our encouragement that these large fish have fallen to the rods of some of our brethren. The fishing from this point to Hawes is very good, the river winding through pastures and meadows, and being wonderfully free from trees, so that it is easy work for the angler.

5   Walter White's " Month in Yorkshire."

Having reached Hawes at last, it will be very convenient for those who intend to fish in the waters of the Hawes Angling Association to stay there. This little market town has many pleasing associations for the writer of this paper. It was here that I was born, and where I spent my early days. Many a time and oft, during my boyhood, have I rambled with my schoolfellows up Blackburn syke, Thornes syke, and others, taking all the trout with our hands, a style of fishing commonly called " graaping." We were rather fond of this kind of sport. There was no angling association then to interfere with our youthful tastes, yet I believe that the river and tributaries contained more fish than at the present time, notwithstanding the fact that the Hawes Angling Association have watchers, and strictly preserve the river, becks, and sykes or burns. From the tower of the handsome new church of St. Margaret, at Hawes, a magnificent view of the country can be had. Looking west are seen Widdale, Mossdale, Cotterdale, and Fossdale; eastward, there is the lovely river wending its way down the valley, and most extensive views of all the surrounding district. As we pass through the market place we find more than one inn at which we can take up our quarters; the White Hart, the Crown, the Black Bull, and the King's Arms amongst the rest.

Returning to matter of special interest to the angler, we reach the Yore, at the point were Gale beck enters it. This beck is now an improving trout stream, and, when sufficient water is found coming down, can be fished to advantage. A walk of a mile and a half along the side of this stream leads to Gale Force, a fall about twenty-four feet high, and as many in breadth. The water flows over a hedge of hard limestone rock, lying on a bed of shale particularly rich in organic fossils. Returning to the Yore and fishing up the river, we find good stream every few yards, with here and there a deep pool affording suitable lodgement for both trout and grayling. I wish here to say that the trout in the Hawes waters are the best; they soon reach a perfection of condition rarely found in the fish we take lower down the river, say below Askrigg or Aysgarth Falls. Continuing our progress up stream, we find, coming into the river on the north bank, another nice beck for trout—Fossdale beck. If we follow this up, we shall pass through the village of Hardraw, a short distance from which is the most remarkable waterfall in the district. The stream, during the lapse of ages, has scooped out a large amphitheatre in the rocks (Hardraw Scar), the lower strata of which being softer than the uppermost, the latter projects a considerable distance. Over the brink, from a height of ninety-nine feet, comes an unbroken column of water, at the back of which is a footpath, so that the cascade may be viewed on every side, In the great frosts of 1739 and 1749, and also this year (1879) icicles so arranged themselves round the falling stream as to make a huge tube, through which the water was seen to flow, Again pursuing pur course up the main river, we come to a point at which Widdale beck joins it. Passing up this stream, we come immediately to the village of Appersett. I consider this to be one of the best of the tributaries of the Yore for trout. With a fair quantity of water there is sure to be sport in this beck, when the trout are doing nothing lower down in the Yore. Last year, I found, when fishing up to this beck, that the fish would not run in the Yore. I fished a short length of this tributary, and took half a dozen nice fish in a short time, one of them being a pound in weight. If I had not been obliged to leave to catch a train, I am sure I should have made a heavy basket by fishing up the Gill as far as Snaizholme Bridge, a point at which another good beck joins the one spoken of, and which is also well-stocked with trout The distance from Appersett is about two miles. A Hawes angler caught a trout just below Snaizholme Bridge weighing two and a half pounds.

Fishing higher up the main stream again for a mile or so we come to a capital beck on the north bank, Cotter beck, a good trout stream. I have fished a short length of it and have killed fish in the Force Pool. Cotter Force consists of a beautiful series of falls, in which the water takes several leaps in rapid succession, forming a beautiful cascade. On the south bank of the main river Mossdale beck contributes its waters. If we follow the stream for a short distance we come to the Lower Mossdale Falls, partially screened by foliage, and decorated by a natural rock-fernery of rare beauty. Half a mile beyond is the Upper Force, which has been described as a beautiful small copy of the celebrated High Force on the Tees.

Here we must end our tour, as we cannot fish further for want of water. True fishermen will find the pleasure afforded by the beautiful district through which we have passed to be indeed great, and to such I shall be happy to give any additional information they may desire.

As a local poet says:—
Where can you find a sweeter spot than this ?
Enchanting ! yes, to breathe the air is bliss.
Nor can you find in Britain's lovely land,
So sweet a spot, to *me,* you understand.
Look at the vale, through which the Yore glides on.
Endowed by Nature's gifts, improved by man ;
Yonder the hills, with moor-game well supplied,
Down in the vale are rural towns descried.
And if you journey to that pleasant place,
Look at the men, too,—with a smiling face
Each seeks his home, contented and at peace.

THE EDEN AT ARMATHWAITE.
BY FREDERICK KENDERDINE.

AN intimate friend, who resides in Westmoreland, agreed to join me in a visit to the Eden, a river he had never thrown a line upon, although residing in the adjoining county. It was the first week in June; not a good time in England, though, according to my experience, about the best for Scotland. On arriving at Armathwaite Station, we observed two other anglers alight, who, we ascertained, had previously engaged the trap and beds. As they did not ride, and we were not acquainted with the place, we followed them, leaving our rods, and luggage, to come with theirs. The principal inn, the "Red Lion," was nearly full, and we had to occupy a double-bedded room, very scantily furnished, our extra clothing and other things which were not required for the day's use being kept on the floor in the corners. Mrs. Stephenson, the hostess, on our making complaints, said that she had only been in the place a short time, and that her preparations for visitors were not yet complete. She, however, did her best to make us comfortable. Our first thoughts being the campaign, we requested that tea might be served at once to give us a good start.

In the meantime we tooted for information, and were staggered at the outset. One informant said we might not fish on the right bank ; another that we couldn't fish on the left; a third that all down the river was strictly preserved. The first and last items of information were found correct.

A ticket of the Penrith Angling Association (charge ten shillings and sixpence for a week) is required. This ticket covers several miles of the Eden, the Eamont up to the bridge near Penrith, and some portions of the Lowther. There are reservations, but as notice boards are not put up, I heard it was customary to fish anywhere unless warned off. The keeper of the water, fortunately, was at an inn with some signed tickets, which relieved us of a difficulty—but I think it is desirable for intending visitors to obtain these by post before leaving home, and thus prevent any unpleasantness.

A quarter of a mile up the river is a residence called Armathwaite Castle, belonging to Lord Lonsdale, who has a considerable estate here, and a fishery including a mile and a half of water. This is let to a tenant who daily has men netting for salmon. The owner of the hotel, who has a little property on the other side, also sends her gardener out for the same purpose. The take this year (1879) has been poor—not more than about two fish a day, though one evening when I was there four were caught. Diseased fish have been rather frequent. I saw one which weighed eleven pounds, while a healthy fish of the same length weighed thirteen.

After tea we took the high road through the village, and turning off at a small farm, came to a weir above the castle, the beginning of the Penrith fishing. For a long distance there is still deep water. Circles were incessantly made by the fish, but it being a perfect calm, although the water was very brown, no fish were put in our creels. The opposite bank is steep and rocky, probably one hundred feet high, and clothed with trees; and after two fields were passed the bank on our side took the same character.

Our principal object in starting on the first evening was to reach a place called Catclints, but rain prevented us from reaching it. It is a perpendicular rock over a deep pool, and to enable anglers to pass along it there are holes chiselled in the rock for the feet, and hooks arc inserted for the hands. Now, to an angler with stock-ings on, and carrying his rod, basket, and landing net (unless he is young and has no nerves), this is no easy task ; but to avoid it, a steep climb and a corresponding descent must be made, in all a *detour* of half a mile. We decided not to face these difficulties, but to take the train to Lazonby, and this we did the next morning.

The " Joiners' Arms" at Lazonby is a clean little inn, close to the river, and use-ful for a glass of beer or lemonade, but there are no bedrooms, or it would do very well to stay at for a few days. At a distance of half a mile on the opposite side stands Kirk Oswald, and judging by the slated roofs among the trees, this seems to be a better place than Armathwaite. The river above the bridge runs through fields free from trees, and is easy to fish, but there are only two or three really good streams. Below, excepting the first field, it is very rocky, and in many places it is not easy to get along. Nevertheless there is grand trout-water all the way down to Catclints, but it is almost essential to wade deep. The river is perhaps eighty or one hundred feet wide. One of the visitors related an amusing tale one evening. He had taken the cobbler of the village out with him. The latter was in the middle of the river having some sport, when the gentleman came up and called out " Thompson, I can't wade there." Thompson looked at his own stock-ings and replied, " Oh yes, sir, come in : I've an inch to spare !" The gentleman, who stands about five feet six inches, while the shoemaker is an immense fellow of six feet and a half, notwithstanding this as-surance, declined to venture.

I had only two full days, my friend having unexpectedly to return. I decided to go with him, for the weather was wet and the river already too large and brown. The fish we caught were few in number, but of a good average size, over half a pound each. Fish of three quarters are commonly taken, and daily some of a pound. Largc baskets are frequently made. A friend of mine caught, on Whit-Monday, fourteen pounds. The flies used are hackles, such as are made by Hutchinson, of Kendal, for the river Kent, on No. 3 hooks. The mottled feather of the partridge, with dark body, is a particular favourite. Dark snipe, with purple body, is also good. I have generally found that Hutchinson's light and dark snipe hackles, with purple, orange, and yellow bodies, will take fish on any river.

Making allowance for the want of furniture in the bedroom, we found the " Red Lion " comfortable enough. The cooking was good and there was a liberal table. The charges are moderate. Horses are kept and attended to by two of the landlady's sons, and I noticed one of the sons went out with visitors. Apparently it is a much frequented place. The company consisted of two gentlemen from York, two from Kendal, two from Manchester, one from Coventry, my friend from Burton, (Westmoreland,) and some others. The " Duke's Head " is an inferior inn, but accommodation can be had there on an emergency.

A DREAM OF SPRING TIME AT PEN-Y-BONT[6].
BY GEORGE DAVIES.

LARTH her ermine mantle changes,
For the emerald of spring ;
Zephyr o'er the moorland ranges,
On his balmy-scented wing ;
Blooms the willow by the river,

Early haunt of busy bees ;
Flows the brooklet singing ever,
'Neath the tall o'er-hanging "trees.

Dappled kine are in the meadows,
Lambs are frisking on the hills ;
Pleasant are the lights and shadows,
Sweet the sound of mountain rills :
Birds sing out of wood and bower,
Musical is earth and air ;
Nature moves with magic power,

6   Pen-y-bont—The Fishing-ground of the Association, on the Dee.

Bids us throw aside our care ;

Woos us to that charming valley,
Though which runs the "Sacred Dee,"
Over rocks with sudden sally,
Or though deeps of mystery;
Where the noble salmon hideth,
Or where leaps the speckled trout, Or grim patriarch abideth,
Which no angler hath found out!

Woos us to the flowing river,
Where it laves the mystic hill,
On whose top the tall pines quiver,
Musical, if seeming still:
Where the spirit of Glendower,
Seems to beckon us away
From the city to his bower;
Come! O come! he seems to say.

THE LOCHS AND RIVERS OF SUTHERLAND.
BY WILLIAM BANTOCK.

IT is generally admitted that no county in Scot-HSJD land supplies either so rich or extensive an arena to the lover of the "gentle art" as Sutherland.

In addition to its being one of the largest counties, its fishing waters are proportionately more extensive. It possesses a great advantage, too, in having an extensive coast. Its shores are washed by the German ocean on the south, by the Atlantic on the west, and by the North sea on the north. To each of those seas, rivers flow, and they are not only very numerous, but are also somewhat unique in their character, in that both their sources and exits are contained within the boundaries of the county; they possess also another distinctive characteristic. We correctly associate the riverine system of a great part of Scotland, and of nearly all England, with very long distances, over which the streams run—and their sources with very modest dimensions, which they are ever increasing in their seaward flow; but these rules do not apply at all to the Sutherland rivers. Any one of these, could it answer the question put to Topsy upon the subject of her bringing up, would hardly reply as she did—"I s'pecs I grow'd!" for, from the beginning of their flow they are full watered,—the whole of them emanating from great lacustrine sources.

As salmon-producing rivers they will, according to their several sizes, favourably compare with any throughout the kingdom; and as regards their angling capabilities, one of them at least has obtained the renown of being superior to all others. It must, however, be understood that they are associated chiefly with salmon angling. Sea-trout (Saltno trutta) of course ascend them all, but although these fish are obtained in the rivers through which they run, still they are best caught in the lochs with which the rivers are connected. Neither do the rivers afford any angling for brown trout (Salmofarid) at all to be compared with that of the lochs.

The rapid and impetuous character of the Sutherland rivers does not supply the conditions which would render them a favourable continuous habitat for trout, which are not slow to recognize the advantages of the more placid and food-producing lochs. In the smaller streams and burns—principally those entering the lochs —very good brown trout may at times, and in favourable localities, be got Char (S. salvelinus) never leave the lochs wherein they resort.

The varieties of fish which frequent the fresh water are of very limited range; but what they lack in that respect is fully compensated by the position they hold at the head of our fresh-water fishes. They are:—salmon (S. salar), sea-trout (S. trutta), great lake-trout (S. ferox), brown or yellow trout (S. fario), and char (S. salvelinus). Happily there is a total absence from these waters of the voracious pike, with the single exception of Loch Migdale, a small loch on the Skibo estate. Nor is even the ubiquitous perch to be found within the range of the county, so far as I am aware. The whole of the Salmonidce referred to are migratory. S. salar and . S trutta are, in every natural condition of their existence, recognized as migrants, and so too, but over a more restricted range, is S. ferox; but in regard to our more familiar friend, S. fario, he departs to a large extent from the customs of his congeners, in consequence of the necessities imposed upon him, whereby he too has his season of migration. The fresh-water loch is both to him and S. ferox precisely what the sea is to the more extended migrations of S salar and S. trutta, namely, their common pasture ground, which they occupy until at each recurring period they are led by their instincts to ascend the rivers and streams, for the purpose of procreation.

The journey by railway to Lairg occupies about eighteen hours. Lairg is an important station to those who are desirous of proceeding further into the county. There is good hotel accommodation there; but, in the height of the tourist season it is often unable to cope with the great stream of pleasure-seekers which constantly passes towards the westerly and northerly parts of the county. By next year the hotel accommodation will be considerably augmented by the addition of the contiguous building, hitherto occupied as a shooting lodge by the tenant of the adjoining shootings, for whom another lodge is in course of erection overlooking Loch Shin. From Lairg, three times a week, mail gigs start for Lochinver and Scourie, respectively in the west and north-west of the county, and to Tongue in the north. There is another grand route available by sea to Lochinver, which will be referred to further on.

Lairg is situated at the foot of Loch Shin, close to where the river makes its exit. This loch, one of the largest in Scotland, and the largest in Sutherland, is upwards of eighteen miles long. At the Lairg end, the fishing is at present only moderate, and in that part it has for several years past lost the prestige formerly acquired by the size and number of trout found there. At the other end there is the fishing station of Overskaig, to which I shall presently refer. Loch Beannach (Blessed Loch), a small loch about four miles fron Lairg, is daily resorted to by anglers, and very fine baskets of trout are got. They generally rise freely to the fly.

The finest angling loch at Lairg is Loch Craggie, and in a less degree Loch Doula, both close together, and about three miles from Lairg. Loch Craggie has deservedly the reputation of being one of the finest, for the quality, as well as for the size of its trout (S. farid). Neither of these lochs is open to the public. They belong to the neighbouring estate of Achany, and are rented with the adjoining shootings, at, it is said, £100 a year. Permission was obtained by a favoured few to fish here during our two or three days' stay at Lairg, at the end of last August. On that occasion two rods brought home from Loch Craggie, one day, fifty-six pounds weight of trout, scarcely one of which was under one pound weight, many were two pounds and three pounds weight, and all of surpassing symmetry and beauty. These trout seem to be a different variety to those obtained from any other loch in Sutherland. They are deep thick-set fish, thickly covered with large brown and orange spots.

At the north end of Loch Shin, and distant from Lairg about sixteen miles, is Overskaig, where there is inn-accommodation for about seven or eight visitors. We were anxious to go there, but we found that they were unable to receive us at the inn for several days, and we had, therefore, to seek other quarters.

The loch fishing at Overskaig is of a very high character. In addition to Loch Shin, there are Lochs Merkland and Griam, angling upon which is free to visitors at the inn. Besides loch-trout, each of these lochs contains **S. *ferox*,** many fine specimens of which are procured. Loch Shin also contains char and salmon. Char abound in scores of the Sutherland lochs, but they are very rare risers to the fly, and have' never been known to be taken by any other lure. But there is a small loch of the finest spring water high up on the shoulder of Ben Hope, where this very shy and beautiful fish is said to take a small grey fly freely. There is another small loch near the Manse of Durness—Loch Borley or Borralie—which is said to contain char only, and where they are got in considerable numbers in October.

Early this autumn (1879) there appeared in the columns of the ***Field*** a series of papers upon the Over-skaig fishings from the pen of " Pelagius," which is worth the attention of those who may desire to visit that locality.

At Shinness, about half-way between Lairg and Overskaig, are to be seen the Duke of Sutherland's reclamations, where His Grace has spent upwards of £100,000 in reclaiming upwards of two thousand acres of land, building farm steadings, and planting suitable belts of wood.

The river Shin, issuing from Loch Shin, pursues a course of about six or seven miles, and falls into the Kyle of Sutherland (which is the upper continuation of the estuary of the Meikle Ferry) a short distance above Bonar Bridge. Passing glimpses are obtained of the river, and a very good view of Achany on the opposite side from the railway between Ardgay and Lairg.

The capabilities of the Shin, as an angling river, have already been described by one whose ability as a writer, and whose experience and success as an angler in his day and generation have been long ago fully recognised. I refer to the gentleman who, under the ***nom de plume*** of "Ephemera," contributed a series of articles to Bell's Life, and published a ***Handbook of Angling,*** and ***The Book of the Salmon,*** two works which will always retain a high position. In his ***Book of the Salmon*** " Ephemera " says :—

I believe that at the present season the rivers of Sutherlandshire will afford more sport to the salmon and sea-trout fly-fisher than any other streams in the empire.

And then he speaks about

The celebrated river Shin, the best in Sutherlandshire, and the best I have ever fished in. Last season (that would be the year 1849, as the work was published in 1850) I killed fifty-four salmon in it in fifty-five hours.

I have also been favoured with recent information about the angling on the Shin by Mr. George Young, the manager of the Duke of Sutherland's fishings at Invershin :—

The Shin is an early river, as an average of four salmon a day has been caught in a mild spring after the nth February—the opening day of the season; but in April and May this number has been exceeded by good anglers, and salmon of thirty-five pounds weight caught. Previous to the year 1865 there was acruive fished regularly every lawful day; yet in the month of July of 1864 two rods caught two hundred and twenty-eight salmon and grilse. Thirty-eight fish was about the largest number of one day's catch. June is hardly such a good month for grilse, as they are small and not so numerous until about the end of that month. The month of August is not so good for angling below the big fall as in July; but there are good pools above it where in this month in favourable seasons it is second to none in the county. I consider the Shin still up to the mark as the best angling and spawning river in the north.

The Shin is let by the month, and the angling alone from the big fall down to the mouth of the river—about a mile and three quarters—produces £500 a year. It should, perhaps, be stated that the above-mentioned angling feats were all accomplished with the fly, which, on the Sutherland rivers, so far as I am aware, is the universal lure used in the capture of salmon ; and long may it remain so !

There seems good reason for the belief that the high character given by " Ephemera " to the Sutherland rivers is still, after the lapse of thirty years, fully maintained ; and if the fostering care since exercised in regard to them be compared with the excessive drain they had formerly to withstand, there is every reason to suppose that they are now larger producing-waters than then.

In addition to its reputation as a salmon-angling and producing river, the Shin has likewise had the good fortune to occupy a position altogether unique, in its identification with the investigation of the natural history and habits of the salmon. To the late Mr. Andrew Young, of Invershin, belongs the honour of having first solved this problem. And, it may be said, so exhaustively, and at the same time so accurately, did he investigate the whole subject, that Mr. Young's ***Natural History and Habits of the Salmon*** (Longmans, 1854) still continues to be the first authority upon that subject

It may truly be said that up to the year 1845, little or nothing was known of the life-history of the salmon. It seems now almost inconceivable that there should have been at so late a period such a dearth of knowledge of the habits of a fish which has ever occupied a prominent position in the food economy of the nation, and has afforded so many facilities for investigation. To the late Mr. Shaw, of Drumlanrig, belongs the honour of having originated the artificial breeding of salmon for the purposes of scientific investigation ; but this statement ought perhaps only to apply so far that Mr. Shaw was the first who made public the result of his investigations. There appears to be good evidence that Mr. Young's experiments were conducted at quite as early a period as those in connection with which Mr. Shaw laboured ; but the latter gentleman was first in the field of literature on the subject. I fear, however, it must be said, that the publication of the result of his researches by no means added to Mr. Shaw's fame as an accurate investigator. About the year 1845 Mr. Shaw published, in pamphlet form, his experimental observations on the development and growth of salmon fry, from the exclusion of the ova to the age of two years. Along with other statements, he asserted that:—

The milt of a single male parr, whose weight may not exceed one and a half ounce, is capable, when confined in a small stream, of effectually impregnating all the ova of a very large female salmon.

Mr. Shaw likewise asserted that the parr, from the period of their being hatched, to their migration, remained in their native element for two years. The theory in the minds of the public at this time, in contrast with the above, was that the fry were parr and smolts within the same year, and that their migration took place shortly after they were hatched—a most absurd conclusion to arrive at, and one which would, in frequent instances, make migrants of the young fish while yet they were attached to their umbilical sacs. It was in order to rectify these erroneous conclusions that Mr. Young (at first through the medium of the periodical press, then in pamphlet form, and afterwards in the book already alluded to,) gave to the public the result of his investigations. He combated Mr. Shaw's male parr theory, by the assertion that the duty referred to was only performed by the more mature male grilse and salmon ; .and upon the migration question he showed that the smolts invariably migrated to the sea after they had attained the age of one year. It need hardly be said that all Mr. Young's conclusions have long since been fully verified. There were many other questions in regard to the salmon very ably investigated by Mr. Young—especially those which had reference to their usually extended periods of migration to the sea, and to the extraordinary development of the fish while there. It may truly be said that the publication of the results of the foregoing researches had the beneficial effect of developing artificial fish breeding for other than mere scientific purposes, from which, also, the aquarium movement afterwards originated. To no other two gentlemen, therefore, does the science of pisciculture owe its advancement so much as to Mr. Shaw and to Mr. Young.

I now propose to consider the fishing grounds of the west and north-west portions of the county. In proportion to the extent of superficial area within which they are situated, they far exceed those of any other district in the United Kingdom. And they are not more remarkable for their extent than they are for the reputation they have acquired as fish-producing and angling waters. Here there is elbow room for all the anglers in the kingdom—not the twelve-yards allotted spaces which we associate with our angling brethren of Sheffield ; but those wherein " distance lends enchantment to the view " of one's next neighbour. There is no scope offered here for the display of selfishness, were it possible to find any good angler possessed of such a spirit.

On one or two occasions I fished a few of the waters of this district, but the knowledge I possessed of such a wide and varied field was not such as would satisfactorily redeem the pledge given in respect of this paper. I therefore placed myself in communication with Mr. McIver, factor of the Duke of Sutherland's Scourie management, and he has with so much kindness, and with such complete information, come to my assistance, that I must acknowledge my obligations to him. This information, too, is the more important as Mr. McIver speaks with a special knowledge of the whole subject within his range.

The Scourie district includes the parishes of Assynt and Eddrachillis, and that part of Durness extending from Durness to the west side of Loch Eriboll. A mail gig runs from Lairg to Loch Inver every Monday, Wednesday, and Friday mornings (a distance of forty-six miles), returning to Lairg on Tuesdays, Thursdays, and Saturdays. The first fishing station arrived at is Aultnakealgach (Cheaters' Burn), distance twenty-five miles from Lairg. The journey from Lairg to this point is a very interesting one. The road traverses Strath Oykel, a very favourable specimen of a Highland strath. About eight or nine miles from Lairg, Rosehall is reached, where the eye is relieved from the landscape of open moor by extensive woods, through which the river Cassley (a tributary of the river Oykel) runs. The course of the latter is afterwards followed for several miles up to the Oykel Inn, close to which there is a salmon-leap, which, when the salmon and sea-trout are running up the river, will repay a visit.

After surmounting the hill above Oykel Inn, the head of the watershed is reached, the flow of the water from this point being westward. Aultnakealgach is shortly afterwards arrived at.

The inn is a small one, containing about eight or nine bedrooms, and is situated on the shores of Loch Borrolan, on the borders of the counties of Sutherland and Ross. In addition to Loch Borrolan, there can be fished at convenient distances from the inn, Lochs Cama, Urigill, and Veattie, the Ledmore and Ledbeg rivers, the stream issuing from Loch Urigill, and some other streams. Mr. McIver says :—

Hitherto residence at the inn has given all parties living there a right to fish in the lochs and burns near it; but as this practice misleads, and a right to fish has actually been claimed under it, a small charge is now thought of to preserve His Grace's rights; but so small as to be nominal, for the Duke is most anxious to increase the number of strangers, anglers, and tourists, and to give them every reasonable facility for fishing and seeing the lochs, rivers, and mountains of Sutherland.

I had the pleasure, when at Golspie, of meeting a gentleman who had just come from these waters, and he told me it was surprising to see the numbers of trout brought in by the six or seven anglers who were staying at this inn, the aggregate weight varying from seventy pounds to upwards of a hundredweight, day after day. It may be judged how productive these lochs occasionally are from an entry in the visitors' book at Aultnakealgach, dated some years back, wherein the writer states that in ten days' fishing, during the month of August, he caught one hundred and five dozen of trout with the fly.

The next inn in Assynt is Inchnadamph, thirty-three miles from Lairg, and situated near the foot of one of the buttresses of Ben More (3,281 feet, the highest mountain in the county), at the upper end of Loch Assynt, and between the two small rivers Loanan and Trailigill, both of which flow into Loch Assynt, the former from Loch Awe, and the latter from the sides of Ben More. These two streams, as well as Lochs Assynt, Awe, and Mulach Corrie, are open to the public. Loch Assynt contains salmon, sea-trout, *S. ferox* and char. The best locality on this loch for salmon and sea-trout is along the rocky shores between Ardvreck Castle and the head of the loch. Very fine specimens of *S ferox* are got in this loch by trolling. In the autumn, salmon run up the Loanan to Loch Awe, upon both of which they are taken with the fly. Upon the occasion of a previous visit to the county, I fished these waters-, and can therefore speak of them in the highest praise. One day upon Loch Assynt I got twenty pounds weight of trout, the best of which was one of three pounds weight. I also fished Loch Awe for an hour one day with good success, until the wind fell and obliged me to desist with about ten pounds of trout. The trout on this loch do not generally exceed herring size, though occasionally they are got of a pound and over ; but as a free rising loch I know of no other in the county equal to it. As many as fifty pounds weight of trout have been got off this loch in one day by one rod. I also fished Mulach Corrie, which lies at the foot of Ben More, above Inchnadamph, and which is probably the highest-situated loch in the county. The day, however, was such a stormy one that I was completely beaten away from it. Two or three trout were got, one of which was about one pound weight They are highly esteemed for their fatness and flavour, the result of their feeding upon the freshwater shrimp, which is said to abound in the loch. Sir William Jardine first made known these trout to science, as gillaroo or " gizzard " trout, from the discovery of the indurated stomachs they possess; but, I believe, more recent investigations have not established their affinity with the gillaroo of one or two of the Irish lakes.

It may be of interest to mention here, that this part of the county has been rendered famous by the defeat and subsequent capture of the Marquis of Montrose, when fighting for the cause of Charles the Second in the year 1650. Montrose, after landing in the Orkney Islands, and traversing the counties of Caithness and Sunderland with his army, had reached Carbisdale, a few miles on the Ross-shire side of Strath Oykel, where he was attacked by the Presbyterian forces led by Colonel Strachan, and utterly routed. Montrose escaped from the field with much difficulty with a few followers, and wandered amongst the Sutherland hills above Strath Oykel. A large reward having been offered for his head, he was, after enduring for a short time great privations, captured by Neil M'Leod, the Laird of Assynt, who conveyed him to his Castle of Ardvreck, whence he was afterwards taken to Edinburgh, and there beheaded[7]. Ardvreck Castle is now a prominent ruin on the shores of Loch Assynt, where it is to be seen shortly after leaving Inchnadamph on the way to Loch Inver. Loch Inver is thirteen miles distant from Inchna-damph. It is beautifully situated at the head of the bay of that name where the Inver joins the sea. The road runs by the shores of Loch Assynt, for nine miles, and for the remainder of the distance along the Inver. The scenery throughout this route is magnificent. The hotel is large and commodious. I am informed by Mr. McIver that the Inver is at present let with the contiguous shootings to Mr. Whitbread, M.P.; but that Mr. Whitbread often sub-lets the lower half of the river to the hotel keeper, who lets two rods on it at ten shillings each per day to parties residing at his house. It is a late river, but in a wet season affords excellent angling in June and July.

To enumerate the lochs in this neighbourhood would be almost an endless task. Some conception may be formed of their number when it is stated that, within a circle of four miles radius, measured from the village of Loch Inver, upwards of fifty lochs are to be found, almost all abounding in trout, and free to the public. Reference to the map will shew how the whole country between the northern seaboard of Assynt and Loch Inver, a distance of about eight miles in a straight line, is literally honeycombed with lochs, on many of which a fly has probably never been cast. Those best known and usually fished here are Lochs Fewn, Beannoch, Clashmore, the Break or Trout Lochs, Crokach, Roe (connected with the Break Lochs and frequented by sea-trout), Loch-na-Break, in most of which trout of superior dimensions, unsurpassed symmetry, and excellent flavour are obtained. Mr. McIver says further:—

7   Brown's History of the Highlands. Vol. II.

In addition to the mail gig, a steamer plies from Glasgow to Loch Inver once a fortnight, and we are now endeavouring to arrange that it ply once a week next season. In addition to loch fishing there is bathing and sea-fishing, with shooting of sea fowl, and altogether it is as pleasant and amusing a retreat in the summer months as any part of the Highlands. It has a telegraph office, a resident medical man, good roads, and very interesting drives in several directions among as wild and romantic scenery as could be desired. The Duke has a very pretty house on the opposite side of the bay, where at least thirty persons could be accommodated, and he now contemplates letting this charming residence as an hotel for anglers and tourists. It contains almost as many apartments as dDunrobin Castle. There is a most productive garden, good offices, and the steamer lands passengers beside it. It is proposed to let with Loch Inver House the river Kirkaig, separating Sutherland from Ross—a fine salmon river with numerous pools about four miles long up to a fall, and the public will thus get angling upon it.

On the north coast of Assynt, already referred to as being so intersected with lochs, there is a small inn at Drumbtg,distant fourteen miles from Loch Inver,and close to a loch of the same name, with numbers of other lochs at one, two, and three miles distance, and all open to the public. And there is a small inn at the Ferry of Kylesku, eighteen miles from Loch Inver and nine miles from Inchnadamph, near which numerous lochs can be fished, and also excellent sea-fishing obtained. There is accommodation here for no more than two visitors. About four miles distant are Glendhu and Glencoul—two sea lochs into which flow large burns, which are frequented by sea-trout. The scenery here is unsurpassed for grandeur and variety by any part of the west coast of Sutherland. There is a waterfall about two hundred feet high, on a stream that runs into the head of Glencoul. It is called Ess coul aline, or the fall of the beautiful backlying glen, and is, when in flood, a very striking object.

Scourie Inn is distant from Lairg forty-three miles. A mail gig leaves Lairg for Scourie upon the same days as for Loch Inver. Near the inn, at a distance of from two hundred yards up to five or six miles, there are numerous yellow trout lochs open to the public, and there are two small rivers and a loch in which sea-trout and salmon are taken. From here also the Island of Handa, distant two miles, and famed for being the breeding resort of millions of sea-fowl, can be visited, and in May, June, and July it is well worth seeing.

The river Laxford, Loch Stack and Loch More, are let with the Reay Forest to the Duke of Westminster. The Laxford issues out of Loch Stack, and has a course of less than three miles. As an angling river there is hardly another in the county that has such a high reputation, and it is, after the Shin and the Naver, the best for salmon, and for sea-trout incomparably the best.

Loch Stack is justly celebrated as an angling loch, especially for sea-trout. It certainly is not surpassed, and probably not equalled, in this respect. It also contains large yellow-trout, char, and probably *S. ferox.* The creels of sea-trout with which it has been credited are almost incredible. Stoddart, in his *Anglers' Companion to the Rivers and Lochs of Scotland* (Wm. Blackwood and Sons, 1853), a book containing much useful information upon the lochs and rivers of Sutherland, says he fished Loch Stack in 1850 in very unpropitious weather, and that in the course of a few hours, without landing net, he captured thirty-one sea-trout, the largest of which was upwards of five pounds weight, several yellow trout—one of three pounds weight—and a char.

Mr. McIver further says :—

Near Rhiconich Inn, situated at the upper end of Loch Inchard, there is excellent fishing both for sea-trout and salmon, as well as for yellow trout. The house is not large, there being not more than five rooms for sleeping. There is excellent sea-fishing here. Rhiconich is forty-two miles from Lairg. Mail three times a week as before-mentioned.

Stoddart says that, on Loch Garbet Beg (near this inn), on the occasion of his visit to the county already referred to, he killed :—

In the course of five hours, thirty-eight sea-trout—several of them three pounders—two salmon, and a couple of new-run grisle, besides several loch-trout of various dimensions.

Enough, surely, to have satisfied Mr. Stoddart for one day.
The fishing season is late—from
June onwards.
Mr. Mclver again says :—

From Rhiconich the mail gig goes on to Durine Inn, dDurness—fourteen miles. There is not much fishing here. The river Grudie is seven miles distant from the inn. The lower part is sub-let by the shooting-tenant to the innkeeper, and salmon and sea-trout are taken. The innkeeper has the right of angling in the Kyle of Durness, where there is good sea-trout and salmon-fishing got by trolling from a boat with minnow or sand eel, and also with the^ fly. There are also distant lakes in which yellow trout can be taken. As there are good roads, the innkeepers all let vehicles. Single horse is. a mile ; four-wheeled carriage and pair, is. 9d. per mile. I believe a boat and gillie average per day about 6s., and ios. a day is charged for a rod on the rivers for salmon-fishing. I think from fifteen pounds to twenty pounds of yellow trout, as a rule, may be taken on the average. Trout generally are under one pound in weight. The lochs are so numerous that I cannot attempt to give you their names. There are many lochs in the county never fished. Expenses at the inns will be about twelve shillings for entertaining, exclusive of drinkables—living in a public room. We have a wet climate—plenty of waterproofs therefore desirable.

No wonder Mr. Mclver shrinks from the task of naming the lochs in his district, for in the parish of Assynt alone there are upwards of two hundred of them; and I believe it to be a fact, that from the high ground above Inchnadamph, and in the neighbourhood of Loch Inver, about a hundred of these lochs can be seen by the naked eye.

In the north and north-east part of the county is situated the Tongue district. It includes the parishes of Reay (in Sutherland), Farr, Tongue, and part of Durness to the ridge west of Loch Eriboll, and is under the management of Mr. Crawford, the Duke's factor at Tongue.

Tongue is thirty-nine miles distant from Lairg. The mail gig arrangements are the same as those to Loch Inver, &c. There is a large number of lochs in this district, and several very fine angling rivers. From a hill close to Loch Craggie, three and a half miles distant from Tongue, about one hundred lochs can be seen. I believe all the rivers are let for angling, and that all the lochs, with the exception of two or three, in the midst of deer-stalking ground, are open to the public.

The principal rivers are—taking them from east to west—the Halladale, Strathie, Naver, Borgie, and Hope. Of these the Naver is by far the best and also the earliest—the six or seven rods upon which, we are told, pay about £100 per rod. Those lochs which have access to the sea, such as Lochs Hope, Naver, &c, in addition to brown trout, **S. ferox** and char, afford excellent sea-trout fishing.

At Aultnaharra, twenty-one miles from Lairg, there is a good inn situated at the upper extremity of Loch Naver, a fine sheet of water (seven miles long) at the foot of Ben Clebrick (3,164 feet), the second highest mountain in Sutherland. The innkeeper rents the fishing on this loch, which contains salmon and sea-trout, and he sub-lets it by the day, week, or month. The early part of the season up to May affords the best fishing, and March, as a rule, is reckoned as the best month. The best salmon-fishing is got not far from the inn. As many as fifty-two salmon have been killed in seven weeks by one rod, and as many as six in a single day. The brown trout-fishing on the loch is indifferent. The best trout-fishing within reach is upon Lochs Meaddie and Loaghal (pronounced " Loyal"), each of which is six miles, and upon Loch Corr or a-Choire, which is seven miles from the inn. There are good roads, and conveyances can be had at the inn. The trout in these three lochs are considered very superior, and they at all times afford excellent angling. The ascent of Ben Clebrick can best be made from Aultnaharra, and from its summit, on a clear day, can be seen the three seas that wash the shores of the county.

In reply to a communication addressed to Mr. Crawford, asking for information in regard to his district, he has brought to my knowledge J. Watson Lyall's **Guide to Sportsmen and Tourists to Rivers, Lochs, &c.** in Scotland, published at 52, Fleet Street, London. This book refers largely to Sutherland lochs and rivers, as well as routes, hotels, &c, and as I am informed by Mr. Crawford that he gave Mr. Lyall a good deal of the information which the book contains about the angling waters in his district, we have good evidence of its trustworthiness. Short paragraphs regarding the angling on Loch Hope during the last season, appeared in the *Field.* These accounts spoke favourably, especially of the sea-trout angling.

The only remaining portion of the county now left for consideration is that part contained within the Dunrobin management, which embraces the parishes of Lairg, Dornoch, Creech, Rogart, Golspie, Clyne, Loth, and Kildonan. This district is under the management of Mr. Peacock, His Grace's factor at Golspie, to whom I am indebted for having brought to my knowledge a very interesting series of articles, entitled ***An Angler's and Sketcher's Ramble through Sutherland,*** which appeared in the Scotsman in July last. They contain by far the best account of the Sutherland lochs and rivers that I know.

The Lairg waters have already been referred to. There are few lochs in this part of the county, compared with those in the districts already described. There are two very important rivers, namely—the Brora and Helmsdale. The railway is available for all the accessible angling waters, and for the hotels within the district. After leaving Lairg the railway proceeds down Strath Fleet, along which runs the Fleet, a very small river, but which, for its size, contains a good number of salmon and sea-trout. The Fleet runs into the estuary of the Little Ferry, the upper portion of which was, early in the present century, considerably shortened by the construction of an artificial embankment in order to form the turnpike road, which since then passes over it at the Mound, a station on the railway. The flow of the river is here impeded and impounded during high tide, and by the construction of sluices in the embankment, is allowed to run down only at ebb tide. There is good sea-trout fishing, and occasionally salmon are got. The fishing is not open to the public. I was kindly permitted to fish here when in the north, and got some fine sea-trout along the embankment. About ten years ago the Duke granted permission to introduce into the Fleet a number of young sterlet, which were brought all the way from the Volga for that purpose. This experiment has not, however, resulted in successful acclimatisation.

At Skelbo, about three miles below the Mound, and quite within the influence of the tide, there is a very remarkable cast,- where, during a certain condition of the tide, salmon are taken with the fly. That fact has obtained for this cast much reputation, as there is probably not another in Scotland, except it be in the Kyle of Durness, wherein salmon are obtained under similar conditions. I remember my younger brother, nearly thirty years ago, when quite a lad, killing nine salmon and grilse here within the period for fishing which one tide permitted. This was done with a medium-sized " Blue Doctor " fly. It is very remarkable that salmon have never been caught here before the second week in July. There has been erected on the Carnack, a tributary of the Fleet, one of the most remarkable salmon ladders in Scotland, which enables salmon to surmount a fall of upwards of sixty feet in height, whereby they now ascend to Loch Buie, from which the Carnock flows. The ladder was designed by the late Mr. Bateson, of Cambusmore, and constructed under his direction. Its length is three hundred and seventy-eight yards, and its width from ten to twelve feet, and the salmon are enabled by it to ascend a precipitous incline of one hundred and thirty-eight yards long, with a gradient of about one in four, by means of a series of twenty-three pools.

A short distance beyond the Mound is the village of Golspie, where, at the Sutherland Arms Hotel, very good accommodation is provided. The situation of this hotel is one of the most pleasant in the Highlands. The Golspie burn runs past the hotel, and within easy walking distance there is a very pretty waterfall, which is arrived at by a succession of small rustic bridges, constructed within a narrow gorge of precipitous rocks (through which the burn has made a course for itself), and amid dense woods ; by all of which accessories it has been rendered a very favourite place of resort. This burn is inclined to be a sad disturber of the peace by the roaring tor-rents it sometimes sends down—the result of very rapid drainage in the Dunrobin Glen, from which it proceeds, as well as from Loch Horn—a small loch within the Glen watershed, which holds numerous but small trout. The effect of its ravages is observed in the "red braes," which a walk up the burn side discloses. The railway now passes through one of these "braes," and is carried across the gorge, a short distance from the hotel, upon a very substantial and considerably elevated bridge. I mused much along the pleasant walk up the burn side to the waterfall. What happy exploits in times long past became associated in my memory with every surrounding object! Did I not recognize every hazel as an old familiar friend, whose stem in my young days I had eagerly clasped, and whose branches at times I subjected to rather rough treatment in order to gain my purpose ? And did I not sorrow over the departure of other trees equally cherished in my recollection—the old gean (wild cherry) trees which the railway embankment had so ruthlessly swept away ? Still the whole locality awoke also in my mind the thought that engineering science had not destroyed its beauties.

Within a mile of the hotel is Dunrobin Castle, the princely Highland seat of the Duke of Sutherland, which has on several occasions, of late years, been graced by the presence of Royalty. The castle has been built on the verge of a moderately elevated terrace, which marks an ancient boundary of the sea, which it now over-looks at a little distance. It has been the residence of the Earls of Sutherland since an early period of the thirteenth century. It has since then played, in the history of the family, many important parts, which are recounted by Sir Robert Gordon, the family chronicler. During the present century it has been on two occasions much enlarged—the last and most important enlargement being finished in 1849, by which it has been rendered the largest and most stately mansion in the north. The gardens and grounds have been laid out upon a scale well worthy of the edifice, and the highly cultivated fields and extensive woods, stretching for miles beyond this magnificent seat, give to the whole locality the aspect of a more southern clime, such an aspect as one is hardly prepared to find associated with the heath-covered hills of the northern Highlands. There is within the castle grounds a very interesting museum of natural and antiquarian history-objects which have been collected within the range of the Duke's property. Permission to visit the museum may be procured through the hotel-keeper.

The only angling grounds available from Golspie are the waters of the Brora, distant about five miles. The Black-water, the principal source of the river Brora, pursues a course of some miles before it enters Loch Brora. The loch is formed by a series of four joined together by a chain of narrow necks, and altogether about four miles in length, from the last of which the river issues, and after a course of about four miles enters the sea at the village of Brora. Hotel accommodation can also be procured at Brora. The angling on the river is let for the earlier months of the season only, as the Duke reserves the fishing afterwards for his guests at Dunrobin. The Brora is one of the earliest rivers in the north of Scotland, and it therefore, during that time, affords by far the best angling. Between the loch and the sea it is, by its frequent succession of grand holding pools and rapids, the very perfection of a salmon river. I was indebted to the personal kindness of His Grace for one or two days' fishing on the river, but did no more than get a few salmon rises, though I captured some fine sea-trout The loch fishing for *S.fario* is the earliest I know of in the county. April, May, and June are the best angling months—May, in a favourable season, is the best of all I should think, at which time very fine baskets may be made. But it is for the sea-trout fishing in the autumnmonths that the loch is best known and appreciated. It is in this respect the best open loch I know of in the county. I fished the loch upon two or three occasions, though only for a limited time each day. I got from five to six sea-trout (several of which were upwards of three pounds weight) upon each occasion, and a considerable number of brown trout, which latter, however, appeared to be somewhat out of condition. I was very fortunate also, upon one occasion in capturing an eight-pounds salmon with the fly, and the tussle we had together on my twelve foot trout-rod in the middle of the loch will long be remembered. I should much like to see a trial of trolling for salmon in the early months of the year made upon this loch in the same way as is adopted with such success upon Loch Tay. The very early run of salmon into these waters has for a long time past been associated in my mind with the very probable success that would attend a few properly conducted experiments of the nature indicated, which, so far as I am aware, have not hitherto been tried at that season and for that object. The favourite bays wherein the salmon resort are well known, and the general depth of water is altogether favourable for that class of fishing.

The scenery about Loch Brora is remarkably fine. There are charming views from His Grace's rustic picnic cottages at each end of the loch, and few Highland scenes can be finer than those which are obtained from the centre of the upper basins where Carrol and Gordonbush supply an amphitheatre of rock and wooded scenery whose beauties no words can depict.

Close to where the river issues from the loch the Duke has for some years past established a salmon artificial-breeding house, with a capacity for hatching up-wards of 300,000 ova. A large number of these ova are procured from the salmon of other rivers throughout the country, and also from the Rhine, it being intended by such means to improve the breed of His Grace's rivers, whither the young fish are despatched as soon as they are able to bear the journey. There are likewise breeding houses established in several other places, from which (including the Brora) about half a million of young salmon are annually put into the various rivers of Sutherland. I was also informed by Mr. Wright, the Duke's private secretary, that about a year ago a number of *S. fontinalis* were introduced into the river Brora at its entrance from the loch, with a view to their acclimatisation. One of the little strangers having had the misfortune to seize one of my sea-trout flies in this neighbourhood, was returned to its natural element as tenderly as possible. It is to be hoped that the introduction of this beautiful species of the *Salmonidce* may prove an entire success.

In passing the Brora Railway Station, a small but very familiar Lancashire scene comes into view, in the shape of some very comfortable brick-built dwelling-houses of Sutherland clay and manufacture—a great rarity in the Highlands.

About twelve miles beyond Brora the river Helmsdale enters the sea at the village of that name. The angling on this river is let out to several rods. The spring fishing is excellent. Last year, up to May 1st, five rods killed two hundred and fifty fish. Helmsdale has, for a long time, been an important herring-fishing station. The fishing season is in July and August, at which time this is an interesting place to visit.

At the head of Kildonan Strath, a further distance from Helmsdale of about twenty-five miles, is the railway station of Forsinard, where there is a small inn, from which several excellent lochs can be fished within reasonable distances. Forsinard has, since the introduction of the railway, acquired high repute as a fishing station. The author of the **Ramble through Sutherland,** before referred to, says that on Loch Leum-a-Chlamhain, Loch Badanloch, and Loch-a-Ruiar, he and two friends in five days killed, with the fly, six hundred trout, weighing four hundred pounds. This gives an average of forty trout of nearly twenty-seven pounds weight per rod per day. It is no wonder after this that " The Rambler" seems inclined to consider that the lochs of this basin afford the best trout angling in Scotland. The trout in this district are red fleshed, and of very fine flavour. Loch Sletill—a small loch a few miles from the inn—has acquired a great name for the size and quality of its trout. They are somewhat capricious risers, but on a favourable day twenty trout may be caught, of an average weight of one pound each. In this neighbourhood the Duke is now converting, as he has already done at Shiness, a large tract of moorland into arable land by means of steam ploughs.

Perhaps a few words may be requisite upon the subject of loch and sea-trout artificial flies. My belief is that orange, fiery brown, scarlet, claret, and blue bodies, with corresponding hackles, gold or silver tinsel, and mallard and teal wings, will best suit the tastes of the Sutherland trout, as there is no doubt as to their fondness for bright colours. The addition of a turn or two of blue jay at the shoulder of these will be an advantage for sea-trout. The sizes should vary from the smallest to the largest sea-trout sizes, in order to suit the conditions of weather. I should be content with fiery browns and clarets dressed with seals' fur. Still smaller flies are requisite for the streams and burns. For trolling from a boat, especially for **S. ferox** the natural bait is considered to be the most deadly, and after that Brown's Phantoms, Nos. 9 and 10. For salmon flies, see "Ephemera," Francis and Stoddart. Many years ago I ventured to predict that when railway communication with Sutherland had been effected, there would be a growing desire on the part of anglers to avail themselves of the facilities for spending their vacations with better prospects of success, and over a more extended area, than could be found elsewhere. That this desire goes on increasing from year to year all who are best acquainted with the county know, and that it is not so great as it would otherwise be, arises, I believe, partly from the fact that several of the best fishing inns are at times inadequate to the demands made upon them for the accommodation of their visitors. The well-earned celebrity, however, which the Duke of Sutherland has acquired in respect of his land improvements, as well as his liberality as a landlord, coupled with the statements of Mr. McIver, both in regard to His Grace's desire "to increase the number of strangers, anglers, and tourists," and the means he is already adopting in furtherance of this object, justifies the belief that the requisite accommodation will keep pace with the growing accession of visitors, whose presence in no small degree contributes to the prosperity of the Duke's princely estate.

I have received from Mr. Wright some interesting notes on the natural history and antiquities of the district, communicated to him by a friend, which are appended.

NOTES ON THE NATURAL HISTORY, ANTIQUITIES, &c,
CONNECTED WITH THE LOCHS AND RIVERS OF
SUTHERLAND.
COMMUNICATED BY P—

Loch Assynt.—The scenery fine. Good view from road of Ardvreck Castle, with Cuinneag (2,670 feet high) in background. Close to castle is Eadarachalda House, burned by Ross-shire rievers, middle of last century. In this neighbourhood the relations of the Cambrian sandstones to the underlying Laurentian gneiss and the overlying Silurian strata may be studied to advantage. Pink quartzites of the latter, abounding in curious annelid burrows, lie near the road, and cap Cuinneag. Besides the common ferns of Scotland, the rarer *Asplenium viride* and *Polystichum lonchitis* occur. The former is found in the rock crevices at Ardvreck ; the Holly fern is abundant behind Inchnadamph Inn. The *Osmunda regalis* grows by the side of the loch beyond the castle. The rare and curious *Dryas octopetala* abounds on the limestone slope below Stronchrubie Cliff, and may be found near the road, on the left, half a mile beyond the church to the westward. Near the caves at Auchmore, the Hart's tongue grows, and the delicate and rare *Hymenophyllum Wilsonii.* For full account of the later fortunes of Montrose, and his connection with Ardvreck

Castle, see Sir Robert Gordon's **Genealogy of the Earls of Sutherland,** pp. 551, *et seq.*

Loch Awe.—Magnificent mountain scenery, of which this loch, with its wooded islands, is the fitting foreground.

Loch Ach-na-tt Uaigh—(loch of the field of graves). These are Pictish sepulchral tumuli associated with numerous hut-circles, and belong probably to a very early'period (the so-called "Stone Age"), as numerous chips, and some implements of flint and chert occur near. Flint is not a local product, with the exception of a very few small nodules from the boulder clay. The chert belongs to the indurated beds of the lower middle oolite at Brora, and to the inferior Lias at Dunrobin.

Loch Badan.—Near Kinbrace, at the junction of the streams from this loch and Achintoul, are the remains of acient dwellings, and very large burial cairns. For the very interesting history of the Ladies Helja and Frankark who lived here, see Orktteyinga Saga, c. xlvii., and **Torfaens,** A.D 1115, *et seq.*

Loch dBuigh.—Salmon do still probably reach this loch by the ladder erected for their ascent to the spawning grounds near.

Loch Brora,—The Pictish tower on the Blackwater, called Castle Cole, stands on the edge of a precipice overhanging the river, the bed of which is there very rocky and wild. Gold has been washed out of the gravel and clay farther down. A more entire specimen of the same sort of fortress has recently been explored at Carrol, on Loch Brora. Stone cups, bronze finger rings, archaic pottery, &c, were found there. Close to this grows the **Viburnum Opulus,** Guelder rose, rare in the north. Across the loch are groups of sepulchral tumuli. Cinerary urns and shale ornaments have been found there, and are now in Dunrobin Museum. Gold was found in the neighbouring stream Allt Smeorail, and good pearls are got from the **Aktsmodon MargaritiferuSy** which abounds in the loch. Near this, at Ashville, are the remains of what seems to have been one of the largest Pictish settlements in Sutherland. On an island stood a hunting-house of the Earls (*vide* " Genealogy " p. 5). Its ruins are still traceable. On the plateau, to the south-west, bounded on the side next to the loch by a steep cliff, there was an ancient hill-fort, of which the walls were dry built and over six feet thick; the enclosed space, now overgrown with peat, extends to several acres. A very finely finished arrow head of flint was found near.

Loch Leum a Chlamhain.—A grand hill-fort, of apparently the same date, occurs near this loch on the top of Bienn-a-Ghriam Beg. It includes several hut circles, and commands a wide view, including the Orkney Islands. It is described as a deer-trap in Scrope's *Days of Deerstalking.*

Loch Lundie.—" Dunrobin Castle, the princely seat of the Duke of Sutherland." One of its earliest names is Drum Raffn, Raffn's Ridge. Its present name may have been given in the time of Earl Robert, and means Robert's Fort or Hold. Since 1235 it has been the residence of the Earls of Sutherland, the present owner being the twenty-first Earl. Repaired and enlarged at various dates, some of which are noticed by Sir Robert Gordon in his *Earldom.* It must have been a place of great strength and importance from early times. Between 184$ and 1850 such extensive additions were made that it is now the largest castle in the north, and probably the most tast-fully ornate and best appointed anywhere. For detailed description, see Anderson's *Highland Guide,* 1863, p. 561. *et seq*. The museum at Dunrobin contains a collection of local mineralogical and geological specimens, ranging from the Laurentian gneiss to the upper oolite. There are also many interesting archaeological relics from the stone age upwards, including a valuable series from the Pictish towers so numerous in the county. The natural history of a wide district is also represented by fresh water and marine fishes, plants, and animals. One room is devoted to the purposes of a general museum, and contains arms, implements, and natural history specimens from many distant lands. Several of the Pictish towers which have been explored are within easy drive of Golspie.

Loch Mulach Corrie.—The Gillaroo.—Is there a "gizzard trout?" Some specimens examined by the writer had no trace of any such organ. Their stomachs contained indeed very small rounded pebbles, but this is not unusual in common burn-trout. If the name be Celtic it is probably derived from *gillie,* a lad, and *ruadh*, red—pronounced *gillarooa,* which is very like gillaroo, and may refer to the redness of the flesh caused by rich feeding on Crustacea and mollusca. So rich indeed are these trout, that they cannot be carried for any great distance. Some specimens sent direct for about sixty miles put one's scientific enthusiasm to a severe test in their dissection. If eaten fresh they would doubtless be of fine flavour. The question of the existence of a " gizzarded trout" is important, and is hereby commended to the consideration of the Manchester Anglers' Association. This loch, being famed as the *habitat* of such a fish, offers a good chance of investigating the matter, but it must be done on the spot.

Loch Naver. —A district extremely rich in archaeological interest. Many Pictish towers (seven within a few miles) occur. Also Eirde-houses or underground dwellings, and a great number of Pictish hut-circles, and associated sepulchral tumuli. The cross over the Red Priest's grave is also worthy a visit, and the famed Loch Mo'Nair, still in repute and resorted to for the cure of mental disease.

Loch Shin.—Near this lie the reclaimed lands, the scene of such interesting experiments in steam cultivation. Few districts will better repay the researches of the mineralogist. The neighbourhood of the Limestone band in the lower Silurian strata is richest.

River Blackwater.—" Kilcolmkill," now called " Gordonbush." This stream runs in a very romantic dell, and, where at one point its course is traversed by a granite vein, it has cut its way under it through the flaggy gncissose rock, and leaps in a fine cascade through its port of escape,

River Helmsdale flows through a very interesting district, rich in antiquities and historical associations as the scene of many clan battles. The castle at its foot is worthy of a visit. The gold field, ten miles from the mouth, is now closed, but at one time over three hundred diggers camped in canvas and turf huts there, and it is believed that about £ 12,000 worth of gold was washed out of its gravels and clays. A good deal of good ground had to be turned up ere the " bottom rock " was reaohed, and the expense of management considerably exceeded the sum raised by small rates paid for digging licence. For these, and other satisfactory reasons, the work was stopped.

AN INTERCEPTED LETTER.
BY AN ANGLER'S WIFE.

Sutherlandshire, August, 1879.

MY dearest Mary ! * * * Well, you see we have come to the end of our three days' journey into the wilderness, and reached this out-of-the-world spot at last. Talk about a place having been made on a Saturday night! this forlorn corner of the earth looks as if it had been manufactured on a washing-day, and as if there still clung around it the original damps and vapours from which it obtained its being.

I expect you will be dying to know all that I have done, said, and suffered since I left civilization behind me. My dear! description is summed up, and the conclusion of the whole matter arrived at in one solemn word— *Nothing* ! Angels' visits, and the currants in Sunday-school tea-party cake are of frequent occurrence, and very numerous compared with the items of interest in this *Ultima Thule.*

However, if I were to give you a full, true, and particular account of one day's doings, it would serve as a very good sample of what existence has been to your unhappy friend for the last fortnight—because to-morrow will be as to-day, only more so! Take my advice and never be induced to marry a man who is fond of fishing; for if you do, you will wish you had never been born.

I *suppose* our four gentlemen possess an average amount of brain, but my faith is sorely shaken when I witness their idiotic and unholy ecstasies over a wretched bundle of scales that they have drawn from its native element by means of a stick and a string ; and I believe that if "every one of their innocent heads were trepanned you would find no more than so much coiled fishing line below their skulls." Before my marriage I knew of C.'s wretched failing, but I thought he would indulge moderately in his intemperate habit. My dear! he fished during our honeymoon, and a man who can do that is hopeless. It is indeed a lamentable and grievous thing to discover that the beloved object of one's devoted affections is incurably mad upon one subject. To give but one instance of the deeper depths to which a man can fall. On our way we travelled through the Pass of Killiecrankie, and the train stopped for some reason or other at the most beautiful part, and we had a grand view of the Pass below. I thought of Claverhouse, and a certain memorable occasion where he figured conspicuously, and looked at C. for sympathy. The glow of enthusiasm ' mantled in his cheek, and the fire flashed in his eyes as he glanced down at the scene and watched the river rolling swiftly below. He opened his lips and said, with all the force and fervour of a feeling heart, "By Jove! isn't that a glorious pool for a salmon!"

Shall I describe to you the adventures of to-day? The recital of my woes would make a stone weep, so I am certain *of your* sympathy at all events. In the first place, we had breakfast at eight o'clock, and I decidedly object to this when I am away for a holiday, as I have no fancy for getting up in the middle of the night. C, who has been more or less in a fidget to get up ever since about five in the morning, is down first, and, having swallowed his breakfast before I have fairly begun mine, proceeds to pack the luncheon basket. G., who is invariably last down, no matter who is late, is leisurely finishing his morning repast. When it is completed he will search for his tobacco pouch, fill it in a deliberate manner, and when he has slowly put it in his pocket, found his pipe, and calmly laced his boots, he will have contributed his share towards the preparations. F. passes the time by playing selections from "Pinafore" on the piano, which sounds like a cracked tea-tray with the influenza. H. assists the performance, and I hand C. the provisions for his basket, thinking disconsolately that I might just as well be paying my usual visit to the queen of the kitchen and ordering dinner.

The morning is wet—the mornings here usually are!— and when the gentle-men set off, their outfit is more useful than ornamental. They are attired in every variety and shape of mackintosh imaginable, in the form of hats, coats, and leggings (not to mention a patent air-cushion), and C. looks like an enormous black beetle.

However, they all possess nobler qualities than their personal appearance warrants, and this is a great consolation.

Of course, just at the last moment G. cannot find his fishing basket, and there is a vast amount of impatience manifested, and a good deal of unparliamentary language launched at him, until it is discovered behind the door, and finally they are off—men, rods, gillie, and baskets, and I am left behind " apart, unfriended, melancholy, slow," for the next ten hours. And *this* is going for a holiday!" My first work invariably is to tidy the room, for it is left in a perfect chaos. Slippers lie promiscuously over the floor, tops of rods litter the little table, and discarded pipe-cases choke the mantel-shelf; the table-cloth is awry ; every antimacassar is pounded into a cotton lump: reels are legion, and are as great a plague as Pharoah's frogs, for there are reels in the bed-chamber ; and tobacco is sown broadcast! The piano is the general receptacle for all the odds and ends that cannot find a resting-place elsewhere, and at this moment it has lying upon it two rod tops, a reel, a Scotch bonnet, a tobacco pouch, a biscuit, a box of phantom minnows, a ball of string, half a newspaper, two time-tables, a pencil, a photographic lens, a novel, a pipe case, a broken match box, and a packet of tobacco. The piano also forms the favourite roosting place for the latest brood of chickens belonging to the establishment. I came in the other morning and found six or eight of them picking up a precarious livelihood from the floor. To judge from the dignified manner in which they walked about, it was i who was the intruder, and not they.

The prospect out of doors is far from inviting. The rain is coming down steadily, and a Scotch mist is slowly blotting out the landscape. The loch is lost in vapour, and the mountains look as if they were coming out of the middle of next week. There are five buildings in the place, and about three cottages. I can see the manse and the kirk, the post-office and the school-house from my window ; these, together with one other house, complete the town. The cottages are built of the roughest material: the more aristocratic have a barrel in the roof by way of a chimney, the rest have only a hole, through which the smoke gets out and the rain gets in. So you perceive that this is by no means a region over-run with streets. People, too, are scarce, and I do not know how the population is to be kept up, for I have only seen four children (whose principal attire is bare legs) since I came. We are fifteen miles from the nearest shop, and when I think of St. Ann's Square my soul is harrowed up within me.

I have written two letters, and read a little, and the rain is coming down as obstinately as ever. The landlord and a cowherd are having a subdued conversation in Gaelic under a cart-shed, and contemplating the scene. Years of this sort of climate no doubt produce a philosophic indifference in the bucolic mind. A be-draggled hen is pecking about under an empty wheelbarrow, and a discarded ginger-beer bottle lying just beneath my window inspires me with a feeling of infinite disgust.

I read a little more, contemplate the outside scene once again, reflect upon the advisability of water-gruel and mustard-plaisters when the gentlemen return ; presently the handmaiden, Christina, brings in my solitary dinner—Scotch broth, fried trout, mutton cutlet, and tapioca pudding. I turn my back upon the window, and take my dinner and a book together. * * *

After dinner I sat at the window to watch for the arrival of the mail cart, and to look at the rain which was coming down in a thoroughly sulky fashion. Still, when it does not pour cats and dogs here one considers the day as almost fine, so I ought not to grumble. The mail arrived about two o'clock, and created a vast excitement in the place. There were horses to change, parcels to deliver, and passengers to alight for refreshment, to say nothing of the letter-bag, in which was centred my chief interest. I did not think much of the passengers to-day. The ladies looked as if they had bought their dresses ready-made, and the men were attired in different varieties of what some third-rate tailor would advertise as " Fashionable Travelling Costumes," *i.e.*} last year's clothes dipped in a glue-pot and then rolled in bran till they all look like a collection of peripatetic meal bags. The other day a German professor came in the car. He was little and fat, and had a moon-face polished by much yellow soap and good humour. He wore long hair and spectacles, and looked as if he were dressed by contract, his clothes were so badly made. He discoursed volubly in broken English to the landlord just outside my open window, and I discovered that he was mad on the subject of jelly-fishes! I was actually comforted to find that there was a deeper depth, and a lower hobby even than fishing.

Presently my letters came, and for the next ten minutes I was lost to the miseries of my position. I was reminded that there is a land of civilization beyond these desolate regions, where people live, and move, and have kettledrums. When I tell you that I have not brought a ***bonnet*** here, you will know the depths of degradation to which I have descended. I feel as far from the pomps and vanities of this present evil world as a stained-glass martyr in a church window.

When I had come to the end of my letters I heaved a sigh of profound regret for vanished happiness, and then read two chapters of a French book by way of improving my mind. Then I watched a man in a cart going from the hotel to a peat-stack in the distance and bringing back turf. It took him thirty-five minutes to go, fill his cart, and return. He stood up in the middle of the cart, and jogged along with his hands in his pockets. He varied the time by singing Gaelic songs, and sucking straws in a meditative manner as he contemplated his horse, which plodded along without requiring any reins to guide it. When I was growing tired of watching the sleepy movements of the peat-cart, I was aroused by the unusual spectacle of the schoolmaster's chimney on fire ! It burnt ten minutes, and life afterwards seemed very flat arid uninteresting. Then I devoted myself to the ***Nineteenth Centtiry*** until five o'clock, when I went upstairs to change my dress, and came down again to my solitary tea, the drinking of which I spun out as long as possible. Then Christina lighted the fire, and I put the room in order against the return of the gentlemen. The other anglers in the hotel came home, and, in loud voices, compared notes outside the window upon the day's sport and the day's disappointment—generally the latter. The outside atmosphere is more than ever like that of a washing-day, where there are fourteen children and all " done" at home. Volumes of mist have rolled up the valley and completely blotted out the last vestige of the loch. It is growing dusk, too—the "gloaming," as I suppose they call it here,—it sounds nice and poetic, you know, but " Where the gloaming is I never made the ghost of an endeavour to discover " still, the reality, in a Scotch inn on a wet day, is the reverse of poetic, and I feel that Mariana's life in the Moated Grange was a vortex of dissipation compared with mine.

I take a book and sit down in the one arm-chair that the room contains. It has seen better days, for its internal arrangements are dyspeptic and out of order, and it feels as if it were stuffed with dbubled-up pokers and old steel forks, instead of springs. I think sadly of my comfortable chair at home, and wonder when its arms will embrace me again.

To crown all, the room is filled with a pungent odour of wood and peat, for the fire *will* smoke ! I dare not poke it to try to improve its constitution, for the front of the grate is so weak that it has to be propped up on one side with a piece of iron, and on the other by a Colman's Patent Mustard tin. The least shake to the structure would bring down peat, coals, mustard tin and bars amongst the poker and tongs, in hopeless confusion. So, with the calmness of despair, I watch the smoke curling slowly out through every available crack and cranny in mantel-piece and fireplace, and reflect that the smuts which result have one advantage, for they serve to re-mind me of Manchester.

The small room is rapidly emulating Cologne, with its " seven-and-twenty separate and distinct smells," for the odour of smoke is pleasantly mingled with that of burnt leather, arising from the slippers of my absent lord, which have been warming for the last two hours. I don't know that a man cares particularly for hot roast-slippers ; but it is the correct thing to air them, I believe. Christina has also brought in a paraffin lamp, which adds one more odour to the perfumes by which I am surrounded. Also, when she opened the door there was wafted in a breath of wet mackintosh coats, fried onions from the kitchen, and tobacco smoke from the coffee-room. There is a girl in the coffee-room, across the passage, who makes day hideous by continually singing " John Peel." She has a voice like a tuneful nutmeg-grater, and the only time when I envy a deaf person is during her daily practising.

So I read and meditate, and just when I am on the point of falling asleep, I hear sounds of the return of my own particular anglers, and come back once more to this world.

An admiring throng of fellow-lunatics from the other room meet them at the door, and contemplate the result of the day's sport with the most absorbed interest. Every man has a pipe in his mouth and his hands in his pockets, and gazes with profound admiration upon a heap of nasty-smelling, shiny fish, which have been emptied out of the baskets upon a dish. My four gentlemen are several degrees dirtier than when they started off this morning, and, if looks would hang them, I would not give much for their lives. C, who is more disreputable in appearance than the rest, is the centre of attraction, for he is weighing each horrid little trout on the scales, and there is great excitement as to the number of ounces shown. I think fishing develops, as much as anything else, the envy, hatred, malice, and all uncharitableness of the human mind ! If a man happens to have caught the biggest fish that day, he has no modest scruples whatever, but announces the fact from the house-tops.

Ah! my dear! the pleasures of fishing are like the prospect spoken of by the Irishman—" No fellow can describe it but him who has seen it, and *he* can't!"

I will draw a veil over the supper, where they ate as if they had not had a meal for a week, and talked as if their lungs were iron, and their throats brass. They disputed about the particular inch in seven miles of water where they " rose that big chap," and their whole conversation was a confused Babel of " rises," " bites," " trolling," and "flies." Amidst "confusion worse confounded," I registered a mental vow that never, no! *never*! under any circumstances whatever, would I set foot again in Scotland bound solely on a fishing expedition.

And after this experience of *one day's fishing,* from my point of view, can you wonder that after three weeks of precisely similar days, I consider the *Sportsman's Guide* to be the most idiotic and the feeblest book ever written, and Scotland the most detestable word in the English language! * * *

THE RAID TO KIRKCUDBRIGHT.
BY THE RAIDERS.

CHAPTER I.—*THE SCENE.*

KIRKCUDBRIGHTSHIRE, or, as it is more frequently termed, the Stewartiy, constitutes about two-thirds of the whole province of Galloway. It is bounded on the north and north-west by Ayrshire ; on the east and north-east by Dumfries-shire ; on the south by the Solway Frith and the Irish Sea ; and on the west by the county of Wigtonshire. Its extreme length and breadth are forty-four and thirty-one miles respectively. Its general outline is irregular, but, as a whole, bears some resemblance to the form or figure of a trapezoid. It contains large tracts of stratified rocks, which are either nearly perpendicular, or slanting towards the north-west, and which consist, sparsely, of the new red sandstone, and chiefly of the ordinary whinstone and the light grey granite. The north-western district, which embraces nearly two-thirds of the whole area of the county, is bold and somewhat rugged and mountainous. Blackcraig, which is situated on the north-eastern boundary of the Stewartry, is nearly 2,300 feet above the level of the sea, and is closely followed in its cloud-aspiring tendencies by many adjacent summits. The various heights along the boundary, and for some distance into the interior on the north, form a part of what is often called the "Highlands of the Lowlands;" and a living Gallowegian writer assures us that at the present day, there are unmistakeable evidences that the original inhabitants of these mountainous districts spoke the Gaelic language. This broad Alpine belt, as it has been termed, stretches across the middle of the Scottish Lowlands, and ascends, as a whole, to lofty elevations ; and extending down to the sea on the west, or running down parallel to Dumfriesshire on the east, forms an imposing semicircle, from which widening and lessening spurs run off into the interior. The south-eastern division of the county, when viewed from this northern mountain range, seems like a great plain diversified by a marvellous variety of light and shade, according to the colour, size, or distance of the heights on its surface. So gradual and gentle, too, is the ascent of this plain from the Bay of Kirkcudbright, that after following the course of the Dee for several miles inland, it is only 150 feet above the level of the sea. And yet nearly one-fourth of this plain is what we would designate as hilly, or rather mountainous; while the greater part of the other three-fourths, though chiefly under cultivation, consists of a rolling and broken surface, and continues, in many parts, its bold undulations down to the estuary of the sea. These heights, though considerably inferior to those of the north-east and western divisions, are far from being insignificant, as many of them reach no mean elevations—and in all parts of the country the uplands chiefly consist of rocky knolls, steep hills, abrupt protuberances, craggy cliffs, and dark summits, which are highly picturesque, and occasionally even sublime.

Such is a brief outline of the ***land features*** of Kirkcudbrightshire. But while the Stewartry is so largely and beautifully diversified with hill and dale, with mountain and rocky declivity, and whilst it abounds, as might be expected from its undulating configuration, with small brooks or burns, it cannot boast of ***numerous*** rivers. Its chief streams are the Urr, the Cree, the Fleet, the Ken, the Deugh, and the Dee.

The Urr, taking its rise in a loch known by that name at the junction of the parishes of Dunskae and Balmaclellan, and receiving a large number of small tributaries on its way, runs for 26 miles in a southerly direction by Castle Douglas and Dalbeattie, and then falls into the Solway Frith. This river generally, but more especially in damp seasons, carries large volumes of water, and furnishes considerable quantities of salmon, grilse, sea-trout, herling, and burn-trout. It runs through the lands of six different proprietors, and is strictly preserved.

The Cree rises on the south-east of Carrick, on the borders of Ayrshire, and flowing south by south-east, falls, after a run of some 25 miles, into Wigton Bay. It receives a considerable number of small tributaries in its course, and is reputed as being well-stocked with salmon, grilse, and other ordinary kinds offish. It is said that the smelt or sparling, which is a very rare fish in Scotland, being only found elsewhere in the Forth at Stirling, is caught in large quantities in this river for a few days of the month of March. This fish, which is both a salt and fresh-water inhabitant, and which measures some eight inches in length, both tastes and smells of rushes. In the upper part of its course the stream runs through a bleak and dreary country, and in the lower through a rich valley and well-wooded slopes and undulations. The angling in this river is partly free, and partly preserved, but it is not difficult to obtain permission to angle over its entire length.

The Fleet, which owes its existence to two small burns known as the " Big " and " Little Fleet," rises some considerable distance to the south-west of the town of New Galloway in the parish of Kirkmabreck. Pursuing its separate course for four or six miles, and receiving several insignificant tributaries on the way, this divided stream unites; and then running in a south-westerly direction, and receiving sundry additional rivulets, it falls into Wigton Bay a little below the small town or village of Gatehouse. There are no salmon in this river, but it is reported as being richly stocked with sea-trout, herling, and burn-trout. Like the Urr, it runs through several landed estates, and is strictly preserved ; but permission can be had from the manager of the bank in Gatehouse to angle on it on the following terms, viz :—-For the whole season two guineas ; for the Mondays and Thursdays of the season one guinea ; for one week ten shillings; for one day five shillings. A certain writer when speaking of the vale of Fleet says,—"The Highlands of Scotland have no scenes of greater beauty, and hardly any wilder hills, than those among which both branches of the river take their rise. The basin of the Fleet for a good many miles above Gatehouse is exquisitely fine. Rough heath-clad hills, indeed, overlook the stream on both sides ; but declivities and plains, opulent in soil, ornate in tillage, and plentiful in groves, form its ' immediate banks' "

The river Ken, which rises on the Blackcraig mountain, to which we have already adverted, flows alternately in a south-east and south-westward direction over a distance of 20 miles, and then falls into its larger neighbour, the Deugh. The streamlets which the Ken receives in its course are very numerous, but individually-

inconsiderable. About three-quarters of a mile before its junction with the Deugh, there is a very pretty, romantic, bold, and dashing waterfall, known by the name of the " College Xoup." Tradition says that in olden days an English nobleman, not far removed from royal blood, became enamoured with the charming daughter of a Scotch farmer in the north-eastern district of the parish of Carsphairn—telling her on more than one occasion of his love, wealth, and rank. She gracefully, but firmly-resisted his alluring protestations of affection each time they were renewed. Determined upon making her his own, either by foul or fair means, he visited her parental home one April eve ; and having again met with a stern denial of the fair one's hand and heart both from her parents and herself, he first mastered the father, and next two sturdy hinds in succession by a few well-aimed blows : and then, gently seizing the maid, he made off on horseback for the south as fast as he could with his lovely prize. This bold exploit had hardly been accomplished when an only brother, who had been pursuing his studies at Glasgow University, arrived upon the scene. Having been told what had just taken place, and feeling that the daring captor would most likely cross the bridge that spans the Ken about a mile to the north, he dashed off in hot pursuit across the rocky and broken land that intervened between the river and the farm. Coming to a margin of the stream at a point where even few of the gods, in sober moments, would attempt to cross, this youth, burning with wrath and filled with classic lore, swept athwarf it at a single bound, shortly intercepted his sister's captor, and after administering to him such a castigation as he never forgot, returned with her in joy and triumph to the farm. The point where this Kirkcudbrightshire student so heroically crossed the Ken, and rescued his charming sister, was ever afterwards christened by the natives with the name of the " College Loup." It is stated that the upper parts of this river are very beautiful. In addition to the burn-.trout which tenant it, and which are reported to be plentiful and of a goodly size, grilse and salmon also frequent it, despite the obstruction bearing the learned name to which we have referred. The fishing on this stream is free, as a whole, and where it is preserved, permission may be had by asking at the proper quarters. The Deugh rises from *three* sources, amid very wild and beautiful scenery, in the north-west part of the parish of Carsphairn ; and running in this divided condition for some considerable distance, the three streamlets unite about three miles to the north-west of the village of Carsphairn, whence the river flows in a south-easterly-direction through fine moorland and hill for nine miles, and then joins the Ken. This river receives a number of small tributaries in its course, and with the exception of a few grand, deep, rock-bound, and shingley pools, runs the whole way over a thin, wide-spread, and rough, rolling, boulder-bed. The burn-trout, which are very plentiful both in the upper and lower reaches, generally run from three to eight ounces in weight, but are not unfrequently caught as heavy as one, two, and even three pounds each. Salmon and salmon trout have access only to the lower reach. The fishing over the whole length of this river is free, except on the estates of Knockgray and Glenhoul. There is an exceedingly wild and grand waterfall of forty feet a little over two miles to the south of the village of Carsphairn, which is called the " Tinkler's Loup.' Tradition says, that in former days, a stalwart travelling tinker visited a farmhouse just on the eve of supper-time. Having travelled a great distance, and being very hungry, he asked the farmer's wife for some of the porridge that stood in some half score of dishes on the kitchen table. The gudewife replied that there was none to spare, as the lassie had only made enough for the ploughmen and shepherds' supper, and that there was no more time to make any more before the men came in. On hearing this, the tinker unceremoniously proceeded to help himself to the porridge; the farmer's wife meanwhile secretly despatched a wee lassie to report to those whom she shortly expected to their evening meal, what was going on at the house. Dish after dish of the porridge speedily went down the tinker's throat ; but just as the last one was following in the wake of the first, the ploughmen and the shepherds appeared on the scene. Seeing some six or eight powerfully-built fellows arrayed against him, and feeling, under the circumstances, that "discretion was the better part of valour," the tinker took to his heels, and running towards the river, bounded over it at this wild cascade, leaving his chagrined pursuers on the other side, to retrace their steps homewards, and wait till a second supper was prepared. From the date of this feat, the spot has been known by the name of the " Tinkler's Loup."

The Deugh, from the point of its junction with the Ken, takes the name of the latter river, and for the next four miles consists of a series of splendid, rough, boulder streams, fringed with huge blocks of whinstone or granite, and of magnificent salmon pools which, every now and then, are shut in by such deep, rugged, and perpendicular rocks, as not only to challenge the approach of the keenest angler, or the most adventuresome quadruped, but which, if ever angled, must have been before the dry land was called " earth," or the waters " sea." Some of these rock-encircled pools are exceedingly wild, picturesque, and grand. In this section of the river the Ken receives a few tributaries, the chief being the Pulmaddy and Pulharrow burns, which, like the main stream, are well supplied with trout weighing from three ounces to three pounds, and even upwards. A little less than a mile above Dairy, the Ken enters a champaign part of the county, through which, for a distance of three miles, it sweeps noiselessly over a shingly bed, in segments and semi-circles which abound with splendid trouting streams and magnificent salmon pools. At this point, which is exactly opposite the clean and pretty little town of New Galloway, the valley-land becomes so flat that the river assumes the form of a series of lochs for three or four miles, which vary from one to three-quarters of a mile in width, and which, now and then, are skirted on both sides with pretty belts of wood. This chain of lakes is reported to be well supplied with large trout, pike, and a variety of other fish, as also salmon in the season. At the head, and on the right bank of the lake chain, stands Kenmure Castle, upon a very pretty eminence, and has a very picturesque appearance, but certainly few architectural charms. To the rear of the castle is the garden, which is enclosed on one side by perhaps the most magnificent buck-hedge in the kingdom, this being from twenty to twenty-five feet in height, and thirty broad at the top, wide enough for a carriage and pair to be driven along it. The whole section of the Ken, from its junction with the Deugh to its subsequent junction with the Dee, extending to twelve miles or thereabouts, is free to anglers who live for the time being at any of the hotels in New Galloway, at the Spalding Arms, which is less than a quarter of a mile distant and on the left bank of the river, or at the Lochinvar Hotel, Dairy, which is two miles farther up the stream.

The river Dee has its sources in something like a dozen rills, some of which pursue an independent course for a considerable distance. The highest of these rills, and strictly speaking the parent stream, rises a mile from the southern boundary of Ayrshire, and pursues a circuitous course for six miles under the names of the Sauch Burn and the Cooran Lane. Receiving at this point the surplus waters of Loch Dee, it then takes the name of the river Dee, and flows for seventeen miles in a south-easterly direction, absorbing a large number of small tributaries on its way. Over the whole of this distance it is said to be a "pretty stream, wending its way through moorland flats" by the foot of hills alike devoid of "verdant foliage or grandeur." Passing by New Galloway about two miles to the westward, this river next flows almost due east for five or six miles till it receives the more plentiful waters of the Ken; and then bending silently, but proudly round, like the arc of a circle, it sweeps in a south-westerly direction, rich in waters and scenic beauty, till it falls into the Bay of Kirkcudbright. This river has the repute of being well stocked with salmon, which are said to be of "a darker colour and fatter quality" than the salmon of any river in the south of Scotland. Like the majority of its tributaries, it is also said to be well supplied with burn-trout. The salmon reaches, as well as some of the trout ones on this stream, are preserved, while the rest are free. Generally, however, angling permission for trout, and not unfrequently for salmon, can be obtained for the preserved sections of the river from the different proprietors.

Kirkcudbrightshire also abounds with lochs, which are more or less plentifully supplied with burn-trout and other kinds of fish, and which are said to vary in weight from a few ounces to several pounds. Permission to angle in almost all of these lochs may be had on the same conditions as on the rivers.

CHAPTER II.—*IN ACTION.*

INTO the glorious country described in the last chapter, five ardent members of the Manchester Anglers' Association resolved to make a raid. It was in the midst of the hardest winter any of them remember that they first began to lay their heads together and to concoct their plans. They talked of journeying in April, and all through the dreary winter months looked anxiously forward to the happy days to come; they took out their rods, looked over their flies, and examined their lines a hundred times during the dark days, and laid them by on each occasion in solemn silence. At last April came, but the winter had scarce begun to relax its hold on nature, and eager as they were, they were loth to defer their raiding for another month. Even when May, "smiling May" appeared, a freezing east wind swept over the earth with its biting breath; the winter snow lay thick on the hills, and lingered in the valleys; the trees had made no sign, no grass had begun to spring, and once more the journey northward must be deferred. By the end of the month a milder period set in, and, like boys dimissed from school, away went our raiders with all the speed the north express could supply.

The outward aspect of these raiders was scarcely uniform—they were sixes and sevens, long and short, thick and thin. Piscator, the commander, was of burly or even ponderous build; Scholar, the lieutenant, as thin as a scarecrow, and half the weight of his chief; Corydon, the pioneer, was to the "manor born," and carried a farmer's thews and sinews; Venator, the rubicund, neither tall nor short, thick nor thin, boiled over with continual merriment; and Peter, the orator, though originally thin, was on the point of commencing that thickening process which sets in when gentlemen approach the certain age which young men call elderly, but older ones designate maturity.

As is the custom of raiders, our company travelled by night, and in over-due time (for they were delayed on the way by an accident which befel another train) arrived at Parton in Kirkcudbrightshire, to which station Corydon had directed them to book. Here, by the provident care of the same officer, a vehicle was in waiting to take the travellers to New Galloway, where their first attack on the trout was to be made. But when the traps came to be counted up, those of Piscator (except his rod, which he never allows to leave his sight) were found to be missing, and the telegraph had to be called into requisition.

Now they are off, and after a pleasant drive of six miles, doubly beautiful to their town-accustomed eyes, they descend at the Spalding Arms, where they find everything in readiness for their reception. Without loss of time they prepared for battle, and issued forth on their watery quest. The poet of the next chapter says that "by sun-down they'd all got their baskets crammed full," and if that account has something of poetical license in it, let us say that it is near enough to the mark. But not in slaying trout did our raiders find their only satisfaction. After the smoke and dust and din of busy Manchester, how serene and balmy the atmosphere of the Stewartry! How inspiriting and elastic the clear sunshine! How lovely the budding hedge-rows, and the mossy banks and woods dotted with pale primroses and sweet violets! The songsters of the woods had once more awakened to new life, and were pouring forth their thrilling strains of melody. The young lambs frisked and gambolled in an ecstacy of delight, the cattled browsed in the fields. The cuckoo gave forth its doleful but melodious note, and the mavis from the shaw saluted his brooding mate. The trees, which were recently so naked and skeleton-like, were fast assuming their beautiful appearance; with branches, lately so bleak and naked, now gracefully bending under the weight of bursting buds and blossoms. The raiders then saw the end of the first day and returned to the inn, with trout in their creels enough to satisfy them, and their hearts softened by these rural beauties.

On the morrow, in obedience to command, they moved on to Dairy, some two miles away, taking up their abode at the Lochinvar Arms, where they found pleasant quarters, comfortable and cleanly rooms, sleep-inviting beds, attentive landlord and landlady, and daughters pleasant to look upon. What more could men desire ?

Half a mile above Dairy, the Ken turns abruptly to the north, and entirely alters its character. Below that place, and between it and Loch Ken, the river is generally a somewhat slow-flowing stream with long deep pools, and here and there a wide shallow ; above Dairy, except in the neighbourhood of the " Tinkler's Loup," already mentioned, where a deep pool a quarter of a mile long fills up a chasm in the tall rocks, it is a dancing stream, broken up into rapid runs, eddies, pools, and shallows in infinite variety. In this stream the raiders found ample room for the whole of them to fish, without interruption to one another; and when evening came, their creels carried greatly more weight than on the former day. Thus, in healthful exercise and delightful occupation the time passed away, and when they met around the dinner table in the evening it was with appetites sharp as hunters', hearts as merry and happy as children's, and heads free from ache or care. Oft did the gentle Piscator replenish the plates of his disciples, oft did the merry Venator convulse his brethren with laughter, and render due progress of the feast impossible.

No friends are ever like those we have known as boys, but these men turned lads once more, and their friendship became as that of boys, to last, let us hope, as long.

" When the dinner was over"—well, that was perhaps not the least pleasant part of the time ; but Scholar, who appears to have taken accurate notes of every word spoken and every song chanted, has told this in another chapter, to which it is now time to turn.

CHAP. III.—*A NICHT AT THE "LOCHINVAR."*

PISCATOR, VENATOR, CORYDON, SCHOLAR, PETER,

Pisc.—Well met, my brethren; we are all here at last, and your creels are laden with many a fish, I'll warrant me. But before we count the trouts, let us to dinner; for I am weary of waiting, and you are all impatient to begin, as I see by your hungry looks.

VEN.—I am hungry indeed ; but first give us drink, and then let us have dinner at once, and we'll eat it cheerfully. I have sped so among the trouts, that I have scarce tasted my luncheon, and others are like me, I know.

OMNES.—Yes, let us to dinner first, and to the weighing the trouts after.

PISC.—Well, now that our meat is eaten, and our hearts be thankful, let me see the fish, and I will judge who is the best angler. Let me have the creels ; what is yours, brother Venator ?

VEN.—Marry, I have done fairly well; here be eight and twenty trouts, all over our limit of size. They look well, see you.

PISC.—Right well done! you have had good fortune, brother. Who is the next
?

SCHO.- -Here is my basket, my loving master. It is heavy as Venator's, and I have twenty-nine fish, great and little.

Pise.—Well done, Scholar! marry, I am glad you have profited so well by my advice and precept. Now, Corydon, what have you ?

CORY.—No sae muckle as the tithers, but I hae a gude feesh o' twa poond, and that's mair than they hae, forby.

OMNES.—Bravo, Corydon! Bravo! That is a thumper!

PISC.—But what is this ? O, fie, Corydon ! Here is a parr. This is an offence against our first statute : " No fisher but the ungrown fry forbears." What is to be done, brethren ?

OMNES.—Fine him glasses round, good master.

CORY.—Stop! stop! Nae so faust, I'll jest tell you nae lees ; that parr was sair hookit, sae I broke his neck to put him oot o' his trouble.

PISC.—Quite right, too, Corydon. What says the play-book ? " There's nothing in the world so noble as a kindly angler."

PETER (aside),—It should have been glasses round, all the same.

PISC.—No treason, Peter. Now, what have *you* ?

PETER.—Not so much, I have had but ill fortune ; I have here but ten trouts, and I lost one great one ; I had a grand fight with him, but had no chance at all, so——

CORY.—Cut it short, Peter.

PETER.—so I lost him,

PISC.—Look you, Peter, that was bad luck, but better fortune to-morrow, my friend. And now for my judgment. I do here pronounce you all equal, for Venator and Scholar had the best water!

OMNES.—Bravo! bravo! bravo! An upright judge!

PISC.—Now, brother anglers, 'tis time we should light up the fragrant weed, or, as Scholar there would call it, the flagrant weed ; and, Mary dear, bring, if you please, a mutchkin of the national drink !

VEN.—Aye, a mutchkin, and see you, Mary, bring it in a measure, (Aside, and winking awfully,) A measure holds twice as much as a crystal!

PISC.—Now, boys, while the whisky is coming, let Corydon sing us the song he writ for us.

CORY.—Weel, if ye maun hae it, ye maun tak it wi' all its faults. Now for my song.

CORYDON'S SONG.

Air—*Modification of "The Farmer's Boy:'*

Cauld winter's gaen, the spring is come, we soon will hear the dgouk,
So anglers all, look up your rods, for we must have an out;
We'll make our way to some famed stream, where there are shoals o' trout,
And we will do our very best to bring lots of them out.

Then to angle we will go, we'll go,
To angle we will go,
Wih rod or line, or wet or fine,
To angle we will go.

We'll tak' our baskets on our back, our geazecoats on our arm,
And we have got good watertights to keep us dry and warm ;
We'll fill our pouch wi' scone and cheese, our flasks wi' mountain dew,
Tobacco and our sneezing mill, wi' that I think we'll do.
Then to angle we will go, &c.

Before we start we'll tak' a drap, and wish each other weel,
And hope, before the day is oot, each man shall fill his creel.
We'll drink success to our ain Club :
Success, come on us shine ! Success go with us on our raid, success for
Seventy-nine ! Then to angle we will go, &c.

Like all true anglers we'll mind this—The wee fry let alane,
For nothing but a gude-sized fish we'll think of takin' hame;
We'll tell our friends when we come back, how we enjoyed the fun,
So now I'll bid you all adieu, for this my song is done. Then to angle we will
go, &c.

PISC.—Well sung, Corydon, thou shalt be our Laureate. And now, Peter, I see
by thy looks that thou art anxious to follow. But here come the drinks. * * * Now that
we have all filled up, except that cold water boy there, let us have a toast. Here's a
hearty draught to you all, success to the Manchester Anglers' Association, and to
our good fishing to-morrow! Now, Peter, for your song.

PETER.—Mine is something that I hope will please you ; it was writ by our
friend, " Crabstick," and is sung to a tune you all know well.

THE RAID INTO KIRKCUDBRIGHT.

AIR—*" Bonny Dundee:"*

'Twas the Manchester Anglers in Council agreed,
That when spring came again they'd go north of the Tweed,
And that weather defying,—or cold, wet, or dree,
They'd take down their rods into Kirkuberee.
They all came together—they came in the night—
Reid, Currie, Heywood, and Vice-President
White ; They waved their rods high, crying " Now we are free,
We're all going a fishing beyond Lockerbie."

They rode till the morn, when the sun was half high,
As they leapt from the train, " to the river," they cry;
They shouldered their rods, and marched off as one man,
With Reid in the rear, and White in the van.
They all walked together that came in the night—
Reid, Currie, Heywood, and Vice-President White ;
They waved their rods high, cried " Hurrah ! we are free
To begin our day's fishing in New Gallowee."

Like skirmishing soldiers they spread themselves out,
And with steel they attacked the bright red-speckled trout;
With such skill they threw over each stream and each pool,
That by sundown they'd all got their baskets crammed full.
They all met together again in the night—
Reid, Currie, Heywood, and Vice-President White ;
They put up their rods, crying " Now we are free ;
We have had a day's fishing in Kirkuberee."

When the dinner was cleared, they sat in a ring,

And then was the time that they'd laugh and they'd sing ;
They fought o'er again all the strifes they'd gone through,
While they quaffed (all but Heywood) the Scotch mountain dew.
They all sat together, half way through the night—
Reid, Currie, Heywood, and Vice-President White ;
And then they jumped up, crying "Now we are free
To be off to our sleeping in New Gallowee."

But all things must end, so the fishing must stop,
As the time surely comes when you drink your last drop ;
So one evening the Chief said " Now, Secretaree,
Please to order our men to turn back from N.B."
They all went together that came in the night—
Reid, Currie, Heywood, and Vice-President
White ; They all hung their heads, crying "Oh, deary me,
We have finished our fishing beyond Lockerbie."

Just a word or two more, for I want to explain,
That as well as the others who came in the train,
Was one whom they all said their leader should be
When they went on their raid into Kirkuberee.
So when you count up those who came in the night,
As well as Reid, Currie, and Heywood, and White,
You'll please to add Colonel John Mawson, C.E.,
Who was boss of the raiders to New Gallowee.

Pise.—Well sung, well sung ; we anglers are all beholden to the good man that made that song. Come, hostess, give us another mutchkin, and let us drink to him.

VEN. (sotto voce)—Aye, in a *measure.*

PISC.—But it was unkind of Crabstick to leave me out till he got to what I may call the appendix. However, I trow well I came in late, and that must be his reason.

Thank you, Peter ; here's to your good health.

PETER.—Thank you, good master, and God speed you.

PlSC.—Now, Scholar, it is your turn, and soon we must to our beds, which are scented with lavender, I warrant But what are you drinking, Scholar ?

SCHO.—I drink the red cow's milk, father, with a merry heart, and may I never drink worse.

PlSC.—Now for your song, then, and don't let us have a milk and water one.

SCHO.—It is not mine own, gentle master, so you will not have milk and water ; but here are a few verses that may suit you ; I learned them, when a boy, from the visitors' book of a little inn in Wales, and cannot tell you who wrote them.

SCHOLAR'S SONG.

You anglers all, both great and small,
Who Cerrig's Inn have sought,
Join in the lay of a rainy day,
To the trout you *might* have caught.

When the wind is high, and a stormy sky
Sets all your arts at nought,
Then, not unpraised, because unraised,
Be the trout you might have caught.

From Coquet's mouth, to the distant South
An angler's strife I've fought;
But fewer still are the trout I kill,
Than the trout I might have caught.

In the deeps they swim, the deeps so dim,
Of mountain pools unsought:
And none shall see, whoe'er they be
The trout they might have caught.

PETER.—Very pretty verses, and well remembered, honest Scholar. May you find him that wrote them !

PISC.—Now, Venator, what have you to say ere we go upstairs, all as sober as judges ? By the way, let us have another mutchkin.

VEN.—Another mutchkin, good hostess, and see you bring it in a *measure.* Like Scholar and Peter, I must sing you what is not mine own. This song comes from the land of songs, and was wrote by a true angler, as you shall say when you hear it.

VENATOR'S SONG[8].
When cauld winter is past, and the green ice is gane,
While ilk curler lays by his bonnie whinstane,
And the win' frae the south comes kindly and warm,
Ah ! then is the time for the fisher to arm,
Wi' his rod and his creel, and be off to the burn
Gushing fou to the brim, wi' deep pools at ilk turn.

When the south-west win' blaws, and the clouds as they pass
Are changing the shade o' the wide-waving grass ;
When the ripplin' waves hurry across the deep pool,
Ah ! this is the time to be steady and cool,
An' to wave your wan deftly, ye're flees mauna whistle,
But fa' on the streamlet like down o' the thistle.

8   This song is reprinted, with the omission of two verses and some alterations in the last verse, from Blakey's **Anglers' Song Book,** 1855, where it appears under the title, " Uncle Will to Uncle John," dated 1702.

When ye've gien twa-three *waps,* an' a fine thumpin' grilse,
Has lap at ye twice and made flutter your pulse ;
When at last ye ha heuk't him, an' he's afF to the deep,
Ah ! then tak' your time, an' let him tak' his sweep ;
Gie him plenty o' line, an'tak' tent o' your graith,
For ye've gut no sae Strang, an' he'll sure tyne his breath.

When wi' fair skilly feshin' ye've warsled him out,
A dainty three-pounder, a bonnie sea-trout,
Frae the brine freshly run, an' just fit for your creel,
Ah ! then is the time that contented ye'll feel,
An' care all forgettin', devoutly ye'll say,
Thank God, that He let me live on till to-day.

PISC.—Bravo, bravo, well sung! I thank you heartily. That song shall send us to happy slumbers. And now let us all to bed, that we may rise early. Good night to everybody ; good night!

OMNES.—Good night, father, and to-morrow you shall show us how to catch a salmon.

CHAP. IV.—*AT THE CLACHAN OF FINTRY.*

VENATOR, PETER, CORYDON.

ENCOURAGED by the delights of their first raid, three of the members of that expedition undertook, in the month of August, a second journey. On the morning of the 11th, Venator, Peter, and Corydon met in royal glee at the station yclept Lenzie Junction, which they named as their trysting place, the two latter furnished with so large a quantity of baggage as to incur a merited reproof from their senior, Venator. Pleasant greetings, and the reproof both over, Lennoxton was soon reached, whence further progress to the Vale of Fintry, nine miles away, must be by trap, which, by the well-ordered providence of Venator, was duly in waiting.

Through this vale flows the Endrick, famous among Scottish streams for its fine-flavoured,and not parsimonious trout. The drive was somewhat slow, being steep ; but the slowness of the locomotion was amply compensated for by the glorious view which the raiders had of the far-famed Glen of Campsie, with the noble Castle of Lennoxton, surmounting a finely wooded hill on the right, and stretching away to the south-west towards Lenzie Junction and Glasgow.

After four and a half miles, the first human habitation on the way is reached, a toll-bar, which effectually bars any further progress until the sum of ninepence is forthcoming. This found, the toll-wife smilingly opens the legal barriers on the highway, and after Peter and Corydon had begged a drink of the gudewife's cow's milk (which was produced as soon as asked for), the three, now on the descending slope of the hill, shortly arrived at the end of their pleasant mountain drive, and were safely landed at the Fintry Inn.

The proprietor of the soil, to whose residence they at once proceeded in order to ask permission to angle, was from home, but being assured by those in charge of the mansion that the request would be granted, they got their piscatorial trappings in order, and walking less than a hundred yards, found themselves on the bank of the Endrick. To their surprise and disappointment the stream was unwontedly small. The late heavy and continuous rains, which seemed to have prevailed everywhere, had not visited the Vale of Fintry. But faint heart never won a fair lady, and a dispirited angler never made a good basket; the anglers, therefore, addressed themselves earnestly to their work, whipping the river for a couple of hours, until it grew dark, losing the while divers lines and casts, or meeting with the sundry mishaps which fishermen encounter in their much-loved pursuit. When they returned to their inn, their creels were somewhat scantily furnished, but their hearts were undaunted. Evening was spent after the manner of raiders, the mountain dew being religiously ordered in the standard " measure,"

Next morning, five o'clock found them by the river, and till breakfast time they fished up the stream. After breakfast they fished down, continuing their efforts till evening again drew nigh.

The sport of the day was not great, but when the baskets came to be exibited Venator showed twenty-six trout, Peter twenty, and Corydon fourteen.

On the morrow heavy thunderstorms put an end to the sport, and the friends found employment in arranging a further raid to the valley of the Girvan, the Fintry, probably on account of the unfortunate weather (it is always so) having scarcely realised expectations,

The story of this new expedition must be told in Chapter V.

CHAP. V.—*THE VALLEY OF THE GIRVAN.*

To Find las Loch they now resort,
That far-famed place for goodly sport;
I've heard it said if fish you'll court,
Large trout you'll kill;
And ne'er a day will you go short
Your creel to fill.

They found the fish there fu' o' mettle ;
Venator's rod they soon did settle,
And snap't it through just like a pettle,
Wi' age worn short; It cost him twa 'oors it to fettle—
An' fit for sport.

When he gets righted he begins,
And aye the ither cast he flings ;
Up jumps a trout, and he him brings—

Guid faith, there's two— Come,
Robert lad, be on your pins,
And land them, do.

He lands them both and gives a cheer,
Venator says, " Now just look here,
I've seen my fish fast disappear
In Cory's creel;
I'll no hae that, not me, no fear!"
He oot did squeal.

Peter was gettin' on gey weel,
An' mony a gron' fish he did creel,
Till ae' great big ane made a wheel,
And drew, him in,
Alas ! poor Peter's fate to seal—
He couldna swin.

Poor Peter thocht his race was run,
His awfu' hinner en' was come ;
Till " Genoch " saw it was past fun,
An' drew him out;
But was obleeg't to cry " Come, Come,
Let go the troot"

Venator sair, sair for him grat,
And Corydon lang mournin' sat;
The boatman said, " I pity that
Puir drookit craw!"
But Peter cried, " Though I'm gey wat,
Til fish awa'!"

The " wormer " scarce could get a rise,
Though lang and lang he threw his flies,
At lang and length his spirit dies,
Sits doon to mourn ;

Soon up again and then he cries,
I'll try the worm.

The worms are out and baited right,
Out goes the line wi' all his might;
And in a jiffey what a sight!
A great one on,
He made one rush, soon ceas'd to fight,
And's landed home.

He was so pleas'd he had a race,
A trout like that deserves a taste ;
The flask is oot, the angler's grace,
" Here's tae ye, man !"
" Now, boys, be quick, nae time to waste,
The fun's sae gran'."

Each man in turn then had his cast,
An' aye the ither troot got fast
Upon the line, and then were past
Right in the creel;
And there they kickt and lept their last,
For lang and weel.

The sun at length got roun'the hill,
The air it changt, got rather chill,
They stopped and counted up their kill—
Just ninety-eight;
Then oot the boat and owre the hill,
For hame made straight.

ST. BOSWELLS AND THE TWEED.

BY HENRY VANNAN, M.A.

THE village of St. Boswells, in the northern end of the county of Roxburghshire, is beautifully situated in a district where every stream, and tower, and hill have been rendered classic by the pen of the great Sir Walter. Its approach from the south is by what is appropriately known -as the Waverley route of the North British Railway. The station at which the traveller is set down is Newtown, St. Boswells, a thriving-little modern village, which has attained some degree of importance since the introduction of the auction system in the'sale of cattle. Here there are two or three of the largest auction marts in Scotland, and some large annual fairs are held in the neighbourhood. St. Boswells proper, however, or, as it was anciently called Lessudden, lies about two miles from the railway station, and close to the right bank of the Tweed. Previously to 1876 I made two or three annual visits to this quarter, staying about five or six weeks each time,—generally from about the beginning of August to the middle of September. Before this I had frequently fished the Tweed at Peebles and Innerleithen, but I was ignorant of its character here, until my attention was directed to it by a brother angler, who warmly recommended St. Boswells, not only for good and varied trout-fishing, but for the intensely interesting nature of its situation and surroundings.

From my own subsequent experience, I also can recommend it to anyone in search of a quiet and beautiful spot wherein to exercise to his heart's content all the subtle deceptions of what has been called, with, I always think, a slight tinge of the sarcastic, "the gentle art." Gentle it may be legitimately termed, but there are anglers, and anglers. Amidst the multitude who come under this designation, there are hundreds whose principles, and practice, are directly opposed to anything entitled to the name of gentleness. To see a regiment of native " artists " in a row upon some river, at the rise of the flood (times and again have I seen such a sight) with worms like moderately-sized eels, and rods and tackle of corresponding proportions, dragging, what they **will** describe as "great lumps of fish," from the water, over their heads, with a bang against the wall behind them ; or switching the prey by main force *in sutnmis arboribus,* to wriggle and dangle as if suffering the last penalty of the law—this is an exception to the gentleness alluded to, either in respect to craft or craftsmen.

I have always believed (and wherever it is practicable, I act upon the belief) that the angler has quite sufficient exercise for his arms and legs at the river-side, and in plying his vocation for the time being, without having superadded to this a long and toilsome walk to and from his fishing ground. Indeed, one's basket often suffers in consequence of the physical energy that should have been expended in keeping the hands acutely sensitive to the slightest touch upon the line, and the eye quick to note the smallest sign denoting the presence of a fish, having been previously dissipated in a rough walk over the hill, possibly keeping up with some gillie or gamekeeper, who strides over the ground very much as if his nether extremities were made of jointed cast-iron. It has invariably been my experience that, when fatigued, my fishing has been careless, and consequently unproduc-tive. One of the great advantages of St. Boswells is its proximity to the water. You can always put on your wading gear at home ; and, for that matter, put up your rod too. Indeed, I have known some who kept their rods up for weeks together. This I much object to. It is a little trouble, perhaps, at the end of the day's work to take down your rod, lovingly straighten out the pieces, and deposit them safely in the bag; when, seeing that you will be on the water bright and early next morning, you could have saved the trouble by leaning it against the outhouse in the garden, or leaving it lengthwise in the lobby. But, not to mention the risk of having the rod broken, a week or two of this treatment will do it more harm than a whole season's work on the other plan. A rod, after a day's fishing with minnow, for instance, and more or less with any lure, takes a particular bend, and if not taken to pieces and carefully straightened, is sure to grow twisted and useless.

About the middle of the village of St. Boswells, a road leads down to the Dryburgh Ford, and the angler cannot do better then begin work at what is locally known as Brockie's Hole.

By this name there hangs, or rather there hung, a " veritable tail." It is related that upon one occasion a farmer of the name of Brockie, while in a state of intoxication, rode his horse into the river here, at a time when it was in full flood, and "roaring from bank to brae." The poor animal at once lost its footing, and its rider his seat, both, in consequence of the deepness of the water, being in a moment plunged overhead. The horse soon came to the surface, and boldly struck out for the opposite bank; not, however, before the farmer, with the instinctive energy of a drowning man, had clutched the object nearest him, which, fortunately, happened to be the horse's tail. To this he tenaciously clung and was towed in safety by the noble creature to the Dryburgh side of the river,—a sadder, but we may well believe, a wiser and more sober man. A huge mass of rock projects into the river at this point, and is indeed the cause of the pool; and the deep, dark, still water affords a fine quiet harbour for the fish after struggling with the current outside, which runs very strongly. I have known of fish being landed here of five and seven pounds weight, but I imagine they were bull-trout.

If the angler object to fishing down stream, he had better walk on as far as Mertoun Bridge and fish his way back. In the main I agree with Stewart as to fishing up stream ; but I do not hold to the opinion so tenaciously as he does ; and what trifling experience I have had of angling as a scientific pursuit, leads to the conclusion that it is very unsafe to dogmatise on the subject at all. Fish—trout especially—are such maggoty creatures (if I may be allowed the use of this expression in its secondary meaning), that they will insist by their conduct upon a large number of exceptions to most rules you can lay down for them. In the broad general principle that, in consequence of their being very sharp-eyed, it is better to keep out of sight, I am a thorough believer; and if it were equally convenient upon all occasions, in the case at least of a burn, I should certainly always fish up. But circumstances may interfere. Fishing up, for instance, may take us away from our train, when fishing down would land us at the station just at the proper time. But even though the angler may find it more convenient to fish down than up on some occasions, there is no reason why he should do what Stewart tells us some of his disciples were guilty of, while all the time they fancied they were following implicitly the precepts of his book.

He says:—

We have met anglers fishing down stream—and this is no suppositious case, but one which we have seen over and over again—with a copy of this volume (the ***Practical Angler***) in their pockets, who complained that they had got every thing herein recommended, and were getting no sport. On pointing out to them that there was one important mistake they were committing in fishing down stream instead of up, they stated that when they came to a pool they fished it up—that is to say, they first walked down the pool and showed themselves to the trout, and then commenced to fish for them.

These were certainly very ignorant anglers ; but the fault lay, not so much in fishing down as in fishing after being in full view of the trout For the most part, perhaps, there is less chance of being seen in fishing up than in fishing down ; but then, no matter how it comes about, if the fish see the angler, the same undesirable result will follow. Were it impossible for the angler to conceal himself when fishing down stream, the result would be that he would take nothing ; and doubtless a better method would be discovered. But every angler of any experience knows that this is not so; and I venture to say that a fisher, when he is supposably ***out of range of the vision*** of the trout, can acquaint himself generally with the nature of the water he is coming to, in fishing down, as well as one coming up at an equal distance on the other side. Then, surely, it is an easy matter to skirt the water at the lower end of pool or stream and fish up. Besides this, the careful and successful down-stream angler, whose first article of belief is to have the best of tackle, and his second, to keep out of sight, will studiously take advantage of every tree or bush that can in the least degree afford concealment, and fish with a longer rod where there is no natural cover. As, when fishing, whether I walk up or down stream, I invariably cast in one way, viz., across, and a little up, it comes much to the same thing, provided I can keep out of sight as well the one way as the other.

I make these remarks in connection with trout-fishing in comparatively small streams, and where the necessity for wading is not great: the conditions affecting a large river are somewhat different. In fishing such a river as the Tweed, and standing in a strong current at a depth of three feet or more, wading up stream is, to my thinking, absurd. Provided you have a good body of water, and can cast a good line, you may fish down with as much success as if you went in the opposite direction. What I contend for most strongly is, the necessity for keeping out of sight Trout will not take the lure, fish how you may, if previously they have seen the apparition of an angler on the bank. If the shadow of your rod be thrown on the water, you must at once change your side, or fishing will be useless. To keep in the shade, everyone who wishes to be successful finds it necessary to kneel, creep, crawl, or sit collier-fashion, as the occasion demands.

The fishing from the village of St. Boswells to what is called the " Long stream " inclusive, ranges over a piece of most excellent water. The banks are like all the banks of the Tweed with which I am acquainted, soft and grassy, and pleasant to fish from; and here, when the river is moderately full, there is not much occasion to wade. Still, I would advise the angler in this district, at all ordinary times, to encase himself in his stockings, otherwise he may lose a deal of good water. We have taken some nice trout in this reach of the Tweed, notably one very fine fish which weighed something over two pounds, at a time when the water was spent to a shadow, and not a fish worth mentioning had been taken for weeks. I caught it late one evening, with. the finest gut ~cast I had in my possession, and a very small teal drake, with a black hackle,—a favourite fly, which I find very deadly at all seasons, and which, with the occasional variation of the red instead of the black hackle, forms one of the flies of nearly every cast I fish with. I remember this individual fish well, the more by token that it was a Saturday night when I caught it, and knowing that a two-pound Tweed trout in good condition makes an excellent repast, I looked forward hopefully to the morrow. But, alas! my landlady, whatever else she was, was no cook ; and she brought in the fish to breakfast so much ***underdone,*** that after one or two mouthfuls I gave it up in disgust. Talking of the cooking of fish reminds one of good old Izaak and his quaint and appetite-provoking recipes. I think also of former fishing days spent upon the Aberdeenshire Don, famous for its yellow trout. There, I had the advantage of a landlady, who, as far as trout were concerned, might have been cook to a prince. I remember well her smoking dishes of beautifully-done trout and whitling. Her method was to split the fish down the back : hence in the case of large fish there was every chance that they got well cooked.

My recollections of fishing days at St. Boswells are very pleasantly associated with a most remarkable angler, resident in the village—William Rankin by name. This man was born and brought up there, and travelled about a good deal in early life. Upwards of thirty years ago, while in London, he lost his sight through small-pox, and after that sad misfortune he returned to his native spot, where he still lives. Naturally shrewd and intelligent on all ordinary topics, he is quite an authority on angling and its accessories ; for, notwithstanding his blindness, he is one of the most successful fishers on the Tweed. He can make all kinds of tackle, and fish with fly or bait equally well; but his favourite lure is the natural minnow. I have never seen this used with such deadly effect as in his hands. He knows every inch of the ground, and walks into the water as fearlessly as if he saw. On my first visit, I prac-tised worm more than minnow-fishing, and I have fished with him for a day when the water has been in good condition—he with minnow and I with worm— but our baskets would never compare, though mine might not be altogether empty. From twenty to thirty pounds is quite a common weight of fish for him to carry home as the product of one day's fishing ; and that in a part of the river, say within a mile or two of St. Boswells, where it is necessarily very much fished. But then the water must be in perfect ply for the minnow, and other circumstances must be favour-able. His most successful time is when the flood is falling, and the river assumes that deep-black, and yet clear colour, which all anglers love so well. He informed me that, during the spring of the present year (1879), on two successive days in April, he killed with *artificial* minnow, nine sea-trout, and two or three river-trout, the total weight being thirty-six pounds. On one occasion, with flies of his own tying, he took out of one stream in the Tweed ten trout, weighing seven and a quarter pounds; on another, below Mertoun Bridge, he hooked with fly eight sea-trout, five of which he landed. He now prefers minnow fishing, because he can make heavier baskets. During two days' salmon-fishing, at the close of November, 1877, he killed on the first day three salmon, weighing twenty-two, thirteen, and ten pounds re-spectively; and on the second, two salmon and four sea-trout—the salmon twenty-two and seven pounds each ; the largest sea-trout seven pounds, and the smallest three. One would think it very awkward work for such as he to wade ashore and land the fish, and so it would be, and dangerous too ; but his plan, unless when he fastens upon a salmon or something very weighty, is not to leave the water at all. He simply runs the fish a little, then winds it close in, and dexterously seizing it be-hind the gills, in an incredibly short space has the minnow disgorged, and the cap-tive safely " landed " in his capacious creel. I have often watched him thus skilfully manipulating in deep water, upon a trout of two or three pounds weight, and have thought that few fishers with the best of sight could have managed half so well.

Besides being an angler, Rankin is a capital rod-maker. His want of sight seems to be in great part made up to him in the acuteness of his other faculties, especially those of hearing and touch. The latter sense enables him to give a better taper and balance to a rod than nine-tenths of ordinary makers can give, who are guided by their eyesight alone. His rods are perhaps not so elegantly finished in respect of varnishing and fittings as some others ; but in every quality that would recommend them to that sensible individual, "the really practical angler," they are much in ad-vance of many very expensive articles which I have handled. When first he made the attempt to add to his income in this way, he was not very particular about the finishing ; and on receiving an order from a gentleman friend for one of his rods, he proposed to get him one from a maker better qualified than he was to finish it. To this the gentleman replied, that he was not at all particular about the finish of the rod, provided he could make one to " finish" the trout. After years of patient industry, and with a little external help in the decorative branch, he can now turn out a very nice-looking article indeed, and one that he himself will thoroughly guarantee—in the hands of course, of a " complete angler "—to " finish " any num-ber of trout No one can fish the Tweed near St. Boswells without getting to know and like Rankin : he is full of information on all local and piscatorial subjects, and always ready to help and advise those who are strange to the waters.

Another local angler is William Younger, son of John Younger, the poet. This man is a capital fly-dresser, and an equally good fly-fisher. I mention him on ac-count of a peculiarity he affects in the arrangement of the flies upon his casting line. Most fishers, I take it, in making up their cast, would put the largest fly at the tail, and, if the others varied in size, would put the next largest in the position of first dropper, and so on. I speak here of comparatively small flies. Younger's practice is to reverse this order, retaining the smallest fly for the point hook. I have argued with him that this is a mistake, because when the line gets the turn of the wrist and the forward impetus, the point-fly, if the weightiest, will best continue the motion, and take the line out farthest and straightest. I imagine also that the weightiest hook in a cast of three or four being placed highest up the line would render the chances of entanglement much more frequent. He contends that he does not find this to be the case, and that his mode is the most deadly in his experience. His reason is that the point or tail-fly being the most important and most deadly, falls upon the water by his method in the softest possible way. There is certainly truth here. The point-hook is generally (though by no means invariably) the most attractive, because, being attached to the line, on only one side, it is less artificial-looking than the others. If I find that the trout are taking a fly whose position on the cast is first or second dropper, and neglecting the point-fly, I change the latter for one of those which seems more attractive ; as I find that the chances of landing fish on this hook are much greater than upon any of the others. The reason of this is not far to seek. If the angler is fishing with three or four flies on his cast, and hooks a fish of trifling size on the highest dropper, well and good—he can lightly toss it out.

> " But should he lure
> From his dark haunt beneath the tangled roots
> Of pendent trees, the monarch of the brook,
> Behoves him then to ply his finest art."

And truly a very fine art it will then become ; for, with six or more feet of gut dangling at the rear of his fish—the loose hooks upon which, by a strange and inexplicable principle of contrariety, seem immediately to awaken to the necessity of fastening upon something, and fasten accordingly—it is a thousand to one the angler loses both his fish and his flies. While admitting the prime importance of dropping the point fly lightly upon the water, I still adhere to my preconceived notion of placing the largest fly of the cast in that position on the line. There cannot be a doubt, however, that in such matters of detail, within, of course, the limits of certain well-defined and well-known rules, the angler's own experience and observation will be his best and safest guide. As regards numbers, I would strongly advocate the course of erring upon the side of safety in having too few, rather than too many hooks ; not necessarily because the sight of a number of flies—if it be true that our aquatic friends really take them for flies—can be such an unusual sight to the fish, but because to the average angler they are a source of frequent annoyance and perplexity. The most skilful and successful angler I ever met with, never used more than a pair. I very seldom fish with more than three.

Passing the " Long stream," below which the Mertoun water begins, and still fishing down on the right bank, the angler will come to a fine bit of water known as the " Cauld Pool," where the current is kept back to supply Mertoun Mill. Between this and Mertoun Bridge there are some capital streams and deep side runs, where fish may always be taken. About a mile and a half below the bridge is some splendid water, running through Lord Polwarth's estate. At this point the river winds gracefully along, and there is a picturesque view of his lordship's beautiful residence—Mertoun House. Here the water is preserved, and the trout, in consequence, are more plentiful, and, as a rule, larger than above. I had heard glowing accounts in the village of the superiority of the trouting in this particular spot, and was eager to try it. Accordingly, I wrote to Lord Polwarth, and received by return of post a most cordial permit, which lasted during the period of my stay. [9] I have always met with the utmost politeness and kindness when I have had occasion, as in this instance, to ask permission for fishing from any nobleman or other proprietor. Liberty to fish would be accorded much more readily than it often is by the riparian owners, were it not for the disgraceful fact that poachers and rowdy-fishers, who carry pots of roe, poke nets, and quicklime, often gain access to the best waters, and in addition to harrying and spoiling the river, damage and break down the fencing. The true hearted and innocent disciples of Walton suffer for their guilty brethren. I feel sure that every true lover of the sport will agree that one of the main objects all properly organized angling associations should keep steadily in view, is the stamping out of everything like illegal and unfair practices in taking fish. The " honest" angler is a quiet, contemplative, orderly, law-abiding, and thoughtful man—I mean thoughtful in as far as the interest of others are concerned. He is not the one carelessly to leave his friend the farmer's gate open, after passing through himself, and thus afford free ingress for the eager cattle into the good man's corn. In crossing the fence or dry-stone dike he is careful not to break it down. If the farmer's furrows

[9] From all I know of his lordship's kind and generous disposition, I feel pretty sure that no gentleman would be refused the like courtesy. I found this water the most productive of any in the neighbourhood, and I therefore took frequent advantage of my liberty.

come down, as they often do, to the river's edge, he will, even at considerable personal inconvenience, and it may be loss, as far as sport is concerned, avoid treading down the grain ; and this, though there may not be a human being within miles of him. And in his war with the finny tribe, though it is true he uses every artifice, yet no **compulsion** is ever resorted to, and the ultimate end of the sport is the legitimate one of supplying the table.

The angler's pastime leads him amongst the most glorious and sublime scenes in nature! and he becomes familiar with these under all their ever-varying aspects, in quite another way from the ordinary observer. He sees them in the early morning, ere the sun has dispelled the vapours from the still cloud-capt hills, or dried the glistening dewdrops from the grass: ere the curling smoke has begun to ascend from the distant cot, or the rustic labourer has risen from his lowly couch ; and while yet no sound is heard save the cheerful voices of the birds hymning their matin song of thanksgiving. And again, in another aspect does nature present herself when, at mid-day, he sits down to rest and refresh himself, after the morning toils. Now the sun has reached his meridian splendour, and all the landscape stands out in the full blaze of the perfect day. The air is laden with the perfume of a thousand wild-flowers ; and every leaf and cranny send forth their myriads of winged inhabitants to dance away their short life in the warm brightness of the summer day. The green hill-sides are clad to their summits with the fleecy flocks, and the oxen wade knee-deep in the rich and verdant meadows. He wanders by the winding stream or stately flowing river, and every bend and turn present him with a new and beautiful picture. He stands beside the foaming waterfall, and as he strains his ear to listen to the fancied voices, remembers that he has read somewhere of a voice which is " like the sound of many waters." Perhaps he threads his way along the bottom of the deep ravine, following the river which glides past—its waters, darkened by the tall, overshadowing trees on either side. In this solemn region he listens to the plaintive voice of the wood-pigeon cooing amorously to his mate, and hears the ringing, blythsome song of the mavis, echoing far away from among the topmost branches overhead ; and all around him, he sees in sheltered crevices and secure nooks and corners, the richest mosses, the rarest ferns, the tiniest and most beautiful of flowers. And all this, be it observed, is viewed by him while he is diligently plying his legitimate sport. He has not gone to look for the beautiful in nature, but practically it has come to him unsought, and by the way, and for this reason probably, it is all the more enjoyable. Finally, when the twilight shadows, stealing across the western sky, warn our angler that it is time to be going homeward, he counts his fish— mayhap, no difficult task, but he is content; for he has had abundant enjoyment, and he looks forward hopefully to better sport another day.

On the title-page of the first edition of Walton's book, within a quaint and original device, he inscribes the words—" The compleat Angler ; or the Contemplative Man's Recreation." To say that Izaak was a shrewd as well as clever man, is only repeating what has been said a thousand times. Evidently he considered that an angler to be " compleat" must be contemplative. The fisher who thinks of nothing but the slaughter of the finny tribe, and has no eye to see, nor soul to appreciate the beauty of the scene that surrounds him, is not a man after Izaak's model, nor worthy of imitation. He certainly is not of the genus " Contemplative," and the loss is all on his side ; for truly he misses one half of the enjoyment. What true fisher has not glorious scenes of natural beauty photographed, as it were, on his mind, these memories being unaffected by the weight of the basket at the end of the day ? The sights and sounds amidst which the angler pursues his harmless recreation elevate and ennoble his mind, furnish material for earnest reflection, and raise his thoughts from the beauty and exuberance of nature to the benignant Author of it all. And such sights and sounds are met with upon the banks of Tweed in sweet profusion.

It is not to such men—though not seldom their love of nature is only equalled by their brilliant success—that we are in any degree to attribute the apparent fall-

ing away in the numbers of our river trout, and the increased difficulty we now
experience in making a good basket. Independently of the influence which the
universal draining of the land has exerted, by causing the sudden rising of heavy
floods, which sweep away the spawn, and the food of the fish—the eggs of aquatic
insects—there are two causes which I think may fairly be held to account for the
change. These are ***poaching antipollution.*** In spite of river acts and river bailiffs,
it is notorious that in our best streams (I am speaking of the North), illegal practices
of the most depopulating character are largely carried on. Netting is one of the most
common expedients resorted to. Stewart says :—

The net used is what is usually called "harry-water net." Nets of this kind are
made so light that they can be carried in the pocket, and so complete in structure,
that a whole pool may be almost cleaned of its finny inhabitants at a single haul.
Tweed and its tributaries suffer more from netting than any other stream in Scotland, and it is most usually carried on in the neighbourhood of towns or villages,
where the poachers can find a ready sale for their trout.

It is generally agreed that the only radical cure for this evil is watching the rivers ; but this, in consequence of the expense attending it, is seldom so thoroughly
carried out as to be efficacious. Pollution is more deadly, certainly more insidious in
its effects than even poaching, and more difficult to deal with. Even under a modified form, a decided deterioration in the race, and a falling off in numbers, must
inevitably take place. Just as among that unfortunate portion of the human family who live under unhealthy conditions, breathing bad air and not getting proper
nourishment, we have disease nearly always prevalent, and deterioration becoming
more apparent in every generation; so that if left to themselves, and not in some degree resuscitated by the infusion of extraneous blood, in course of time they would
die out; so under the conditions at present existing in many of our fishing rivers,
were it not for the constant flow of pure water from unvitiated tributaries into the
main current, and the introduction of strong, healthy fish from the same sources,
the finny race would soon cease to exist in them. The disease which, to such an
alarming extent, has affected both the salmon and the river-trout this year (1879),
is, I believe, more than probably due to this cause ; and if means be not taken to

enforce existing statutes on the subject, or new laws made which shall ***effectually*** check pollution, we may live to see our finest streams untenanted by either trout or salmon.

Before visiting the Tweed at St. Boswells, I had fished the Don in Aberdeen-shire for several seasons in succession, almost exclusively with worm, using what is commonly known as " Stewart tackle." Whether it was owing to some peculiarity in the river, or the kind of seasons, I cannot say ; but I found that the same tactics did not suit the Tweed nearly so well, and as I was generally more successful with the fly, I practiced that style of fishing more frequently on the latter river.

Stewart, in his ***Practical Angler,*** admits either three ox four hooks on his worm-tackle. I think anglers will generally find it more advantageous to have three only : more than this number necessitates the use of a larger size of worm, which is decidedly to be eschewed. Were it in any degree a rule that a large trout must have a large bait, this would alter the case. Unfortunately, however, the rule is more frequently—the larger the bait the smaller the fish. I would not like to say that the converse of this is universally true, but I often find that the largest trout are taken with the smallest, pinkest, and most lively worms, possibly because to them such seem the daintiest morsels ; whereas, if one chances upon a too-large and uninviting bait, and, just to use it up, makes a throw, it is ten to one that it captivates only some " paunchy" and audacious minnow, or wretched parr. Those anglers who follow Stewart exactly will, in baiting the tackle, pass the hooks quite through the body of the worm, leaving all the three or four points and barbs fully exposed. This, I am afraid, is a mistake. Skilful worm-fishing, as at present practised, is generally car-ried on in clear water; consequently, that the deception may be more perfect, it is absolutely necessary to conceal the hooks, at least as far as is possible; otherwise the best fish will be scared away, remaining, after a rapid inspection of the somewhat abnormal-looking reptile, at a safe and respectful distance, and indulging in reflec-tions, the tendency of which will not be to add to the weight of the angler's creel. Another disadvantage attending Stewart's method of putting on the worm is the liability to catch upon obstacles, such as stones, weeds, sunken branches, and green slime. To obviate this, the best way is to use a smaller size of hook than that with which the tackle generally to be had in the shops is dressed. At the same time, the worm has to be frequently examined, as there is always a tendency on the part of the hook to work its way into sight. Stewart, who was admittedly a prince among anglers, and whose book, I believe, has done more for the education of the brethren, in all branches of the art, since its first publication in 1857, than any other work which has appeared in the present century, admits "that the exposure of so many hooks is calculated to scare away some trout that would otherwise take the bait."

The most deadly hook for making the tackle is a small size of sneck-bend, but the great drawback in using it is its liability, with any sudden jerk, to break off at the bend. The round-bend will answer the purpose pretty nearly as well, and is perhaps a safer hook to use. I generally tie them for my own fishing with a smaller size of hook than that in general use, with the lowest a size larger than the upper two, taking care to attach them to long and fine threads of picked gut. The best kind of worm for this size of Stewart tackle is what is known as the marsh worm, which is found in abundance in ordinary garden soil: those should be selected which are about two inches long. They areeasily recognised by their pale, bluish colour, though when scoured they become of a beautiful pink. When newly dug, they should be put into a basin of clear cold water, which will cleanse them from any dirt that may adhere to them. A few handfuls of fine moss, from which all impurities have been removed, should then be placed in a jar, after being rinsed through water several times, and well wrung by the hands. On this, when teased out so as to cover the bottom of the jar, the worms should be spread, care being taken to exclude all *mangled* or *broken* ones, as they only contaminate the rest. In a few days they will scour quite pink, and become a very deadly lure for trout. They also attain a nice degree of toughness, and can, if sufficient care be taken, undergo the strain of casting without the risk of being injured. The only other worm worth mentioning is the brandling, easily distinguishable by the yellow rings round its body: it is found in rich leaf-mould or in dunghills. Some fishers set great store by this bait, but I have never found in my experience that it approached the " pink " worm in point of attraction ; besides, it is difficult to toughen, and when pierced emits a most offensive odour. In worm-fishing with the tackle, no hook that has done some execution one day should ever be used a second time; for independently of the points being blunted, the dressing of the hook gets frayed and loosened from the shank by rubbing against the teeth of the fish caught, and nothing is more provoking than to strike a good fish and lose it, in consequence of the hook slipping down off the gut. The angler in such circumstances richly deserves his loss for his temerity. In setting out for a day's fishing I never like to have less than eight or a dozen of the tackle in my book. Not unfrequently *one* will do the work of the day, even when trout are taking freely: but most commonly a good many are lost through circumstances over which the angler has little or no control.

I have known anglers whose practice it was after taking their fish off the hook, to put them alive into the basket, and leave them there slowly and miserably to gasp themselves to death. This I consider a piece of wanton cruelty, and I take the present opportunity of protesting against it. It is surely quite an unnecessary prolonging of their sufferings, even if it be conceded that they do not *feel* very acutely ; and as far as I know, it can answer no reasonable purpose. My own custom is to kill the fish as soon as it is caught, and on all grounds,—the angler's own safety included—this is the best course to follow. I remember when fishing a reach of the river Don one day, in company with a friend, who might be distant from me about sixty yards, seeing him engaged with a fish which he finally succeeded in getting ashore. At that distance I could not distinguish the size of the fish, but I was struck with the length of time he was occupied in manipulating upon the creature, before he commenced to cast again. Presently, he came slowly down towards me with his rod under his arm, his hands held in front of him in a kind of appealing attitude, and a somewhat rueful look on his countenance. A single glance explained the situation ; the fact being that, contrary to all accepted notions on the subject, the *fish* had caught the fisher. He was fishing with the three hooks, the lowest of which only had fastened in the fish—,a nice trout of over half a pound—and instead of killing the animal at once, he was attempting first to disgorge the hook; when with a sudden wallop the fish succeeded in imbedding one of the loose hooks in the fleshy part of his thumb, right over the barb. I at once cut away the gut and threw down the fish ; and happening fortunately to have a good knife, one of the blades of which had a lancet point, I managed, after a little surgical operation, to dislodge the hook, not, however, without inflicting some pain, as was evinced by sundry wincings on the part of my patient. We had just commenced fishing, consequently, if my friend had been alone, his day's sport would have been done for, and that through an accident which a little care and forethought would have prevented. It was during one of my vists to St. Boswells, in a deep dark pool opposite the village of Maxton, that I had my first run with a salmon. Anglers not "unfrequently have to bear the taunts of their non-piscatory friends that " the big ones *always* get away." Where is the angler, I would like to know, of any experience, who cannot recall the loss of many and many a *big* one ? Why, the big ones, in these days of fine tackle and shy fish, have of course.the best chance to get away. That they *frequently* do make their escape I frankly admit; that they *always* get away, I strongly deny ; though in my case— alas! that I should have the tale to tell—I lost my fish. But, not to anticipate, I had been wading down the middle of the river, about a mile below the Mertoun bridge, one Saturday after-noon, among the first days of September, fishing fly, not over successfully, in con-sequence of the sparkling and fiery brilliancy of the sun overhead and the absolute cloudlessness of the sky, when I sat down on a little gravelly island in mid-stream, to rest and refresh myself; and also to change my cast, and wait for the beginning of the twilight shades, and the turn of fortune. I had been using a cast of very small flies, and on looking over my book, I came upon some of a considerably larger pat-tern—average-size trout flies they were, such as one would use when the fresh was clearing off, or when there was a good "curl" on the water, or, as was now the case, in the evening. These, a relation of mine—a keen angler—had got dressed from some special feathers, by a crack tier of hooks in Aberdeen, and they had found their way somehow into my book. I selected one with a brownish-yellow wing, a sort of tawny moth-looking fly, and attached this to my line as the tail hook: the other two I did not change. Thus accoutred, with strong, well-tried rod of thirteen feet; silent reel, holding sixty yards or thereby of line in its coil, carefully tapered with two or three lengths of twisted gut, and that again with single strands of grad-ually decreasing thickness, down to the finest on which the hooks were fastened; and with no thought beyond a good-sized, well-conditioned trout for supper, as my creel was most uncomfortably light, I made for the pool to which I have alluded before. Having soaked the new hook a little, straightened the gut by drawing it once or. twice through my fingers, and examined the line generally, I waded cautiously in, through a little, sandy shallow—*just made for landing fish*—which gradually sloped away to unknown depths in the pool beyond. By this time it might be six o'clock. The sun was still sending his beams slantingly athwart the stream, but a lofty embankment on the opposite side effectually screened the cast; and, joyful sight to the somewhat jaded angler, signs were not wanted in sundry dimplings of the water, that the fish were now on the feed. Not without a little twitch of nervous anticipation, such as one sometimes feels when he arrives at a favourite spot which is sure to yield him one or two good ones, did I cast straight out for the deepest part of the black, silent water. A good cast it happened fortunately to be ; that is to say, I managed to reach the spot aimed for, and the point-fly alighted as gently as I could have wished. No sound, no splash, no breaking of the surface followed ; but, in-stinctively, as the hook was sucked down by something that was *not* the current, the point of the rod went up, and he was on ! I was about as much surprised as the fish would probably be; and, strange as it may appear, at the moment, I woud have much preferred it to be a good trout, which, if I had secured, I could have tapped on the head, and laid to rest in the creel, no one daring to call me in question. For, be it remembered, my permission was only for trout; and I felt that I might be sus-pected of aiming at higher game, more especially as I saw a man on the opposite side, whom I believed to be one of the gamekeepers, come up and ensconce himself behind a tree, evidently bent on seeing what the stranger was about. At best, if I caught the fish, I should certainly deliver it to the rightful owner, and thereby, I, personally, would not be much of a gainer; and incidentally, I might to an indefinite extent be a loser, if the animal, which had given occasion for these thoughts, like a flash, to dart across my mind, should lead me a dance, and indulge in such unseem-ly and unnecessary behaviour as would endanger my rod and line, neither of which was of such a kind as I should have selected for salmon-fishing. Accordingly, as soon as I felt his dead weight, I struck rather forcibly, intending to see whether the hook—a mere midge for a salmon—was properly fastened, and if not, to be off with him at once. But the hook was firm, and up he came to the surface, shewing the round of his back and his dorsal fin ; and after shaking his head indignantly, as a terrier might do with your handkerchief, he headed away down stream in gallant style—a fish of fifteen or twenty pounds—having evidently made up his mind for a run to Berwick-on-Tweed, or the sheltering lee of the Holy Isle; whence, judging from his appearance, he had but recently arrived. This, however, it was not my intention to permit, as my line would *scarcely* have uncoiled so far: accordingly, when he had run out about fort}' yards, I gradually pulled him up, as he was getting into broken water, where I could not well follow him. Round he turned, and back he came as gracefully as might be, and so swiftly that I had difficulty in winding in. He repeated this two or three times, during which I was sometimes on the bank, and sometimes in the river; sometimes wading in shallows, and sometimes following him into water much too deep, as I soon found to my cost by the increased weight of my stockings. Finally, after a struggle which lasted considerably over an hour, he seemed to be getting exhausted, and I led him towards the shallow bay for the purpose of attempting to land him. Several times he turned tail upon the bay and dashed back into the deep water, each time, however, with less vigour. On the last occasion when I was wearing him in, he turned perpendicularly upon his nose, evidently for the purpose of rubbing it against the gravel at the bottom. Most anglers will know what this means ; but in my case I could not prevent it, as I dared not put more strain upon the tackle than it was already bearing, otherwise breakage would have been inevitable. On his coming up, I saw between my line and his snout, a small branch attached, which had not a reassuring effect. Immediately after this, on my making another attempt to get him to the side, and probably increasing, though but slightly, the strain upon the line, the hook, having no doubt worn and widened its catch, suddenly spurted out, and the salmon and I parted company. After such a *denouement* what can one say ? " There's many a slip 'twixt the cup and the lip!" and equally so 'tween the salmon and the fishing basket. Very true, O king of fishes! And some are disposed to relieve their minds in such a case by a few *strong,* if inelegant expressions; while others would be inclined to drown their disappointment in the manner indicated in lines attributed by Stewart to a certain humorist, "a friend and associate of anglers":—

> The flask frae my pocket
> I poured into the socket,
> For I was provokit unto the last degree ;
> And to my way o' thinkin',
> There's naething for't but drink in',
> When a trout he lies winkin' and lauchin' at me.

I will not say that I was not" provokit," or to what degree I was. I certainly felt a good deal put out. After a struggle that had lasted a couple of hours, perspiring as I was at every pore, and soaking wet, through going beyond my wading depth, the termination was not a pleasing one to reflect upon. But I feel strongly that anglers should never brood over their disappointments, but endeavour to take them philosophically. By this time the moon was up ; my line seemed uninjured, and I marched in for a " last appeal;" hooked a fine yellow trout of over a pound, which in ordinary circumstances I should have handled with great caution; expended my pent-up feelings by at once dragging him ashore, *nolens volens;* packed up, and took the road homewards—a loser in one sense ; but a gainer practically, in an experience that has stood me in good stead on many a subsequent occasion. On examining my casting-line by daylight, I found the lower part of it twisted, as if it had been done by a machine.

Excellent trouting may be had by going from St. Boswells up the Tweed, on the Dryburgh Water. This ground begins at a place called Monk's Ford, about three-quarters of a mile above the Suspension Bridge, and extends to the " Long stream " mentioned before ; in all, a distance of at least two and a half miles. It includes some splendid streams and pools. The first—Monk's Ford—is a capital piece of water for trout: then follow in order, coming down the river, " casts " locally known as the Battery stream; Bay-hill (spanned by the Suspension Bridge) ; the Boat-hole; the Island ; Haws Craig; the Burn-foot; Brockie's-hole ; the Gullet-stream ; Berkie Haugh; Haugh-side, and the Long-stream. It will be seen that this stretch of fishing, as well as what has been described before, lies within easy and comfortable access of the village, and it will take the angler who is new to the district a considerable time to get thoroughly acquainted with the ground. Should he wish, however, any day to change the scene of his *depredations,* he can get readily to a good part of the Teviot, by taking the train from Maxton Station to Roxburgh, a distance of a few miles ; or he can walk four miles south of St. Boswells to the Aill Water, which figures in Scott's *Lay of the Last Minstrel,* as the " foaming tide " stemmed so gallantly by the stout Sir William of Deloraine, when on his midnight ride from Branksome Tower to "Melrose's holy pile," to seek "the monk of St. Mary's Aisle."

Unchallenged thence passed Deloraine
To ancient Riddell's fair domain,
Where Aill, from mountain freed,
Down from the lakes did raving come ;
Each wave was crested with tawny foam,
Like the mane of a chestnut steed.
****

Never heavier man and horse
Stemmed a midnight torrents force.
The warrior's very plume, I say,
Was daggled by the dashing spray;
Yet, through good heart, and our Ladye's grace,
At length he gained the landing place.

I have never seen the Aill raging after this fashion, but its wide channel must contain a large quantity of water when the river happens to be in full flood, and its swift current will make it, I can imagine, at such times, very dangerous to ford. The lakes alluded to in the poem are those which constitute its source, viz., Headshaw, Essen-side, and Shielswood, &c. They are situated among the Selkirkshire hills, in the neighbourhood of Ashkirk, and all contain trout. The Aill is a tributary of the Teviot, which it joins from the left bank at the village of Ancrum: both rivers contain good trout, and are well worthy the attention of the angler.

I assume that no disciple of Walton will ever visit St. Boswells without at intervals laying aside his rod thoughtfully to luxuriate among the interesting and suggestive scenes that surround him. The nearest of them in point of distance—though properly it should be mentioned last—is Dryburgh Abbey. Along the whole length of the back of the village there runs a pleasant path, sloping steeply to the water's edge, from which the most picturesque and charming view's of the Tweed may be had; and right across on the left bank of the river, the venerable ruin of the Abbey is seen, embosomed among stately trees. To get to it, one must either go by the highroad, or the river-side as far as the Suspension Bridge, and then cross. Interesting as a relic of antiquity (it was founded about 1150), it is rendered doubly so as the burial place of Sir Walter Scott, who was interred there, in St Mary's aisle, on the 26th September, 1832, in the tomb of his ancestors, the Haliburtons of New-mains, who at one time owned the Abbey. It seems fitting that he who in his lifetime touched with his magic wand the towers and streams, the hills and glens for many a mile around, giving to them an interest at once historical and romantic which we would not willingly let die, should be laid peacefully to rest amid the scenes he loved and sung, and with " Tweed's silver stream" flowing silently near him. Melrose Abbey, also near the Tweed, lies about four miles from St. Boswells. If the visitor wishes to see it at its best, he will view it at the time Sir Walter recommends in his admirable poetical description :—

> When the broken arches are black in night,
> And each shafted oriel glimmers white;
> When the cold light's uncertain shower
> Streams on the ruin'd central tower;
> When buttress and buttress, alternately
> Seem framed of ebon and ivory;
>
> When silver edges the imagery,
> And the scrolls that teach thee to live and die;
> When distant Tweed is heard to rave,
> And the owlet to hoot o'er the dead man's grave,
> Then go—but go alone the while—
> Then view St. David's ruin'd pile."

It has been often remarked that the ancient monks, who were doubtless allowed to choose the sites for their abbeys, selected them with such taste and judgment as *we* could scarcely imagine surpassed. In almost every instance these buildings stand on, or near, the banks of some famous river; and, viewing the matter from an angler's standpoint, it must have been for other reasons than the scenery alone that this came to be the case. Wise, and full of forethought, were those ancient fathers

; for beyond a doubt they had ascertained the capacities of the river for trout and salmon, long ere the foundation-stone of the proud abbey had been laid,—it may be by royal hands. A wise man once said, "Say not thou the former days were better than these." True, perhaps, for many things; but not so, I.think, for angling. Where is the fisher who would not like a day on the Dryburgh water, if he could have it as it was in those far-off summers, when the sound of the workman's hammer, and the voices of the busy craftsmen rang out over the river, as storey after storey of the ponderous masonry rose into view ; or as it might appear in the long years after, when the cowled monks were seen in the early morning dragging the nets at their "salmon haul" to prepare for Friday's *Fast* ?

From Melrose, the distance to Abbotsford is only three miles to the westward, and admission to view the house may almost always be obtained. Perhaps the most interesting of all the apartments is Sir Walter's study. In it may be seen his writing-table with a few books on it, and his simple arm-chair, apparently much as when he last used them. The largest apartment is the library, which contains a collection of about 20,000 volumes, many of them very rare and valuable. In the different rooms to which the visitor is admitted there are many relics deserving of inspection—ancient arms and armour, and many other objects to which a deep historical interest attaches. Last and certainly not least are the body-clothes worn by the old man previous to the illness which carried him off: these, as most nearly connecting us with the honoured dead, all must love to see.

Many other beautiful and romantic scenes are to be met with in the neighbourhood of St. Boswells, which the angler when in that quarter will do well to visit; but as *they* cannot readily be missed, I may safely leave him to find them out at his leisure.

THE BIBLIOGRAPHY OF ANGLING.

BY CHARLES ESTCOURT, F.C.S., F.I.C.

I CANNOT, from the mere bulk of the matter, treat subject upon the lines of the definition of the word ***bibliography.*** Bibliography is said to be the science of books. In the brief space at my command I can do little more than treat of the exteriors, or titles, of books upon angling: to treat of the contents would require many papers. What I have to say is necessarily gleaned, to a large extent, from the works of others; and though, in the main, my theories and facts will, I believe, be found fairly correct, yet more or less of error must creep in, when, as is the case with the present writer, one is compelled to accept statements made by Other observers.

I find that the first-known list of angling books was compiled in 1811, by Mr. Ellis. It contains 80 works. This list was revised in 1836 by Mr. Pickering, and the number of works was increased to 180. In 1840 Mr. Wilson, in ***The Rod and Gun,*** gave an abbreviated list of 100 works on fishing. In 1847 Dr. Bethune edited an American issue of Walton and Cotton. In this work he printed an appendix, with ballads and papers upon American fishing, and more valuable still, a bibliographical preface with a list of angling works, including in all three hundred. In 1856 Mr. Russell Smith, the well-known bookseller, gave us the then most complete list of British and American works on angling. It enumerated 264, exclusive of those relating to natural history. The next catalogue of fishing literature was compiled by Mr. T. Westwood, whose charming work upon Walton and his editions ought to be read by everyone. This catalogue was published in 1861 by the ***Field,*** and, up to the year 1874, was the most complete of its kind, enumerating a much larger number of angling and kindred works than could be found in any previous list. Mr. Westwood laid the literature of all lands under contribution, and we have placed fairly before us the indices of national character as it may be gathered from the character of the sports of the people. In this list are found works in many languages; Norway, Spain,

Sweden, Denmark, Holland, Italy, America, France, Germany, and Great Britain all come before us in the interesting position of contributors to the literature of the gentle art. The order in which they stand in relation to the work done is that in which I have enumerated them. Thus, Norway is the lowest with one work, while Germany stands out prominently with eighty-eight works. America, which both Blakey in 1856, and Westwood in 1861 included in their catalogues, only contributed to this literature fourteen works. When we consider how many years have passed since the Independence Day of the Americans first dawned upon them, we English people cannot but feel pleased to infer that all their ideas upon the subject of angling, and almost all their reading upon it, must have been derived from the mother country, this mother country possessing in 1861 no less than four hundred and seventy works upon fish and fishing. From the first use of the printing press up to the present year, Britain has indeed held the proud position of instructor of all civilized nations in the gentle art of angling.

The most recent work upon angling bibliography, and probably the most complete, is a work published in 1874, at Haarlem, compiled by Bosgoed. It contains notices of books upon every conceivable subject connected with fish or fishing. It, however, owes its existence very largely to the rare English work I have alluded to, compiled by Westwood. I am not able to say how far it is correct as regards the list of works published since Westwood's.

For the purpose of showing more clearly the exact position of each of the more prominent angling countries, I have analysed (and this you will admit is my proper *rôle*) the publishers' lists and catalogues, up to the month of September, 1879, with the following results :—

	Britain.	Germany.	France.	America.
Real Angling Works	411	64	41	12
Natural History, which includes Ichthiology, Pisciculture, &c............................	50	18	15	3
Poetry and Rhyme................	37	...	...	...
Reports...............................	59	6	4	...
Total.......................................	557	88	60	15

In preparing this list I have placed under the name of each country those books which are printed in the language of that country. Observe how pre-eminently Britain is proved to be the country of angling! France has only one-tenth of the number of books which we possess upon the subject of angling proper. Germany has only one-sixth ; America has only, up to the present date, produced twelve works upon angling proper, though it must be admitted she has done much in improving the methods for the artificial propagation of the best breeds of fish, if not much to improve the modes of fishing ; as to the Greek and Latin nations, whether ancient or modern, their list of such works does not exceed one-twentieth of our number. Besides angling works proper, Great Britain can boast of poetical works, and works upon the Natural History of fish, more numerous than those of all other nations added together.

When we examine these various works as to the value of the information given, and also as to the date at which each country displayed a knowledge of the gentle art, another striking fact presents itself. Although the ancient Greek and Latin writers (owing to the circumstance that they flourished, as well as perished, long before *our* rise) have given the earliest evidences of a knowledge of" angling, still no nation of modern times has given so early a proof as Britain of the advance of civilization which is indicated by an acquaintance with " Ye fyssynge wyth an Angle."

Proceeding, as far as possible, chronologically, I will begin with the earliest mention of angling in the works of profane writers. Homer, who is supposed to have flourished 1,000 years B.C., says (see literal translation of the *Iliad,* 16th Book, where Patroclus kills Thestor) :—

As when a man sitting upon a jutting rock draws with a line and hook a large fish entirely out of the sea.

Some writers upon the bibliography of the gentle art have quoted the above passage, rendered into verse, as follows:—

As from some rock that overhangs the flood,
The silent fisher casts the insidious food ;
With fraudful care he waits the finny prize,
And sudden lifts it quivering to the skies.

Practical anglers may, perhaps, take exception to this method of landing the fish, but, as is evident, we must not blame Homer, but the versifier who fitted the method to the measure.

Theocritus, of Syracuse, 270 years B.C., wrote a series of Idylls, thirty-six in number, which, it is supposed, formed the groundwork for the *Bucolics* of Virgil. In the twenty-first Idyll is a description of the life of Greek fishermen. A few lines from this will serve to show that artificial bait are amongst those things which are fairly included in the wise saying, "There is nothing new under the sun." The Greek fisher is telling of a dream he had, and says:—

Suspended by a rod I gently shove
The bait *fallacious,* which a huge one took ;
Sleeping we image what awake we think—
Dogs dream of bones, and fishermen of fish.

In Virgil (19 B.C.) we find (Georgics) in a description of the progress of agriculture and the work peculiar to each season, these lines, as rendered by Dryden:—

> Then toils for beasts, and lime for birds were found,
> And deep-mouthed dogs did forest walks surround—
> And casting nets were spread in shallow brooks;
> Drags in the deep, and baits were hung on hooks.

In Ovid's works (9 A.D.) we find the next mention made of angling. He says, for instance (***Ars Amatoria,*** Dryden's translation):—

> The wary angler in the winding brook
> Knows what the fish and where to bait his hook.

Again he shows a knowledge of the rod proper, for the literal translation of another part says :—

> While he is angling for fish with his ***quivering*** rod.

As another example of the freedom taken by versifiers with both letter and spirit of the original, I may quote the literal translation of one of the many angling metaphors to be found in Ovid's works. Ovid says :— The wounded fish can be held by the hook it has seized.

Dryden's versification is as follows :

> The fish, once pricked, avoids the bearded hook,
> And spoils the sport of all the neighbouring brook.

Ælian (117 A.D.) is the first writer of antiquity who makes mention of the use of the artificial fly in fishing ; and it is remarkable that for many centuries later, the use of the artificial fly appears to have been totally forgotten. In his ***De Natura Animaliuni,*** fifteenth book, this writer says —

The Macedonians who live on the banks of the river Astreus, which flows between Berea and Thessalonica, are in the habit of catching a particular fish in that river by means of a fly called Hippurus. The predilection of the fish for this fly does not induce the angler to attempt their capture by impaling the living insect. Adepts in the sport have contrived a taking device to circumvent them; for which purpose they invest the body of the hook with purple wool, and having adjusted two wings of a waxy colour, they drop these abstruse cheats gently down stream, and the scaly pursuers, who hastily rise and expect nothing less than a dainty bait, snap the decoy and are immediately fixed to the hook.

Oppian (198 A.D.), a Greek writer, whose work upon the fishes and fishing of the Ancients is, I am glad to say, to be found in our Chetham Library, gives some very interesting matter. The three last books treat exclusively of the art of fishing. In a translation by J. Jones in 1722, a passage in this book describing anglers generally is thus rendered :—

> By those who curious have their art defined,
> Three sorts of fishers are distinct assigned ;
> The first in hooks delight, here some prepare
> The angler's taper length and twisted hair:
> Others the tougher threads of flax entwine,
> But firmer hands sustain the sturdy line ;
> A third prevails by more compendious ways,
> While numerous hooks one common line displays.

I much fear this last line indicates rather poaching with the otter, than the use of Stewart's tackle.

Enough has now been said to show the knowledge which the Ancients possessed of angling, and we may proceed to deal with our more modern friends—though even they now seem ancient enough to us—I mean our ancestors of the 15th to the 17th centuries. The first-known angling work of what I designate modern times (because I am now to deal with printed works and the result of the printing press), was the ***Booke of St. Albans.*** This book we all know well by name, but, from the rarity of the original, and of its reprints of the 16th and 17th centuries, and also of the 1827 reprint, very few I fear know more of it than the title-page. It was a compilation of all known facts relating to English sports generally, made by a lady of rank, Dame Juliana Berners. The first edition was printed by Caxton in 1486, but did not contain the book upon fishing. The ***Booke of Fysshynge wyth an Angle*** appears for the first time in a reprint of the ***Booke of St. Albans,*** printed by Wynkyn de Worde at Westminster, in 1496. It is interesting to note that, as the first book ever printed in England issued from the press in 1474, there appears to have been already a demand for printed books on angling twenty-two years after the introduction of the new method of disseminating literature. No paper of this kind would be complete without a slightly extended notice of this work. It is the prototype of all angling books since written, and I am inclined to trace the origin of the title " gentle," which our art by well-acknowledged right now possesses, to the fact that the first angling book known to us was written by a lady, a gentle lady, for she was not only of rank, but was prioress of a nunnery, and famous for her learning and accomplishments.

This lady gives as her reason for not publishing the book in a separate form, the following, which I have translated into the vernacular:—[9]

And for the cause that this present treatise should not come to the hands of each idle person, which would desire it, if it were imprinted alone by itself and put in a little pamphlet, therefore I have compiled it in a greater volume of divers books, concerning to gentle and noblemen, to the intent that the foresaid idle person which would have little measure in the said disport of fishing, should not by this means utterly destroy it.

It is interesting to observe how completely this work has given the type of a fisherman to all succeeding writers. Thus we are told of the advantages of fishing over all sports:—

9   The woodcut and a portion of the treatise are to be found in Hawkins' edition of Walton. The woodcut is especially curious as an illustration of the state of the art at that period.

If his sport fail him, the angler at the least hath his wholesome walk, and merry at his ease, a sweet air of the sweet savour of meadow flowers, that maketh him hungry' And if the angler take fish, surely then no man merrier than he in his spirits.

In the **Experienced Angler,** by Colonel Venables (two centuries after Dame Juliana had written), we find in the preface the following :—

The minds of Anglers being usually more calm and composed than many others, especially Hunters and Falkners, who too frequently lose their delight in their passion, and too often bring at home more of melancholy and discontent than satisfaction in their thoughts. But the Angler, when he hath the worst success, loseth but a Hook or Line, or perhaps (what he never . possessed) a Fish—and suppose he take nothing, yet he enjoyeth a delightful walk by pleasant rivers, in sweet pastures, amongst odoriferous Flowers, which gratify his Senses, and delight his Mind.

The artificial flies described in the edition of 1496 of the **Booke of St. Albans,** are so much like those given in Walton, that the latter may fairly be credited with having frequently studied Dame Juliana's instructions. Exclusive of some little-known reprints of this work, no other book upon fishing appeared until 1590, when Leonard Mascall published his **Booke of Fishing with Hooke and Line.**

In 1597, Brereton wrote a small quarto, entitled **Wits Frenchman, or, a Conference between Scholler and Angler,** but I cannot find any account of its contents. In 1596 W. G., identified as William Gryndall, wrote and published a quarto on **Hawking, Hunting, Fowling, and Fishing.** That this book dealt with fishing as an important feature of its contents may be inferred from the fact that it had a square woodcut on the title page representing a man with several hooks on the ground beside him. From this date, angling works began to increase so much that space will permit me only to name those which precede old Izaak's **Compleat Angler.** In 1606 we have a book by Gardiner upon **Angling Spiritualised.** In 1613 J. D., since proved to be John Denny, a Somersetshire gentleman, wrote a poem, entitled *The Secrets of Angling,* which contains in good verse all the information obtainable in the best manual, even of the present day. This book is even rarer than the **Booke of St. Albans,** but it was reprinted by Mr. Arber in 1877, in a book called by him the **English Garner.** I give the following selections as an evidence of the progress of angling in 1613.

> See where another hides himself as shy
> As did Actaeon, or the fearful deer,
> Behind a withy, and with watchful eye
> Attends the bite within the water clear,
> And on the top thereof doth move his fly
> With skilful hand, as if he living were.
> Lo ! how the chub, the roach, the dace, and trout,
> To catch thereat do gaze and swim about.

The following mention some few of the qualities desirable in an angler :—

> Then followeth Patience, that furious flame
> Of Choler cools, and Passion puts to flight;
> As doth a skilful rider break and tame
> The courser wild, and teach him tread aright:
> So Patience doth the mind dispose and frame
> To take mishaps in worth and count them light;
> As loss of fish, line, hook, or lead, or all,
> Or other chance that often may befall.

> Next unto this is Liberality—
> Feeding them oft with full and plenteous hand ;
> Of all the rest a needful quality
> To draw them near the place where you will stand.
> Like to the ancient hospitality
> That sometime dwelt in Albion's fertile land,
> But now is sent away into exile

Beyond the bounds of Isabella's isle.

The next good gift, and hardest to endure,
Is fasting long from all superfluous fare;
Unto the which he must himself inure,
By exercise and use of diet spare ;
And with the liquor of the waters pure,
Acquaint himself if he cannot forbear.
And never on his greedy belly think,
From rising sun until alow he sink.

The author's idea of liberality appears rather like what in the present day one would call making a decent investment. It is, in fact, " baiting a swim." The tools which an angler requires are enumerated as follows :

Light rod to strike, long line to reach withal,
Strong hook to hold the fish he haps to hit;
Spare lines and hooks whatever chance do fall,
Baits quick and dead to bring them to the bit:
Fine lead and quills, with corks both great and small;
Knife, file, and thread, and *little basket* fit;
Plummets to sound the depth of clay and sand,
With pole *and net* to bring them safe to land.

The first line suggests the well-known maxim, " fish fine and far off," which first took its present shape in Cotton's second part of the *Compleat Angler* (Chap V.). The creel (as a "little basket") and the landing-net here first make part of the requirements of the angler.

In 1614 a partial reprint of the *Booke of St. Albans* appeared under the title *of Jewell for Gentry*. In 1651 came Thomas Barker, with his *Art of Angling, and various Secrets of Angling,* which was reprinted in 1820. This writer was certainly credited by Walton with having given him much information upon fly fishing.

Thus Thomas Barker and Izaak Walton have respectively written, one a prose, and the other a verse introduction to *The Experienced Angler* of Venables, signed "J. W.—T. B." **Barker's Delight** was the title of a later work published in 1659. It is dedicated to Edward, Lord Montague. A portion of the dedication runs thus :—

If any noble or gentle angler of what degree soever he be, have a mind to discourse of any of those ways and experiments, I live in Henry the VII.'s Gifts, the next door to the Gatehouse in Westminster, my name is **Barker,** where I shall be ready, as long as please God, to satisfy them and maintain my art during life.

This sort of challenge almost carries us back to the age of chivalry again. Meanwhile, between Barker's two books comes Walton's **Compleat Angler,** the book which was to revolutionise the general feeling with which angling was regarded, and which was to raise the pursuit to the dignity of an art. So well has it succeeded, that during the lapse of upwards of two centuries, a distinct class has been gradually growing into being. This class, by its love for nature, and the almost enforced simplicity of its habits, arising from the pursuit of the gentle art, has done more to minimise the evil effects of the artificial life peculiar to large cities than any system of ancient Sparta could have done.

As another example of the truth of the saying that "there's nothing new under the sun," I may mention, in connection with Walton's book, that it is suggested that Heresbach, a person holding a high position in a continental court, was the originator of the types of Walton's famous "Piscator," "Venator," and "Auceps." This Heresbach wrote a work entitled *De Venatione Aucupis et Piscatione,* in which his characters talk, much as Walton's are made to talk, about their several sports. Although it is true that this work was not translated into English, yet it is not unlikely Walton had seen it.

I may here introduce a question which has much interested me during the preparation of this paper, and which must be of much interest to practical anglers. This is :—When was the reel or winch first used for trout fly-fishing ? No writer upon angling in the century (the 17th) now under review gives us any information upon this point. In Walton (1653) we find that he speaks of its use in salmon-fishing.

PISCATOR.—Note also, that many use to fish for salmon with a ring of wire on the top of their rod, through which the line may run to as great a length as is needful, when he is hooked. And to that end some use a wheel about the middle of their rod, or near their hand, which is to be observed better by seeing one of them, than by a large demonstration of words.

For trolling and pike-fishing the winch appears to have been in use from the time of Dame Juliana downwards. In Nicholas Cox (1686) we find the first mention of its use with *large* trout, or salmon. With one exception, which I shall name further on, its real use does not appear to have been recognised by any writer until the present century, as in 1797, in Sir John Hawkins' edition of Walton, revised by Hawkins, Jun., it is mentioned in the notes of Hawkins as something new and only to be used for large trout, or salmon. Walton himself did not use it for trout-fishing, and had a very primitive method of dealing with a fish which he found too big:—

VENATOR.—Oh me ! look you, master, a fish ! a fish—Oh, master, I have lost her.

PISCATOR.—Ay marry, sir, that was a good fish indeed ; if I had had the luck to have taken up that rod, then 'tis twenty to one he should not have broke my line by running to the rod's end, as you suffered him. I would have held him within the bend of my rod (unless he had been fellow to the great trout that is near an ell long, which was of such a length and depth thut he had his picture drawn, and now is to be seen at mine host Rickabee's, at the *George,* in Ware), and it maybe by giving that very great J Trout the rod—that is, by casting it to him into the water—I might have caught him at the long run; for so I use always to do when I meet with an overgrown fish; and you will learn to do so too hereafter ; for I tell you, Scholar, fishing is an art, or at least, it is an art to catch fish.

Cotton does not agree with this method, though he has no better method to offer. Thus in the *Compleat Angler,* Part II.:—

PISCATOR.—I must here also beg leave of your master, and mine, not to controvert, but to tell him that I cannot consent to his way of throwing in his rod to an overgrown trout, and afterwards recovering his fish with his tackle : for though I am satisfied he has sometimes done it, because he says so, yet I have found it quite otherwise.

And now, having arrived at my climax, as it were, in treating of English Angling Works, I should like in passing, to mention some striking evidence of the popularity of our art, and its founder, Walton. In 1864 Westwood, in his history of the Editions of Walton, says that up to that date no less than fifty-three editions had been printed, and since that date I find there have been seven more ; altogether sixty editions. All these prove that whatever may be said of some of our aids, such as the May-fly, our art of angling is not so ephemeral as many other sports.

To conclude the subject, so far as British Angling Works are concerned, I must deal very briefly with the remainder of these. There were published altogether in the sixteenth century, twenty-eight angling works proper in prose, and four in verse. I cannot leave this century, which for the angler is fraught with interest, without calling especial attention to three famous books which appeared. First comes *The Experienced Angler,* by Colonel Venables (famous in his day for the capture of Jamaica). His first edition, to which I have before referred, appeared in 1661, and one passage, containing valuable hints to anglers upon the respective merits of up and down stream fishing, will, I think, bear quotation, even in this enlightened age :—

Fish are frightened with any, the least, sight or motion; therefore by all means keep out of sight, either by sheltering yourself behind some bush or tree, or by standing so far off the River's side, that you can see. nothing but your flie or flote ; to effect this, a long Rod at ground, and a long Line with the artificial flie, may be of use to you. And here I meet with two different opinions and practices; some always cast their flie and bait up the water, and so they say nothing occurreth to Fishes sight but the Line : others fish down the River, and so suppose (the Rod and

Line being long) the quantity of water takes away or at least lesseneth the Fishes sight; but the other affirm that Rod and Line, and perhaps yourself, are seen also. In this difference of opinions I shall only say, in small Brooks you may angle upwards, or else in great Rivers you must wade, as I have known some, who thereby got the Sciatica, and I would not wish you to purchase pleasure at so dear a rate ; besides, casting up the River you cannot keep your Line out of water, which we noted for a fault before; and they that use this way confess that if in casting your flie, the Line fall into the water before it, the flie were better uncast, because it frights the Fish ; then certainly it must do it this way, whether the flie fall first or not the Line must first come to the Fish or fall on him, which undoubtedly will fright him: therefore, my opinion is that you angle down the River, for the other you traverse twice so much, and beat not so much ground as downwards.

The next book, ***The Anglers Vade Mecum,*** by James Chetham, of Smedley, near Manchester, appeared first in 1681. The allusion in this book to subjects of much local interest will sufficiently justify the full quotations which I make. Upon the vexed question of the mixture of silk and hair in lines, Chetham appears to be the first writer who objects to the method. He says :—

The mixing Hair and Silk I esteem no ways good for Lines; but if your Lines must be very strong, make them all of Hair, or all of Silk that is white, because it is strongest, and will not rot so quickly as colour'd Silk.

Then he gives, as a proved success, a recipe for an ointment to lure fishes, in which he also describes *the manner* of using, and no one now even need doubt its utility, under the proper conditions, which I have italicised:—

Of Man's Fat, Cat's Fat, Heron's Fat, and of the best Assa-faetida, of each two Drams; Mummy, finely powdered, two Drams ; Cummin-feed, finely powdered, two Scruples; and of Camphor, Galbanum, and Venice Turpentine of each one Dram ; Civet-grains, two. Make, according to Art, all into an indifferent thin Oyntment, with the Chymical Oyls of Lavender, Annise, and Camomil, of each an equal quantity ; and keep the same in a narrow-mouthed and well-glassed Gaily-pot, close covered with a Bladder and Leather; and when you go to Angle, take some of it in a small pewter Box, made taper, and anoint eight inches of the Line, next the Hook therewith, and when washed off repeat the same. This Oyntment which, for its excellency, I will call Unguentum Piscatorum mirabile, prodigiously causes Fish to bite, if in the *hand of an Artist* that angles within water, and in proper Seasons and Times, and with *suitable Tackle and Baits fit and proper for the River,* Season, and Fish he designs to catch. The Man's Fat you may get of the London Chyrurgeons, concerned in anatomy, and the Heron's Fat from the Poulterers, in London ; the rest are to be had from Druggists or Apothecaries, and this Composition will serve you two or three Summers' angling. I forbore (for some reasons) to insert the same in my fifth edition; but now since it's divulged, value it not the less, but esteem it as a jewel. They that would try other Experiments, not before inserted, and be curious, let them consult a Book, called, "Modern Curiosities of Art and Nature," page 178. But upon *frequent Essays,* this last hath the preeminence, and is found to excel them all.

This is, with the exception of the *Secrets of Angling,* the only book which gives indications of the belief of its author in the efficacy of the ointment it describes. In the same book we find the following :—

When you Angle at Ground in a clear water, or dibble with natural flies, *Angle going up the River:* but in muddy water or with Dub-flie *Angle going down the River*.

On artificial and dub-fly angling, the author again says :—

The flie is always to be on the very surface or top of the water, and you are to *Angle going down the River.*

And again:—

To Fish fine and far off is the great Rule in all manner of Flie Angling.

This author also gives an opinion upon the use of a wire ring at the top of the rod, and a wheel in the middle, for great salmon angling, almost in Walton's own words. The Irwell is mentioned as one of the principal rivers in England, but no reference is made to the Mersey. We are informed that the trouts of the Irk are accounted excellent fish, and that river is in several places described as a good stream for anglers. In one place, after saying that no eels he ever met with were to be compared, for deliciousness of taste, to the eels caught in a small river in Lancashire, called the Irk, he proceeds :—

Which is composed of three small Brooks that have their conflux near unto Middleton Hall, when it assumes the name of Irk, and thence descends through Blakely and Crumpsall, &c, to Manchester.

Mr. J. Eglington Bailey in a note in the **Manchester City** News, February, 1879, gives other details in connection with Chetham which will much interest anglers.

The last book published during the seventeenth century which I shall name is *The Gentleman's Recreations,* by Nicholas Cox, treating of hunting, fowling, fishing, and agriculture. The first edition appeared 1674. In it we find the first mention of the use of the winch in trout fly-fishing. He speaks of Walton, rather patronisingly as it seems, as " a very ingenious man, an excellent angler," probably little thinking that Walton would be remembered and loved long after Nicholas Cox was forgotten by all but the bibliographer.

Pepys, in his Diary, March 19th, 1666-7, shows that he had not escaped the love of sport which then prevailed :—

This day, Mr. Caesar (the lute master) told me of a pretty experiment of his, of angling with a minikin, a gut-string varnished over, which keeps it from swelling, and is beyond any hair for strength and smallness. The secret I like mightily.

In the early part of the next century (the 18th) lived two remarkable men. One of them we know was an enthusiastic angler as well as a fine poet, for Thomson in his *Seasons* proved both propositions at once. In " Spring " he says :—

> Now, when the first foul torrent of the brooks,
> Swelled with the vernal rains, is ebbed away;
> And, whitening, down their mossy-tinctured stream
> Descends the billowy foam: now is the time,
> While yet the dark-brown water aids the guile,
> To tempt the trout. The well-dissembled fly,
> The rod fine-tapering with elastic spring,
> Snatch'd from the hoary steed the floating line,
> And all thy slender watery stores prepare.
> But let not on thy hook the tortured worm,
> Convulsive, twist in agonising folds;
> Which, by rapacious hunger swallowed deep,
> Gives, as you tear it from the bleeding breast
> Of the weak, helpless, uncomplaining wretch,
> Harsh pain and horror to the tender hand.

******

> Just in the dubious point, where with the pool
> Is mix'd the trembling stream, or where it boils
> Around the stone, or from the hollow'd bank
> Reverted plays in undulating flow,
> There throw, nice-judging, the delusive fly;
> And, as you lead it round in artful curve,
> With eye attentive mark the springing game.
> Straight as above the surface of the flood
> They wanton rise, or urged by hunger leap.
> Then fix, with gentle twitch, the barbed hook:
> Some lightly tossing to the grassy bank,
> And to the shelving shore, slow-dragging some,
> With various hand proportioned to their force.

The poet Gay, who makes up this brace of distinguished men who were poets and loved fishing, also gives proof of his intimate knowledge of the art. In his
poem, **Rural Sports,** he says, in describing the artificial fly :—

> Mark well the various seasons of the year,
> How the succeeding insect race appear,
> In their revolving moon one colour reigns,
> Which in the next the fickle trout disdains.
> Oft have I seen a skilful angler try
> The various colours of the treach'rous fly;
> When he with fruitless pain hath skim'd the brook,
> And the coy fish rejects the skipping hook.
> He shakes the boughs that on the margin grow,
> Which o'er the stream a waving forest throw ;
> When if an insect fall (his certain guide)
> He gently takes him from the whirling tide;
> Examines well his form with curious eyes,
> His gaudy vest, his wings, his horns, and size ;
> Then round his hook the chosen fur he winds,
> And on the back a speckled feather binds;
> So just the colours shine through every part,
> That Nature seems to live again in art.

> Far **up the stream** the twisted hair he throws,
> Which down the murmuring current gently flows,
> When if or chance or hunger's powerful sway
> Directs the roving trout this fatal way,
> He greedily sucks-in the twining bait,
> And tugs and nibbles the fallacious meat.

Apropos of worm-fishing, the poet says :—

Around the steel no tortur'd worm shall twine,
No blood of living insect stain my line ;
Let me, less cruel, cast the feather'd hook
With pliant rod athwart the pebbled brook ;
Silent along the mazy margin stray,
And with the fur-wrought fly delude the prey.

It will thus be seen that *up-stream* fishing had its advocates long ago. I shall only name two more works of the last century, and these only because I have had the good fortune to obtain the perusal of them. The first of these books is called ***The Gentleman Angler,*** and is said to be "by a gentleman who has made angling his diversion for upwards of twenty-two years." It is dated London, 1726. The great value of this work is, that in it, for the first time in any printed book, we are instructed how to ring our rod and to use a winch in fly-fishing, or fishing of all kinds.

It will be very convenient to have Rings, or Eyes, (as some call them) made of fine Wire, and placed so artificially upon your Rod from the one End to the other, that when you lay your Eye to one, you may see through all the rest; and your Rod being thus furnished, you will easily learn from thence how to put Rings to all your other Rods. Through these Rings your Line must run, which will be kept in a due Posture, and you will find great Benefit thereby. You must also have a Winch or Wheel affixed to your Rod, about a Foot above the End, that you may give Liberty to the Fish, which, if large, will be apt to run a great way before it may be proper to check him, or before he will voluntarily return.

In the Glossary is given a definition of " To Veer," which, it is said, signifies "to let out your Line from your Wince or Reel, after you strike a large Fish, lest in checking him too suddenly, he breaks his Hold on your Line."

In the same book is an angler's song, which is really novel in style, and indicates a profound experience of life. The quotation of a few stanzas will suffice :—

THE ANGLER'S SONG.

To the tune of " A Begging we will go. "

Of all the Sports and Pastimes
Which happen in the year,
To Angling there are none, sure,
That ever can compare.
Then to Angle we will go, &c.
******

Then you, who would be honest,
And to old Age attain,
Forsake the City and the Town,
And fill the Angler's train.

For Health and for Diversion
We rise by Break of Day, While Courtiers in their Down-beds,

Sweat half their Time away.
And then unto the River
In haste we do repair,
All day in sweet Amusement
We breathe good wholesome Air.

The Gout and Stone are often bred
By lolling in a Coach;
But Anglers walk, and so remain,
As sound as any Roach.

At night we take a Bottle,
We prattle, laugh, and sing;

We drink a Health unto our Friends,
And so God bless the King.

The other work is ***The British Angler'***, and was written by John Williamson, Gent. It is dated London, 1740. The frontispiece is well worth examination, as it represents a lady angler occupying a prominent position, the lady having indeed, in Thames parlance, " the best swim." There are three more illustrations, which are of fishes, and are, as usual, more remarkable for originality than truth. A unique feature in this work is, that at the end of each chapter there is a condensed version of it in rhymes, which the author says are partly copied from ***The Innocent Epicure, a Poem on Angling,*** 1697. Upon silk and hair lines he says :—

Choose well your Hair, and know the vig'rous
Horse, Not only reigns in Beauty, but in Force;
Reject the Hair of Beasts, ev'n newly dead,
Where all the Springs of Nature are decay'd.
Be sure for single Links the fairest chuse,
Such single Hairs will best supply your Use;
And of the rest your sev'ral Lines prepare,
In all still less'ning every Link a Hair.

If for the Fly, be long and slight your Line,
The Fish is quick, and hates what is not fine ;
If for the deep, to stronger we advise,
Tho' still the Finest takes the Finest prize.
Before you twist your upper Links take care
Wisely to match in Length and Strength your Hair ;
Hair best with Hair, and Silk with Silk agrees,
But mix'd have great inconveniences.

All the famous recipes for fishing ointments, including "Unguentum Piscatorum mirabile," are copied direct from Chetham (of eighty years before) with the most unscrupulous disregard of ***meun*** and ***tuutn.*** We have the now trite maxim handed on to us, "fish fine and far off." We are told—

It is a Custom with many to fish for a Salmon with a Ring of Wire on the Top of their Rod, through which the Line may run to as great a Length as is necessary when he is hooked. And to that End some use a Wheel about the middle of their Rod or near their Hand.

Again we are informed that—

The River Irk, in Lancashire, is famed for very excellent Eels.

And also that—

The Irwell is one of the principal Rivers (for angling) in England.

Singular to say, until this date we find no mention made of the Mersey in angling works, and then only in a work entitled, *The Art of Angling, Rock and Sea Fishing,* by Dr. Brookes. This book, which was published in 1740, went through more editions than any angling work, except *The Compleat Angler.* It went through fourteen editions, the last in 1811. It is in the main copied from Chetham, and probably owes its popularity to the instructions in sea-fishing which it contains. It may not be uninteresting just to quote the special allusions made in this book to Lancashire waters. Thus on page 42 of the edition of 1799, we find :—

The Eel-brood, which in Spring months swim in the sides of the Mersey as high as Warburton, are caught by the poor People, in Scoops, in order to store fish ponds, or scald, or make Eel-pies with.

The Mersey gudgeon seems to have grown especially large, for he says—

The Gudgeon is generally five or six inches long, sometimes in the Mersey eight or nine.

We are also told that—

The Lamprey, called by Dr. Plat "The Pride of the Isis," is found in the Mersey.

Special enactments which are to prevent the taking, killing, or destroying salmon under eighteen inches from. the eye to the middle of the tail, and also making close season for salmon in the Mersey, from the 12th of August to the 23rd of November, are quoted. After three pages devoted to the natural history of the salmon, the author proceeds to say that the Mersey is among the chief rivers in England which yield this excellent fish. What follows will, I fear, appear so fabulous, that I must in self-defence quote the words of the 1799 edition :—

The Mersey greatly abounds with Salmon, which in the Spring strive to get up that Arm of the Sea, and with difficulty evade the Nets which the Fishermen spread to catch them before they get to Warrington Bridge, at which Place the River becoming more narrow, and the Landowners having an exclusive right, each Proprietor by his Agents catches Salmon, which in the Whole amounts to above one thousand pounds a year; by which means the Towns of Warrington, Manchester, and Stockport are well supplied, and the Overplus sent to London by the Stage-coaches, or carried on horseback to Birmingham and other inland Towns. In the Month of October they go up to the smaller rivers as far as they can, to spawn. At that season of the year many Salmon get high up the river Mersey, where some few are caught by angling.

Just fancy that, Manchester Anglers! you who go to Norway or Canada in pursuit of your favourite sport! But to continue—

By far the greatest Part of them is destroyed by Poaching fellows with Spears, though the fish are at that Time of little or no Value. Thus most Harm is done to the Breed of Salmon ; and it were to be wished that the Justices of the Peace would a little more exert themselves, and imprison these idle Poachers.

Again we find that—

Near Flixon in Lancashire, they fish for Salmon in the night-time, by the light of Torches or Kindled Straw. The fish mistake the light for the Day-light, make towards it, and are struck with the Spear or taken with the Net.

We are further told that bull trouts, salmon trouts, salmon peale, or scurf (all which appear to be names denoting one species) "have been caught near Warrington, which have weighed near twenty pounds each." Although the author has copied nearly the whole of the practical angling from Chetham, he does not (at any rate not in the edition quoted) give the famous " man's fat" ointment a place. One other indication of his sound practical sense occurs in the following rule which he lays down :—

If at any time you happen to be overheated with Walking or other Exercise, avoid Small Liquors, especially Water, as you would Poison; and rather take a Glass of Brandy, the instantaneous effects thereof, in cooling the Body and quenching Drought, are amazing.

In the eighteenth and nineteenth centuries, up to 1861, the year included in Westwood's catalogue, the number of British angling books proper was three hundred and seven, while in poetry and rhyme in the same period there were twenty-seven works relating to the subject. Since 1861 I find, by examining publishers' catalogues and other lists, that seventy-six new works on angling have appeared in Britain, and that during that period six works have been added to our stock of angling rhymes. All this is exclusive of magazine or newspaper articles, or papers devoted to sport.

Next in order of antiquity comes France. Her earliest contribution to fishing literature apparently consists of a poem in which Gauchet (who was almoner to Charles the Ninth) describes the pleasures of the fields, including fishing amongst them. The first edition of this book appeared 1583. In 1598 appeared a work on sea and fresh-water fishing, by Ch. Gamon. Until 1660 no other work upon angling seems to have seen the light in France, and one wonders what caused so imitative a people to stand still for more than half a century. The wonder is greater when one considers that in England it was a century prolific of good angling works, and also that our Monarch and his courtiers were on sufficiently familiar terms with France at that time (being unwilling visitors there), to offer our Gallic relations many favourable opportunities of learning the gentle art. However, be the reason what it may, we do not find before 1660 (the Restoration year) any further mention of angling in French works. At that date a book, much like a French "Nicholas Cox," was published at Paris. Then, until 1709, no new work appeared. After the last date anglingworks published in that country became more numerous, but with all its advantages, that of nearness especially to the fountain-head of angling, France has not even at this date contrived to reach more than one tithe of the number published in Britain.

Germany has done much more than France for angling literature, and possibly a sort of subtle connection may exist between the pedigree of a people and its fondness for angling. If this be so the Germans have more claim to kindred with us than any other nation. The first work met with in catalogues is dated 1559; then 1581, 1582, 1612, 1680, 1685, 1690, 1692, and 1696, each gave a German book, either wholly or partially devoted to angling. In the following century there were published twenty works on angling, and in the present century I find upwards of thirty-five more. It will thus be seen that, although she is a long way behind us, Germany still outstrips all other competitors.

The earliest American book upon angling of which I can find any record is called a " Memoir (an authentic historical) of the Schuykill Fishing Company of the State of Schuykill, from its establishment on that romantic stream near Philadelphia, in the year 1732, to the present time." It was published in Philadelphia in 1830. Dr. Bethune says, "this is an amusing account of a very ancient fishing club, founded by a few of the original settlers. In the list of names are many of high distinction, and the association still exists." Few, if any, angling works were published in America during the eighteenth century, and indeed as already stated, taking the whole of American angling literature, it only includes up to this date twelve books upon the subject proper, and three upon the natural history of fishes. The angling books include one by Mr. Pryme, entitled, I go a-Fishing. This is one of the most charming books I have ever read. What Mr. Pryme has done for American Angling Life, Mr. W. Henderson has more recently done for Britain, in his beautiful book entitled " My Life as an Angler." The subject of pisciculture is of such importance, that a reference to the work which has already been done in America in the matter of artificial fish-breeding ought not to be omitted here. They have there carried out the system under Livingstone Stone (whose work will well repay perusal), to a perfection and on a scale scarcely possible in this country. I may, however, in this connection call attention to the good work done here by Buckland and by Francis. The latter in his book upon *Fish Culture* describes the trouble taken to introduce new species of fish into Britain. There is another direction in which good work might be done towards increasing the number of *valuable* fish, I mean by the destruction of both fry and spawn of the worthless fish, which, without increasing our food supply or sport, eat up the feed of more worthy water tenants. In parts of the United States a notable example of this necessity exists. At particular times, a fish called the Shad runs up the river in immense numbers (as it did years ago in the Severn), the movement being known as "The Run of Shad." In *Domesticated Trout by* Livingstone, there is given a description of the effect of the shad season upon life in the boarding-houses, from which I quote the following :—

Shad are nature's pin-cushions for bones. They are built of the refuse stuff that was left after all the rest of the fish were concocted. The interior of a shad looks like a fine tooth comb or a wool card, and the best way to get the meat out is to use a tooth-pick. A little later in the season and the shad will make their appearance. When they come, they come a good deal; there is many of him ; he is multitudinous. We are not read up as to where the shad lives before he comes this way, but he boards where they set a poor table. When he first puts in an appearance, he is extremely emaciated. He is so thin that his skin don't fit him, hence the phrase, "thin as a shad." You can't get anything thinner than a spring shad, unless you take a couple of them, when, of course, they will be twice as thin. They look much like a porgie,—about twice as much, but they are not so high-scented. Shad fishing is a lucrative business. If the fisherman has good luck, they will net him considerable or he will net them considerable, we are doubtful which. They are fast. They don't stop to loaf any more than a thorough-bred pill, but just keep right on about their business.

A person to like shad wants to eat them often, at near intervals, once every twenty-four hours for eleven or nineteen weeks. The champion place for getting up an appetite for shad is at a Brooklyn boarding-house. The thing there is reduced to a science.

As soon as shad becomes cheap and plenty, the landlady announces at the breakfast table that she will have shad for dinner. The boarder immediately goes to his room and puts on the poorest shirt he has, and when he comes to dinner he has provided himself with a magnifying-glass, which makes the bones look larger, a small basket to put the bones in, a toothpick, and a pair of tweezers. When one eats shad he wants to eat it; he don't want to talk or discuss the state of affairs in France, as he will get so full of the bony parts that he will sigh for a little more Bourbon[10]. When he swallows a bone, all he has to do is to take his tweezers and pull it out; after one learns this art it is simple and even graceful. It is calculated that during the shad season a good shad-eater will get from ten to fifteen bushels of bones from what shad he eats. After the last shad is destroyed, he tears off his shirt, sandpapers off the ends of the bones which are sticking out through his skin, dons clean linen, and is himself again. If we have in our remarks said aught that looks as though we had wandered from the truth, we are willing to vouch for correctness by furnishing all sceptics with a written affidavit.

The list of works which follows will, with the addition of Westwood, bring our catalogue of fishing books up to the month of September, 1879. They are arranged under the heads, Angling Proper; Reports and Natural History; Poetry, and Works other than British : and the price, publisher's name, and dates are given where possible.

---

10 Americanism for native whisky.

The Codes Of Hammurabi And Moses
W. W. Davies

QTY

The discovery of the Hammurabi Code is one of the greatest achievements of archaeology, and is of para-mount interest, not only to the student of the Bible, but also to all those interested in ancient history...

Religion   ISBN: *1-59462-338-4*

Pages:132
MSRP $12.95

The Theory of Moral Sentiments
Adam Smith

QTY

This work from 1749. contains original theories of con-science amd moral judgment and it is the foundation for systemof morals.

Philosophy ISBN: *1-59462-777-0*

Pages:536
MSRP $19.95

Jessica's First Prayer
Hesba Stretton

QTY

In a screened and secluded corner of one of the many railway-bridges which span the streets of London there could be seen a few years ago, from five o'clock every morning until half past eight, a tidily set-out coffee-stall, consisting of a trestle and board, upon which stood two large tin cans, with a small fire of charcoal burning under each so as to keep the coffee boiling during the early hours of the morning when the work-people were thronging into the city on their way to their daily toil...

Childrens   ISBN: *1-59462-373-2*

Pages:84
MSRP $9.95

My Life and Work
Henry Ford

QTY

Henry Ford revolutionized the world with his implementation of mass production for the Model T automobile. Gain valuable business insight into his life and work with his own auto-biography... "We have only started on our development of our country we have not as yet, with all our talk of wonderful progress, done more than scratch the surface. The progress has been wonderful enough but..."

Biographies/   ISBN: *1-59462-198-5*

Pages:300
MSRP $21.95

The Art of Cross-Examination
Francis Wellman

QTY

I presume it is the experience of every author, after his first book is published upon an important subject, to be almost overwhelmed with a wealth of ideas and illustrations which could readily have been included in his book, and which to his own mind, at least, seem to make a second edition inevitable. Such certainly was the case with me; and when the first edition had reached its sixth impression in five months, I rejoiced to learn that it seemed to my publishers that the book had met with a sufficiently favorable reception to justify a second and considerably enlarged edition. ...

Pages:412

Reference   ISBN: *1-59462-647-2*   *MSRP $19.95*

On the Duty of Civil Disobedience
Henry David Thoreau

QTY

Thoreau wrote his famous essay, On the Duty of Civil Disobedience, as a protest against an unjust but popular war and the immoral but popular institution of slave-owning. He did more than write—he declined to pay his taxes, and was hauled off to gaol in consequence. Who can say how much this refusal of his hastened the end of the war and of slavery ?

Law   ISBN: *1-59462-747-9*   **Pages:48**

MSRP $7.45

Dream Psychology Psychoanalysis for Beginners
Sigmund Freud

QTY

Sigmund Freud, born Sigismund Schlomo Freud (May 6, 1856 - September 23, 1939), was a Jewish-Austrian neurologist and psychiatrist who co-founded the psychoanalytic school of psychology. Freud is best known for his theories of the unconscious mind, especially involving the mechanism of repression; his redefinition of sexual desire as mobile and directed towards a wide variety of objects; and his therapeutic techniques, especially his understanding of transference in the therapeutic relationship and the presumed value of dreams as sources of insight into unconscious desires.

Pages:196

Psychology   ISBN: *1-59462-905-6*   *MSRP $15.45*

The Miracle of Right Thought
Orison Swett Marden

QTY

Believe with all of your heart that you will do what you were made to do. When the mind has once formed the habit of holding cheerful, happy, prosperous pictures, it will not be easy to form the opposite habit. It does not matter how improbable or how far away this realization may see, or how dark the prospects may be, if we visualize them as best we can, as vividly as possible, hold tenaciously to them and vigorously struggle to attain them, they will gradually become actualized, realized in the life. But a desire, a longing without endeavor, a yearning abandoned or held indifferently will vanish without realization.

Pages:360

Self Help   ISBN: *1-59462-644-8*   *MSRP $25.45*

The Rosicrucian Cosmo-Conception Mystic Christianity *by Max Heindel*   ISBN: *1-59462-188-8*   **$38.95**
The Rosicrucian Cosmo-conception is not dogmatic, neither does it appeal to any other authority than the reason of the student. It is: not controversial, but is: sent forth in the, hope that it may help to clear...   New Age/Religion Pages 646

Abandonment To Divine Providence *by Jean-Pierre de Caussade*   ISBN: *1-59462-228-0*   **$25.95**
"The Rev. Jean Pierre de Caussade was one of the most remarkable spiritual writers of the Society of Jesus in France in the 18th Century. His death took place at Toulouse in 1751. His works have gone through many editions and have been republished...   Inspirational/Religion Pages 400

Mental Chemistry *by Charles Haanel*   ISBN: *1-59462-192-6*   **$23.95**
Mental Chemistry allows the change of material conditions by combining and appropriately utilizing the power of the mind. Much like applied chemistry creates something new and unique out of careful combinations of chemicals the mastery of mental chemistry...   New Age Pages 354

The Letters of Robert Browning and Elizabeth Barret Barrett 1845-1846 vol II   ISBN: *1-59462-193-4*   **$35.95**
by Robert Browning and Elizabeth Barrett   Biographies Pages 596

Gleanings In Genesis (volume I) *by Arthur W. Pink*   ISBN: *1-59462-130-6*   **$27.45**
Appropriately has Genesis been termed "the seed plot of the Bible" for in it we have, in germ form, almost all of the great doctrines which are afterwards fully developed in the books of Scripture which follow...   Religion/Inspirational Pages 420

The Master Key *by L. W. de Laurence*   ISBN: *1-59462-001-6*   **$30.95**
In no branch of human knowledge has there been a more lively increase of the spirit of research during the past few years than in the study of Psychology, Concentration and Mental Discipline. The requests for authentic lessons in Thought Control, Mental Discipline and...   New Age/Business Pages 422

The Lesser Key Of Solomon Goetia *by L. W. de Laurence*   ISBN: *1-59462-092-X*   **$9.95**
This translation of the first book of the "Lemegton" which is now for the first time made accessible to students of Talismanic Magic was done, after careful collation and edition, from numerous Ancient Manuscripts in Hebrew, Latin, and French...   New Age/Occult Pages 92

Rubaiyat Of Omar Khayyam *by Edward Fitzgerald*   ISBN:*1-59462-332-5*   **$13.95**
Edward Fitzgerald, whom the world has already learned, in spite of his own efforts to remain within the shadow of anonymity, to look upon as one of the rarest poets of the century, was born at Bredfield, in Suffolk, on the 31st of March, 1809. He was the third son of John Purcell...   Music Pages 172

Ancient Law *by Henry Maine*   ISBN: *1-59462-128-4*   **$29.95**
The chief object of the following pages is to indicate some of the earliest ideas of mankind, as they are reflected in Ancient Law, and to point out the relation of those ideas to modern thought.   Religiom/History Pages 452

Far-Away Stories *by William J. Locke*   ISBN: *1-59462-129-2*   **$19.45**
"Good wine needs no bush, but a collection of mixed vintages does. And this book is just such a collection. Some of the stories I do not want to remain buried for ever in the museum files of dead magazine-numbers an author's not unpardonable vanity..."   Fiction Pages 272

Life of David Crockett *by David Crockett*   ISBN: *1-59462-250-7*   **$27.45**
"Colonel David Crockett was one of the most remarkable men of the times in which he lived. Born in humble life, but gifted with a strong will, an indomitable courage, and unremitting perseverance...   Biographies/New Age Pages 424

Lip-Reading *by Edward Nitchie*   ISBN: *1-59462-206-X*   **$25.95**
Edward B. Nitchie, founder of the New York School for the Hard of Hearing, now the Nitchie School of Lip-Reading, Inc, wrote "LIP-READING Principles and Practice". The development and perfecting of this meritorious work on lip-reading was an undertaking...   How-to Pages 400

A Handbook of Suggestive Therapeutics, Applied Hypnotism, Psychic Science   ISBN: *1-59462-214-0*   **$24.95**
by Henry Munro   Health/New Age/Health/Self-help Pages 376

A Doll's House: and Two Other Plays *by Henrik Ibsen*   ISBN: *1-59462-112-8*   **$19.95**
Henrik Ibsen created this classic when in revolutionary 1848 Rome. Introducing some striking concepts in playwriting for the realist genre, this play has been studied the world over.   Fiction/Classics/Plays 308

The Light of Asia *by sir Edwin Arnold*   ISBN: *1-59462-204-3*   **$13.95**
In this poetic masterpiece, Edwin Arnold describes the life and teachings of Buddha. The man who was to become known as Buddha to the world was born as Prince Gautama of India but he rejected the worldly riches and abandoned the reigns of power when...   Religion/History/Biographies Pages 170

The Complete Works of Guy de Maupassant *by Guy de Maupassant*   ISBN: *1-59462-157-8*   **$16.95**
"For days and days, nights and nights, I had dreamed of that first kiss which was to consecrate our engagement, and I knew not on what spot I should put my lips..."   Fiction/Classics Pages 240

The Art of Cross-Examination *by Francis L. Wellman*   ISBN: *1-59462-309-0*   **$26.95**
Written by a renowned trial lawyer, Wellman imparts his experience and uses case studies to explain how to use psychology to extract desired information through questioning.   How-to/Science/Reference Pages 408

Answered or Unanswered? *by Louisa Vaughan*   ISBN: *1-59462-248-5*   **$10.95**
Miracles of Faith in China   Religion Pages 112

The Edinburgh Lectures on Mental Science (1909) *by Thomas*   ISBN: *1-59462-008-3*   **$11.95**
This book contains the substance of a course of lectures recently given by the writer in the Queen Street Hall, Edinburgh. Its purpose is to indicate the Natural Principles governing the relation between Mental Action and Material Conditions...   New Age/Psychology Pages 148

Ayesha *by H. Rider Haggard*   ISBN: *1-59462-301-5*   **$24.95**
Verily and indeed it is the unexpected that happens! Probably if there was one person upon the earth from whom the Editor of this, and of a certain previous history, did not expect to hear again...   Classics Pages 380

Ayala's Angel *by Anthony Trollope*   ISBN: *1-59462-352-X*   **$29.95**
The two girls were both pretty, but Lucy who was twenty-one who supposed to be simple and comparatively unattractive, whereas Ayala was credited, as her Bombwhat romantic name might show, with poetic charm and a taste for romance. Ayala when her father died was nineteen...   Fiction Pages 484

The American Commonwealth *by James Bryce*   ISBN: *1-59462-286-8*   **$34.45**
An interpretation of American democratic political theory. It examines political mechanics and society from the perspective of Scotsman James Bryce   Politics Pages 572

Stories of the Pilgrims *by Margaret P. Pumphrey*   ISBN: *1-59462-116-0*   **$17.95**
This book explores pilgrims religious oppression in England as well as their escape to Holland and eventual crossing to America on the Mayflower, and their early days in New England...   History Pages 268

QTY

The Fasting Cure by *Sinclair Upton*　　　　　　　　　　ISBN: *1-59462-222-1*　**$13.95**
In the Cosmopolitan Magazine for May, 1910, and in the Contemporary Review (London) for April, 1910, I published an article dealing with my experiences in fasting. I have written a great many magazine articles, but never one which attracted so much attention... New Age/Self Help/Health Pages 164

Hebrew Astrology by *Sepharial*　　　　　　　　　　　ISBN: *1-59462-308-2*　**$13.45**
In these days of advanced thinking it is a matter of common observation that we have left many of the old landmarks behind and that we are now pressing forward to greater heights and to a wider horizon than that which represented the mind-content of our progenitors... Astrology Pages 144

Thought Vibration or The Law of Attraction in the Thought World　ISBN: *1-59462-127-6*　**$12.95**
by *William Walker Atkinson*　　　　　　　　　　　　　　　Psychology/Religion Pages 144

Optimism by *Helen Keller*　　　　　　　　　　　　　ISBN: *1-59462-108-X*　**$15.95**
Helen Keller was blind, deaf, and mute since 19 months old, yet famously learned how to overcome these handicaps, communicate with the world, and spread her lectures promoting optimism. An inspiring read for everyone... Biographies/Inspirational Pages 84

Sara Crewe by *Frances Burnett*　　　　　　　　　　　ISBN: *1-59462-360-0*　**$9.45**
In the first place, Miss Minchin lived in London. Her home was a large, dull, tall one, in a large, dull square, where all the houses were alike, and all the sparrows were alike, and where all the door-knockers made the same heavy sound... Childrens/Classic Pages 88

The Autobiography of Benjamin Franklin by *Benjamin Franklin*　ISBN: *1-59462-135-7*　**$24.95**
The Autobiography of Benjamin Franklin has probably been more extensively read than any other American historical work, and no other book of its kind has had such ups and downs of fortune. Franklin lived for many years in England, where he was agent... Biographies/History Pages 332

Name	
Email	
Telephone	
Address	
City, State ZIP	

☐ **Credit Card**　　　　☐ **Check / Money Order**

Credit Card Number	
Expiration Date	
Signature	

Please Mail to:　Book Jungle
PO Box 2226
Champaign, IL 61825
or Fax to:　　　630-214-0564

ORDERING INFORMATION

web: *www.bookjungle.com*
email: *sales@bookjungle.com*
fax: *630-214-0564*
mail: *Book Jungle PO Box 2226 Champaign, IL 61825*
or PayPal *to sales@bookjungle.com*

Please contact us for bulk discounts

DIRECT-ORDER TERMS

**20% Discount if You Order
Two or More Books**
Free Domestic Shipping!
Accepted: Master Card, Visa,
Discover, American Express

www.ingramcontent.com/pod-product-compliance
Lightning Source LLC
Chambersburg PA
CBHW080905020726
47502CB00008B/2355

* 9 7 8 1 4 3 8 5 3 4 8 7 9 *